SHIELD-MAIDEN: GAMBIT OF SHADOWS

THE SHADOWS OF VALHALLA, BOOK II

MELANIE KARSAK

CLOCKPUNK PRESS

❀ Created with Vellum

For my dear friends, old and new.

SHIELD MAIDEN
GAMBIT OF SHADOWS

THE SHADOWS OF VALHALLA

MELANIE KARSAK

GLOSSARY

Ervie (born Hervor), daughter of Jarl Mjord and Blomma, twin sister of Loptr, foster granddaughter of King Hofund of Grund

PEOPLE AND PLACES

Arheimar, ruled by Prince Angantyr
Bolmsö, ruled by a council of elders
Dalr, ruled by Jarl Leif
Götaland, ruled by King Gizer and Queen Kára
Grund, ruled by King Hofund
Hárclett, ruled Jarl Eir
Hrímgnúp, ruled by Jarl Raghild
Jutland, ruled by King Harald
Silfrheim, ruled by Jarl Hakon and Jarl Halger
Skagen, King Harald's city in Jutland

Uppsala, ruled by King Jorund

HEROES OF GAUL

Alaric, chieftain of Dunhen
Dunhen, village in the holdings of King Hrollaug
Elan, druidess of Dunhen
Garin, chieftain of Nordkehdingen
Princess Hergarth, daughter of King Hrollaug
Holmgarth, King Hrollaug's seat
King Hrollaug, king of the Gauls
Chieftain Hrothgar, Elan's uncle
Lady Ilsa, sister of King Hrollaug
Prince Kjar, son of King Hrollaug
Nordkehdingen, village in the holdings of King Hrollaug
Trave, name of a river, lake, and village of the Gauls
Wulf, Elan's cousin

HEROES OF GÖTALAND

Eyfura, daughter of King Gizer and Queen Kára
Gizer, king of Götaland
Kára, queen of Götaland
Sons of King Gizer and Queen Kára: Gauti, Bjarki Bearskin,
Dag, Kettill, and Thorir
Wigluf, son of Öd, warrior of Götaland

HEROES OF GRUND

Arngrimir, son of Jarl Leif and Lady Eydis

Blomma, deceased mother of Ervie and Loptr, adopted
daughter of Hofund and Hervor

Dissa, sister of Jarl Eir of Hárclett, second daughter of Jarl
Eric and Bryn

Eir, jarl of Hárclett, first daughter of Jarl Eric and Bryn

Gida, daughter of Sigrun and Trygve

Hakon and Halger, jarls of Silfrheim

Hárclett, ruled by Jarl Eir

Hervor, deceased wife of King Hofund and adoptive
mother of Blomma

Hofund, king of Grund, adoptive father of Blomma

Leif, Jarl of Dalr, husband of Lady Eydis, cousin of the
first Hervor

Loptr, son of Jarl Mjord and Blomma, twin brother of
Ervie

Sigrun, shield-maiden of Grund, wife of Trygve

Trygve, warrior of Grund, husband of Sign

HEROES OF THE HUNS

Hlod, firstborn son of Prince Heidrek of Grund and
Princess Sifka of the Huns

Humli, king of the Huns

Sifka, daughter of King Humli

Heroes of Jutland

Ama, elderly woman in Skagen
Arvid, Canute, Eluf, Gunnar, Halstein, Sithric, and Torgun, men in Angantyr's warband
Angantyr (born Heidreik), son of the deceased Princess Helga of Jutland and Prince Heidrek of Grund, jarl of Arheimar
Aud, queen of Jutland
Erika, daughter of Jarl Erlaug
Gisla, daughter of Jarl Erlaug
Harald, king of Jutland
Halfdan, son of King Harald and Queen Aud
Jarls of Jutland, Jarl Erlaug, Jarl Thorson, Jarl Njal, Jarl Torel, Jarl Knud
Magnus, Angantyr's wolf
Morda, gythia in Arheimar
Sigrit, maiden attendant to Svafa
Svafa, mother of the first Hervor, great-grandmother of Prince Angantyr, Loptr, and Ervie, widow of Angantyr and Orvar-Odd
Tove, maid in Arheimar

Heroes of the Myrkviðr

Arnar, housecarl for King Ormar
Asa, spirit of the Myrkviðr

Auðr, shield-maiden of Eskilundr

Eskilundr, seat of King Ormar

Freydis, daughter of Arnar and maid in Ormar's hall

Hrolf and Hrogar, craftsmen in Eskilundr

Jarl Geir, jarl in the Myrkviðr

Old Sten, villager in Eskilundr

Ormar, king of the Myrkviðr

Mythological Characters and Gods

Æsir and Vanir, two tribes or factions of the Norse gods

Alfheim, realm of the elves

Freyja, Vanir goddess associated with love and fertility, known for her affinity for cats

Freyr, Vanir god associated with sex and fertility

Frigga, Norse goddess, wife of Odin

Gullinbursti, the golden boar of Freyr

Hel, daughter of Loki and goddess of Hel

Jǫrð, Norse goddess of the earth, mother of Thor

Jotun, term for giant. Not literally giants, but more likely a metaphor for strong, otherworldly supernatural creatures

Jotenheim, realm of the giants

Loki, Norse god, adopted son of Odin, a trickster

Nantosuelta, Gaulish goddess of nature, earth, fire, fertility, and bees

Nidavellir, realm of the dwarves

Norns, Urd, Verdandi, and Skuld, women who
weave fate

Odin (Grímnir, All-Father), father of the Norse gods

Skadi, jotun from the forest married to Njord

Surtur, fire giant from the realm of Muspelheim

Thor, Norse god of thunder, son of Odin and Jǫrð, wields
the hammer Mjolnir

Wights/Vætt, nature spirits. Can be associated with
certain area of land (such as a farm), body of water, etc.

TERMS

Bifrost, a rainbow bridge that connects the worlds

Blót, a ceremony with sacrifice, a rite

Dísablót, a ceremony held in honor of the dísir

Dísarsalr, temple of the dísir

Dísir, female goddesses, spirits, and ancestors

Disting, an annual market

Fylgja, a sense of self that exists outside the body which
may be used to control animals

Gothar, plural name for priests

Gothi, male priest

Gythia, female priestess

Hamingja, the wisdom, spirit, and luck of our ancestors
passed on to the next generation

Hnefatafl, a board game similar to chess

Hof, another name for a temple

Hugr, the sense of self or individual, like a soul
Jarl, equivalent to earl
Náströdr, a place of punishment after death
Odensjakt, Odin's hunt or the Wild Hunt
Skald, equivalent to a bard or poet
Seidr, a form of Norse shamanism/magic
Skogarmaor, an outlaw or criminal banished from society
The Thing, a meeting of kings and jarls and to decree law
Úlfhéðnar, another word for berserkers
Völva, a seeress with magical abilities

CHAPTER 1

A pair of ravens cawed from the trees overhead. Rain pattered down lightly, dampening my clothes and making water beads cling to my horse's mane like gemstones. A light fog blanketed the forest. The scent of ferns and loam effervesced from the forest floor. In the distance, thunder rumbled.

The unsettled nature of the forest matched my heart.

I was leaving behind everything I had been searching for.

I was leaving behind the *person* I'd been searching for. *Ormar.*

For what?

Because everyone I loved was in danger.

And not just from the Gauls. The Gauls were the enemy they knew was coming. They weren't expecting the gambit afoot in the shadows.

The horse snorted and shook his head, sending droplets everywhere.

His mood matched my heart.

"Sorry, horse. I'm no more pleased than you are."

It had been almost two days since I'd left the Myrkviðr. What I would find waiting when I returned to Harald's lands, I didn't know. But in my heart, I felt a tug. Angantyr needed me. Even Loptr called to me. I couldn't escape their pull.

And yet…

A deer bolted from a thicket and sprinted across the path ahead of me. Spooked, the horse whinnied and reared. I moved to tighten my grip on the reins, but I was too slow. I landed with a thump on the ground and then rolled down a hill toward a jumble of rocks. Reaching for anything to slow my collision with the stones, I grabbed at roots and ferns and tried to straighten my fall, but it didn't help. I quickly rolled toward the rocks, unable to slow my descent. I was hurtling toward a disaster, and there was nothing I could do to stop it.

I bashed hard into the rocks. There was a sharp pain in my ankle as one leg collided with the stones. Then, I hit another rock with my head. After that, everything went dark.

IT WAS NIGHT WHEN I WOKE.

It took me a moment to piece together what had happened.

Then, I felt hot breath on my forehead.

I looked up.

The horse stood over me, touching my head gently with his lips. He knickered apologetically at me.

Feeling a sharp pinch, I gently touched my forehead, my fingers gingerly feeling my eyebrow. At the slightest touch, I felt a twinge of pain. My head was cut open, my eye had swollen partially shut, and there was blood on my face.

"By the Norns," I muttered in frustration. "I hear Hlod's people eat horses," I told the horse. "Keep that in mind the next time you decide to throw me because of a deer."

The horse knickered once more but didn't leave my side.

Aching in more spots than I dared count, I tried to sit up only to discover my legs had twisted weirdly as I'd collided with the rocks. Both legs had been jammed *under* the boulders.

I wasn't worried before.

Now, a flicker of panic shot through me.

It was dark, drizzling, and I was a long way from anyone or anywhere.

Righting myself as best I could, feeling a pinching ache in my wrist and the smarting sensation of cuts on my hands, I braced myself so I could pull my legs free. Holding onto the dirt with my fingertips, I tugged. The boot on my left foot resisted but finally pulled free. My other foot, however, was wedged oddly and firmly in a groove. My ankle throbbed from the movement, a sharp pain shooting to the top of my head. The ache made my teeth vibrate.

Not good.

"If my ankle is broken..." I warned the horse, who neighed once more in what seemed like an apology.

Shifting, I pulled again.

Pain shot from my ankle up my leg, making me wince. I bit my bottom lip, preventing myself from crying out.

Still, the leg didn't come free.

"Okay, potentially broken. Maybe just sprained, but definitely stuck."

Bracing myself with my other foot, pressing it against the stone, I held onto whatever roots I could find. I closed my eyes and then gave the leg a firm yank.

There was an odd popping sound, then stars danced before my eyes.

Pain shot from my foot to the top of my head.

And once more, everything went black.

WHEN I OPENED MY EYES ONCE MORE, THE SUN WAS shining. Slants of sunlight beamed down through the leaves of the trees toward the forest floor. The rays shimmered golden, motes glimmering in the beams of light. I studied the leaves, the wind gently moving the branches. Autumn had come. The leaves were turning red and yellow. The sunshine broke through the canopy, shining into my eyes.

Overhead, the birds were singing.

Awake. The sun is awake. I am awake. The girl is awake. And the vætt has come once more.

"Another inch to the left, and you would be lying in poison oak," a sprite-like voice called from behind me.

I tipped my head back to find Narfi sitting there.

"Narfi?"

"Why are you lying on the ground?"

"I'm stuck. My ankle is either broken or severally injured. Narfi, where have you been?"

"Nowhere," the boy told me with a grin as he went to investigate.

"What do you mean, nowhere? When Ormar's people took me, where did you go?"

"Where did *you* go?"

"They took me to Eskilundr."

"To Eskilundr? Really? That's a surprise. The burned king didn't kill you."

"No."

"But his people usually kill everyone."

"That's what I've heard."

"I guess that means you're one of them now."

"One of them?"

Narfi nodded. "One of Jǫrð's children, a daughter of shadows."

"Shadows?"

"Of course! Ormar's people are just shadows in the forest. Now you're one of them, the forest's shadows."

"What do you know of it?"

Narfi grinned at me. "Did you meet King Ormar?"

"I did."

"And what did you think of him?"

I paused. I thought *everything* of him. "Appearances are deceiving. Now, enough chatter, and help me. I'm stuck."

"You're right. Appearances *are* deceiving. You're not stuck. You just need to choose."

"Choose?" I asked, wiggling to see if I could find a way to free my foot. It wasn't budging.

"Yes, about which world you want to be in."

"What are you talking about?" I asked, my tone sounding more annoyed than I had intended.

"Well, you have one foot in the land of the dwarves and one in the realm of men. If you want to rejoin the realm of men, you need to tell the dwarves to let go of your foot."

"Dwarves *do not* have hold of my foot. It's stuck between the rocks."

I studied my boot. My foot was firmly wedged under a boulder. The force of my fall must have pushed the foot into the tiny gap.

"Is that so? Then pull it out."

"I tried, but it's wedged, and there is something sharp in there. Maybe if I dig around the foot a little," I said, then scooted closer to see, but my leg from the knee down was inside the hole, and there was no way to say for sure what I was stuck on.

"Of course there's something sharp! Dwarven nails and teeth."

"Stop telling stories, and help me get my leg out."

The boy climbed onto the boulder under which my leg was pinned. "How can I help you if you won't help yourself?"

I frowned at him. Ignoring the boy, I moved into position to pull myself out once more. I pulled again, but a terrible pain wracked me. I felt dizzy.

"You have to ask the dwarves to let you go," Narfi told me again.

"That's ridiculous."

"You wield a dwarven blade and can summon an army of wights. How is what *I'm* saying ridiculous?" he asked with a laugh.

I paused a moment. "Fine," I said, then looked toward my leg. "Brothers of the Niðavellir, please release my leg. There is war and terror loose in my lands. I must put your steel to good use defending it."

Narfi chuckled. "That wasn't so hard," he said, then clapped his hands once—loudly. "Now, let me help," the boy said and jumped down. He went behind me, put his hands under my armpits, grabbing me by the shoulders. "The dwarves will set you free. You will see. Now, on three. One, two, three!"

I pushed my body away from the stones and pulled my leg while Narfi tugged. Whatever sharp thing was blocking me had come loose. I yanked my leg free.

"Aye, gods," I whispered, pulling the leg back. I could feel my ankle throbbing.

Moving gently, I undid the lace on my boot and slowly pulled it off. Touching the bone, I tried to feel if the ankle was broken. My foot and ankle were bruised. My ankle had swelled considerably. Why now? I was headed to war. How would I be of use to anyone with a sprained ankle?

"Needs ice, but it's not the season for it. There is a stream that way. The water is cool. Let me help you up," Narfi offered.

Leaving my boot off, I rose slowly, leaning against the boy. When I set my injured foot down for a moment, I quickly discovered that it would not bear my weight.

I winced and bit my lip, not letting myself cry out.

"It's not broken," Narfi told me.

"Help me to my horse?"

Narfi nodded. "He really is sorry."

"I'm sure he is."

"I mean, it's not his fault that deer ran out."

"No, then whose fault is it?"

The boy chuckled. "The deer's, of course."

"Of course. And how do you know about the deer anyway?"

Narfi merely chuckled.

I hobbled my way to the horse. Leaning on Narfi and relying on my good leg, I grabbed my saddle. Using my good foot, I pulled myself up. My ankle protested by throbbing with every move.

Narfi stood looking up at me, his hands on his hips.

"Want to ride to Skagen with me?" I asked him.

"Why would you ride to Skagen?"

"To meet with my cousin."

"But Angantyr is not in Skagen."

"How do you know that?"

He grinned.

"Okay, then where *is* Angantyr?"

"In Arheimar."

"Why isn't he in Skagen?"

"There is nothing left in Skagen."

"They said there was a fire…"

"The wights whipped wildly as the Gauls called their fire gods. Not much but shells of buildings left. You need to go to Arheimar."

"All right. Want to ride with me to Arheimar?"

He paused as he considered. "I'll ride with you for a time. Go there. I'll hop on," he told me, pointing to the jumble of rocks under which my leg had spent the night.

I nodded then coaxed the horse to the stones so the boy could climb on more easily. He grabbed a handful of mane and pulled himself up in front of me.

"That way," Narfi said, pointing. "That will get us to the stream."

"All right," I said, then clicked to the horse to walk on. "Thank you for helping me."

"I couldn't leave my favorite shield-maiden stuck between two worlds."

"Your favorite, eh? I'm fortunate you came along when you did."

"Yes, you are."

"It seems like a very big coincidence."

"It does."

"You know, you could tell me who you really are."

"You mean like how you are *really* Hervor?"

"I'm Ervie."

"Very well, then I am Narfi."

I sighed. "All right, *Narfi*."

"But you should name the horse. He likes you, and he feels bad that you fell."

"Should I call him Narfi?"

At that, the boy laughed. "No."

"Then what should I call him?"

"Call him Ormar. That way, you won't forget about the king."

"I won't forget about the king."

"Are you sure?"

"I'm not naming the horse Ormar."

"Hmm, then maybe call him Utr."

"Utr?"

The boy nodded.

"Like the vætt of Bolmsö?" I asked.

"Yes, exactly like that."

"I already have enough wild sprites coming out of the forest to help me. I won't evoke the name of another."

"But the horse likes the name, don't you, Utr?" Narfi asked the horse, patting his neck.

The horse snorted in reply.

"See, Ervie? Utr is here to keep you safe."

"Really? The horse just threw me into a pile of rocks? And, may I remind you, Utr of Bolmsö was there when my maternal grandmother and uncle were killed during their war against the first Hervor."

"Would your life have been better had Jarl Solva lived?" he asked, referring to my maternal grandmother, Blomma's mother.

"Well…"

"You see, the vætt of Bolmsö *did* have your best interest at heart. Vætts can see the past and future, don't you know? And they always protect their wards."

"How do you know so much about vætts?"

At that, Narfi just giggled and giggled.

I sighed, then clicked to the horse. "Come on, Utr. Let's go."

WE STOPPED AT THE STREAM, WHERE I SOAKED MY ANKLE until the swelling calmed. Dampening some cloths, I wrapped the injury, and we set off again. We traveled throughout the day and into the night, finally settling for a campsite not far from a stand of pine trees.

"Fetch some firewood," I told the boy while I

prepared the camp, leaning on a walking stick as I worked.

With each awkward movement, I cursed my luck. Every step I took toward Arheimar was painful. What good would I be to anyone if I could barely walk when I got there?

Settling down on the ground, I prepared the space for the campfire. Once Narfi brought the first load of wood, I built a fire. Soon, the flames were going strong. I rewrapped my now purple-and-yellow ankle with the cool, wet cloths. My fingers grew cold from the effort. Autumn was upon us. I could smell the winter in the air. This was not the time to launch a battle, and the Gauls knew it. This had been strategic. No one wanted to be away from home during harvest season. There was a narrow window in which our people would be able to take their revenge. Unless Angantyr moved quickly, that window would close.

And then, there was Hlod.

Thus far, the Myrkviðr had served as a barrier between my cousin and the Huns. But Ormar's words echoed in my heart. It wasn't the Myrkviðr they were after. Hlod was Heidrek's son. That meant he was a true heir to Grund, Bolmsö, and could even make a claim to Harald's lands through his father. The Huns threatened everyone I loved. If Hlod found a way to move his forces through the Myrkviðr—which it appeared he soon would—Angantyr had a bigger problem.

I needed to warn Angantyr, but my heart and soul belonged in the Myrkviðr.

Aye, Norns, how you weave.

"You're quiet," Narfi said, a needling tone in his voice.

I looked up at the child. "It's a long ride, and my ankle hurts," I said, then opened my saddle bag, pulling out a round of bread which I split between the boy and me.

"Oh," Narfi said as he sat cross-legged before the fire. "I thought you were thinking about the Myrkviðr."

"I *was* thinking about the Myrkviðr."

"Why did you leave?"

"I must warn my cousin."

"Too late for that. Skagen is already burned," Narfi said, his mouth full.

I frowned at him.

He giggled, then said, "You want to tell him about Prince Hlod."

"How do you know about Prince Hlod?"

"*Everyone* knows about Prince Hlod."

"No. No one knows about Prince Hlod."

"That's not true. Someone does."

"Who?"

"Me, as I already said. Hlod is a wolf-blood. I know

him and his horse people. They are riding toward Bolmsö. Their horses will race down the mountains and across the water, galloping until they reach that ancient isle. Unless, of course, someone stops them."

"Of all the things Hlod could take, Bolmsö is the least of my concerns."

"It should be the chief of your concerns, Reindeer Princess. The people of Blomfjall and the people of Bolmsö are one people."

"What do you mean?"

Narfi simply shrugged and then added, "I suppose Hlod could come for Grund...and your brother."

"Yes."

"Or he could go for Arheimar."

"Yes."

Narfi shrugged. "He's foolish to take those. Bolmsö is the most beautiful."

"And how would you know that?"

"I listen to legends. Don't you?"

"Sometimes."

Narfi giggled. "You drink too much ale to listen properly to the skalds, Reindeer Princess."

"Perhaps."

"I don't see you drinking it now," he told me as I lifted my water pouch.

I paused, then shrugged. He was right. My regular imbibing of ale and mead had tapered off during my stay in the Myrkviðr. My clarity of mind had helped me in my training with Auðr. But more, that empty pit inside me that craved the numbness drinking had brought was gone.

"No need for it," I said, then handed the boy the water skin.

"You are not the same Reindeer Princess who entered those woods."

"No."

"But *they* will expect you to be."

"I—"

"In fact, I would guess some of them have eagerly awaited your return—at least, the *old* you."

"What do you mean?"

"Or maybe not," Narfi said, then giggled. "Have anything else to eat?"

I dug into the pack and pulled out another parcel. I opened it to hand to the boy, along with some cheese and nuts.

"Thank you," he said, then munched happily, leaving off his teasing.

But his words had found a place in my heart.

I was *not* the same woman who had left.

While no one would mind the changes that had come over me, there was one person whose life, whose dreams, would be altered by the transformations in me.

I closed my eyes and pressed my hand against my forehead.

Dag.

"Ah, now you remember," Narfi told me in singsong but added nothing more.

CHAPTER 2

When I woke the following day, Narfi was gone. Thinking he had wandered off in search of berries, mushrooms, or mischief, I slowly struck down the camp and made ready to ride, but the boy didn't reappear.

Hobbling with my walking stick, I went to the forest's edge. "Narfi?" I called into the woods, startling a flock of sparrows roosting in the trees. "Narfi!"

Gone away. He's gone away. The boy has gone away, they chirped at me in annoyance.

I stared out into the woods.

As unexpectedly as he had come, he was gone once more.

I went to the horse.

"What do you think? Is the child some vætt of these woods? Is he playing tricks on us?" I asked the horse.

"I'm leaving, Narfi," I called to the woods again, but there was no reply. "Let's ride for Arheimar, Utr," I told the horse, hoisting myself onto my saddle. I made my way out of the forest and trotted down the narrow paths until I met the road where I had left Angantyr all those months ago.

Turning the horse south, I tapped my heel and set off at a trot.

Soon.

I would be there soon.

I RODE THROUGHOUT THE DAY, RESTING AT NIGHT, THEN SET off again the next morning. My ankle ached horribly. The swelling had gone down some, and the pain was not as piercing, but I was still unable to walk without the aid of a stick to lean on.

Given my condition, I was relieved when I finally saw signs that I was nearing Arheimar.

The road trailed across rolling green countryside dotted with horses toward a bustling city seated in a valley alongside a river. I paused at the peak overlooking the city below. Here, two massive carvings stood on either side of the road: one of Freyr and the other of

Freyja. My gaze went to the goddess. How many years I had called to her only to be ignored.

Freyja.

I waited.

Still, I felt nothing.

I looked out over the landscape. Red poppies, purple asters, and bluebells dotted the tall grasses. The water's surface on the winding river reflected the sky overhead. There was a small grove of apple trees just outside the city. I saw children playing there. And on the breeze, I could smell the tang of ripe apples.

Jǫrð. Everywhere I look, I find you.

My gaze shifted back to the city. The city was walled, the palisades manned. I could see the roof of the great hall with its horseheads on the beams.

I clicked to Utr, then made my way toward the gate. When I arrived, I found the entrance closed.

"Who approaches?" one of the watchmen called.

"I'm Ervie, cousin to Angantyr," I called back.

"Apologies, Reindeer Princess. Open the gates."

When the gates swung open, I saw a boy rushing off toward the jarl's hall.

I guided the horse into the city. It was a bustling place. At the market near the city's gate, I saw goods of all sorts being sold: leather, armor, steel, food, and animals. As I rode toward the jarl's hall, I passed the temple to Freyr. From within, I smelled the scents of burning herbs. I would need to visit them later to seek out a healer but not now. I needed to speak to Angantyr. As I made my way to the hall, I spotted something odd in the square nearby.

Three bodies hung from frames. They had been positioned in the shape of runes. Their blood had been given to the gods. I eyed the men's dress. Gauls. How had the Gauls come here? Why?

I brought the horse to a stop before the hall.

"Reindeer Princess," a young stable hand said, greeting me. "Welcome to Arheimar. I will see to your horse."

"Thank you," I said, then pulled the long walking stick from my things. Gripping it, I slid off the horse, wincing as I landed. I grabbed the rest of my things, then turned to go to the hall.

As I made my way to the door, a bolt of gray rushed from within.

"Magnus," I said, bracing myself with my staff when the wolf jumped up. The wolf set his paws on my shoulders then licked my face. "It is good to see you too," I said, scratching his ear.

"Ervie, may Freyr be thanked," Angantyr called, joining me. His eyes scanned me from top to bottom, taking in my staff. "You're hurt," he said, his tone serious.

"Got thrown. It's just a sore ankle."

Angantyr embraced me carefully. "May the gods be thanked for returning you now."

"Are *you* well, Cousin? What happened? The Gauls..." I said, looking back over my shoulder at the sacrificed men.

"I'm alive, but barely. Come. Let's get you off that foot, and I will explain," he said, then turned to one of his men. "Torgun, fetch a healer from the temple and have a chamber readied for Princess Ervie."

"Yes, Prince," the man said, then hurried off.

"Let's go inside," Angantyr said, then walked slowly beside me.

When we entered, I found many of Angantyr's warriors there, as well as some familiar faces from Skagen. These were men who'd survived the attack on Harald's city. Many of the warriors from Skagen had been injured.

The warriors stood around the long, narrow firepit that ran the length of the hall. At the back of the room was a small platform on which two chairs were seated. The pillars of the hall were carved with horse designs. Horse skulls and shields hung on the walls.

Angantyr led me to a private room just off the side of the hall, closing the door behind him.

When I entered, I discovered one of Harald's men, Canute, a grizzled, silver-haired warrior, seated there. He had a fresh sword wound stretching from his brow to his cheek. He had narrowly kept his eye. Along with him were four of Angantyr's chief men—Halstein, Eluf, Arvid, and Gunnar—and the priestess Elan.

"Elan," I said.

"Princess," she replied, standing. She had a nervous expression on her face.

"Reindeer Princess," Canute said, giving me a slight bow.

"Canute, I am glad to see you alive. May the All-Father be thanked."

"Almost short an eye," the man said. "But only almost."

I inclined my head to him, then greeted the others similarly.

Angantyr turned to the others. "If you don't mind, I would speak to Ervie alone."

The others nodded, then departed. When Elan moved to go, Angantyr motioned for her to remain.

Angantyr poured me a mug of ale and handed it to me, gesturing for me to sit.

I lowered myself slowly into the seat, propping the walking stick on the chair beside me.

"Ervie, you are injured. Your foot, your face...even your hands," Elan said.

"The horse spooked over a deer...or a vætt. I'm not entirely sure which."

"A vætt?" Angantyr asked.

"I'll be fine," I said, waving my hand dismissively. "I trained in the dísarsalr, remember? The ankle is not broken. It will mend."

Angantyr frowned, then said, "My messenger told me he didn't find you. How did you know to come to Arheimar?"

"The Myrkviðr has its own ways. Cousin, what has happened? They say Skagen is burned."

"It was a planned attack," Angantyr began, "arranged by Kjar before we even departed the Gaul's lands. Kjar murdered his father and took his throne. When he was done, he came for Harald. And here in Arheimar—"

"The princess," I said with a gasp. "Where is Hergarth?"

Angantyr paused.

"Dead," Elan said.

"Dead?"

"They struck on the full moon," Angantyr told me. "Kjar's warriors burned Skagen, and Hergarth tried to murder me. If it were not for Elan, I would be dead."

My eyes wide, I turned to the priestess.

"Your gods spoke to me, Reindeer Princess. I saw a dream," she said, then shuddered. "I woke in the night and went to check on Angantyr only to find Hergarth poised to stab him. The moonlight glimmered on the knife in her hand," she said, then shook her head. "I am not ashamed to say it now, but I saved the man I love from a certain death."

"Gaulish warriors were waiting just outside Arheimar for the princess. She and Kjar planned the attack before Hergarth was sent to us," Angantyr told me.

"But your marriage..."

"It was no marriage," Angantyr said gruffly. "Frigga as my witness, we were never man and wife."

"The princess and her brother were close in ways our customs do not approve of," Elan told me.

"Do the Gauls know Hergarth is dead?" I asked.

"I don't know. They must assume," Angantyr said.

"And Skagen?"

"Much of the city is razed, including the great hall and the temple. Some people survived, but many did not. The Gauls came in full force and attacked in the night. Gizer was already gone. There was only Harald, Halfdan, Aud, and..." Angantyr said, his voice catching.

Elan reached out for his hand.

My chest grew tight. "Svafa?"

Angantyr sniffed, then wiped his hand across his lips. "Little Sigrit, the maid who attended Svafa, said...she said that Svafa stood, sword in hand, between the maiden and the raiders so the girl could escape. Svafa sacrificed herself so the child could live."

I sat perfectly still for a moment, letting the words sink in.

Svafa was gone.

Somehow, the world seemed less bright for it. But Svafa had died a warrior. Now, she was with her daughter and those she loved in Valhalla.

Angantyr's pain, however, was palpable.

"I am sorry, Cousin," I said, swallowing hard. "She is with Hervor now."

He nodded, then dashed a tear away.

"Did they attack elsewhere? Jarl Erlaug…"

"No. They came for Harald."

"What will you do?"

"I have sent ships and riders. Time is not on our side, but we must rally at once. I have sent to Gizer, Hofund, and even King Jorund in Uppsala. I have asked everyone to meet on the isle of Samso by the full moon. From there, we will plan our attack."

I lifted my mug. "Then may Freyr be with us, Cousin. We will see them all avenged. Skol."

"Skol."

CHAPTER 3

Settling back into my seat, I considered how to tell my cousin the news weighing on my heart—the real reason I was there. The events that had occurred in my absence were mind-boggling. Svafa had been like a mother to him. While he and Harald had a strained relationship, the man's death would upend Angantyr's life. Not to mention, the deaths of Queen Aud and Halfdan would wound him. Angantyr's world had turned upside down, and as a result, the rule of Harald's lands had fallen into Angantyr's lap.

How could I deliver more bad news? As it was, we would need to ensure Angantyr had the throne firmly in hand. If Hlod came and there was civil war...

"The kingship... Are you worried about rebellion amongst the jarls or competition for the throne?" I asked.

Angantyr looked thoughtful, then said, "Harald had his difficulties. Many jarls whispered behind him. But, may Freyr be thanked, those jarls who did not support Harald have sent word of their allegiance to me."

Angantyr was being humble. I was relieved but not surprised. The jarls respected Angantyr. He had led them to battle and was known to be just and fair—as his grandmother, Hervor, had been.

"Good," I said simply.

"What of you, Ervie? Aside from the bumps and scrapes, are you well? We have all worried for you. Did you find what you were looking for?" Elan asked.

Angantyr lifted Elan's hand and kissed it. "You are right to ask. I'm sorry, Ervie. My mind is…distracted."

"You have much to consider, Cousin."

"Did you find King Ormar?" Angantyr asked.

"I did," I said. Unbidden, a smile danced across my lips.

Angantyr did not notice, but Elan raised an eyebrow at me and then smiled lightly.

"And what the gods sent you for?" Angantyr asked.

"I was trained to use my father's sword," I told him. "That, and in the ways of the people of the Myrkviðr."

"I hope this means we have an emissary to the king after this. Will you be accepted by their people again?"

"Yes. I hope to return to them. The truth is, we will all need one another very soon."

"Have the Gauls tried to attack the Myrkviðr as well?" Angantyr asked.

"Not the Gauls," I said, then inhaled deeply. "I hate that I have ridden here only to bring you more bad news."

"You do nothing without consideration first, Ervie. If there is news I must hear, then tell me."

I took a deep breath and then began. "Ormar's people have faced many attacks on their eastern border. But it has only recently become clear by whom and why. Have you heard of a people called the Huns?"

"Gizer has spoken of them. They are a nomadic horse people to the east."

"They are led by their prince, Hlod, and they are pushing west. Thus far, they have not been able to pass the Myrkviðr, but they are determined to find a way."

"Does King Ormar need reinforcements? Is he asking for help?"

"There is a dís who protects the Myrkviðr, but her charms cannot hold Prince Hlod forever. He is *special*. But it is not the Myrkviðr he seeks. It is his birthright."

Angantyr's brow scrunched up as he scowled. "What do you mean, Ervie?"

"Cousin, I've met Hlod, fought him. He... He has amber-colored eyes and calls himself a son of Heidrek."

Angantyr was still for a long moment, then asked, "He claims to be my father's son?"

"Yes. Son of Heidrek and a Hunnish princess."

Angantyr sat back in his seat. His eyes went to the small brazier sitting on the center of the table. He stared at it for a long time, then said, "My father has many bastards. I met some of them in Skagen. It was an unspoken thing between us, brothers but not brothers. Harald paid a lot of silver to keep people quiet. But this is something other."

"Yes. He is the grandson of the Hunnish king."

"And by rights, an heir to Grund and Bolmsö. And if Heidrek had lived, my father would have taken the throne upon Harald's death—Halfdan or not. This Hlod could try to stake his claim here as well."

I nodded.

"How long do I have?" Angantyr asked.

"Not long."

"We must get the Gauls in hand as quickly as possible, then. I plan to ride as soon as the jarls and their men arrive."

"You should leave some men in Arheimar... just in case," I told my cousin. "Ormar's warriors have the way barred for now, but Hlod keeps raiding, and Ormar is injured."

"Injured? How badly?"

I sucked in my bottom lip and willed my emotions not to betray me. "He will recover."

"Does Ormar have any sons?"

"No."

I could see Elan looking at me, but I didn't meet her gaze. Angantyr usually didn't miss the shifts in my mood, but he was distracted. The loss of Svafa weighed heavily on him. Until he avenged her death and that of those he cared for, nothing would be right with him. But that focus would make him blind to other things.

"How is he, Ervie? Can we work with him? Will he ally with us?" Angantyr asked.

"He is stubborn and difficult, but he will see the benefit of an alliance—with some convincing."

Angantyr nodded. "Good."

"Prince Angantyr," a voice called from the door. "The gythia is here to see to Lady Ervie."

Angantyr turned to me. "Let us leave you now. There is time for talk of war tomorrow."

With that, Elan and Angantyr departed. After they had gone, a dark-robed priestess, her face painted with kohl, runes sketched on her forehead, entered. "Reindeer Princess. I am Morda. I understand you are injured."

"Just a twisted ankle."

"And a black eye and scratched arms, hands, and who knows where else. And here, they told me you trained at the dísarsalr," she said with a smirk.

"Yes, I did."

"Then you already know what I am going to tell you."

"It is worse than it looks."

"It is. Now, let's adjourn to a chamber and see what we can do to patch you up so you can continue limping and lying without damaging your foot forever."

CHAPTER 4

The priestess and I made our way to a small but comfortable chamber that Angantyr had readied for me. The great hall of Arheimar was cozy, much like Ormar's hall. The place was always open to the people. As jarl, Angantyr had endeared his people to him. His hall felt like a home, as did the chamber he'd designated for me. The room had one small bed tucked into a nook in the wall. One end of the room was decorated with a wooden relief depicting an eight-legged horse—Sleipnir, the child of Loki. A brazier burned at the center of the room. Beside it were two chairs. As the priestess got to work heating water and crushing herbs, I lowered myself into one of the chairs. I knew she was making a paste for my wounds, based on the smell of the dried leaves and berries.

I carried many of the same herbs in my pack, but I had been in too much of a hurry to bother to tend to myself.

She set a tonic over the fire to warm, then wet a cloth. "Your eye looks like the sunset in winter: deep purple, dark blue, and yellow. This will sting, but we must clean the wound."

I closed my eyes and then braced myself.

"They tell me you were in the Myrkviðr. Is that true?"

"It is."

"And these wounds? Were you injured in battle? Few go to the Myrkviðr and survive."

"I'm afraid these bruises come from nothing so honorable. I was thrown by my horse and battled with a jumble of rocks."

The priestess chuckled. "Then the Myrkviðr turned you back."

I tried to smile, but the tonic stung. "Not quite."

The priestess blotted my brow. "Okay. You can open your eye now. Let me clean these scratches, then I will apply an ointment."

She pushed up my sleeves and began working on my hands.

"Then you *did* make your way to the hall of the king?"

"Yes."

"What did you find there, if you don't mind me asking?"

I paused a moment, considering the priestess. Had she been any other woman, I would have thought her a gossip. But she was a gythia. Naturally, she would be curious about those who lived on the borders of her world.

"They are a forest people, close with Freyr and Jǫrð."

"With Jǫrð?" she asked. "The mother of Thor is barely remembered these days. It is good to know she is honored. I will not ask how you survived your trials in such a place. You are the daughter of Mjord and Blomma, after all. The most ancient blood in our world runs through your veins. But you must tell me something…"

"If I can."

"Why have they kept their borders closed to us all these years?"

"The same reason we closed ours to the Gauls."

"But the people of the Myrkviðr are the same as us. The Gauls are foreign."

I paused. She wasn't wrong. We *were* one people, as I had pointed out to Ormar. "King Ormar has no wish to be dragged into the problems of our world. He is like the eccentric who lives in the mountains outside the village: one of the village but apart. All things considered, he is not entirely wrong to turn our people away. He has no wish to be involved in war. Keeping themselves separate has protected them from many of our conflicts. As it is, he has his own problems. The Huns beat on his borders."

The priestess paused. "The Huns?"

I nodded.

"I have seen visions," she said, setting aside the cloth. "Horses on the plains and…" Her gaze narrowed. "To our east, there is a border village. The gods whisper about it. I have seen *you* there."

"Me?"

She nodded. "I was not surprised when they told me the Reindeer Princess had come. The Gauls have broken our world here, but in my dreams, fires burn in the east. You must be wary, Princess."

"As long as I don't run into any more jumbles of rocks, I should be fine."

At that, the priestess laughed. "Let us hope. Now, that ankle," she said, then reached down and gently removed my boot.

The ride had done little to help my foot. I was not surprised to see that the ankle was swollen, and the rest of my foot now purpling like a fruit. The priestess gently felt the bones. Her brow scrunched up as she worked. Finally, she sat back.

"I don't believe it's broken. I would tell you to rest,

but the warhorns are already calling. I will bind it as best I can and advise you to prop it up when possible. You will be able to walk on it soon if you treat it gently." She pointed to my bow, which I'd lain on the bed. "That. Not the sword. Keep your distance. You are a warrior, but your body is mortal. Remember that, Princess."

"I understand," I told her, feeling a pinch of frustration in my stomach. *Why now?* The refrain kept repeating over and over in my head. *Why now?*

The priestess got to work wrapping my ankle, then applied salve to my cuts. How had a simple tumble managed to cause so much damage?

I was lucky that Narfi had come along when he did.

Or was I?

The child was not human. That much was certain. A vætt of the Myrkviðr, or of the borderlands between our world and Ormar's, perhaps. Or maybe...from elsewhere. Either way, he seemed to have his own agenda. Had causing me to fall been part of it?

I frowned. "Wise one, a question, if I may?"

"Of course."

"If a vætt is tied to a piece of land...say, for instance, a river, can it leave that place? Could the vætt of a river appear hundreds of miles away from its home?"

"You evoked the name of Jǫrð. As her followers know, the earth is all one. Snow melts and becomes streams, streams flow into rivers, rivers flow into oceans and become the lifeblood connecting this fast world. The land is interconnected, the meat and bones of a singular body."

"What if a vætt is charged with a duty, such as protecting an object or person?"

"Then it will go where that object or person goes."

"I see. Thank you, holy one."

The priestess chuckled. "You are plagued by shadows, Reindeer Princess."

"And rock piles."

She laughed. "Yes, and rock piles," she said, then rose. "I have mended things as best I can. Mind what I've said. Rest. As much as you can, rest. There is a tonic here that will ease the pain from within. I trust you already know the herbs."

I nodded. "Yes. Thank you for your healing hands... and your advice."

She inclined her head. "Stay safe in the lands of the Gauls, Princess. We will need you in Arheimar again."

"Your dreams?"

"My dreams," she said with a nod. "May Freyr and Jǫrð keep you." With that, the priestess packed up her things and left.

After she had gone, I sat with my ankle propped up by the fire. I poured myself a cup of the tonic and then sat back, sipping the hot brew. I ruminated on her words.

All my life, I had heard stories about the vætt of Bolmsö. It had manifested in the time of Hervor and had fought at her side. That vætt had one purpose: to protect the island's rightful jarl. And the last time he had manifested, his name was Utr.

CHAPTER 5

I took some rest in the chamber, then rejoined the others in the great hall, limping along with my walking stick. The tonic the priestess had given me included healing herbs and roots and berries that made my head feel light and lessened the pain.

When Angantyr saw me, he smiled in greeting, but a worried flicker also shot across his face as he eyed my wounds.

Why now?

Magnus trotted beside me, his tail wagging.

Moving slowly, I settled in on the bench beside Angantyr and propped my foot up on a stool.

"The priestess has seen to your wounds?" he asked, eyeing me over.

"I am well enough, Cousin. You don't need to worry."

"Perhaps not, but I will anyway," he told me.

I chuckled.

The jarls and their warbands arrived throughout the day. Those jarls who lived on the coast would sail directly to Samso. Warriors began to collect in the city of Arheimar by the hundreds. By nightfall, Arheimar was teeming with people. The three jarls with holdings closest to Angantyr met with my cousin in the hall.

I lingered, listening to their stories.

Skagen had been reduced to little but ash. The ships had burned at the port. The Gauls had attacked by land and sea, half of their forces crossing into the city from the south. The rest had sailed in, sacking the harbor.

Harald had lost everything, including his life.

Why hadn't he seen the attack coming?

Had there been no warning?

Angantyr listened to the jarls as they shared their thoughts on the best attack route against the Gauls.

"Angantyr," Jarl Njal, a hulking man, began, "won't the Gauls expect us to sail the river?"

Angantyr nodded. "They will. We must make our plans with this in mind."

"Will King Hofund come?" Jarl Torel asked.

Angantyr shifted. "Grund has promised forces."

Canute, Harald's warrior, merely grunted.

Grund promising forces meant Hofund had not said if *he* would come. Surely, he would, though, wouldn't he? It was well known that Hofund had lost his heart for battle after losing his sons and wife, but still. Angantyr was his grandson, and Harald had been a good friend and ally. In any case, Loptr would be there—I hoped. That said, Hofund could easily send Jarls Hakon and Halger in his stead. The twin jarls were a menace and always looking for a reason to fight, whereas Hofund and Loptr were less inclined.

"The Gauls... What do we know?" Jarl Knud asked.

"Jarl Erlaug sent word that the Gauls have spies all along the river," Angantyr said. "And they have a large warband encamped in the forests outside of the village of Nordkehdingen. They are waiting for us."

Jarl Knud nodded. "That presents a problem. The river is the easiest way into their lands."

"Yes," Angantyr agreed.

"But if their forces are waiting for us in Nordkehdingen, doesn't that leave their capital undefended?" I asked.

Everyone turned toward me.

"Indeed, it does," Angantyr said, a smile spreading across his face.

I looked toward Elan. "Is there a way into the capital besides the river? Something by land?" I asked.

"There is a way, but it is not easy," Elan said. "There are marshlands to the east. They are impassible to most. But the people who live in Trave know the way."

"Can we find a guide?" Jarl Njal asked.

"As I said," Elan said with a grin. "The way is impassible to most. But I am from Trave. Bring me a map."

We spent the rest of the night poring over the map of the lands surrounding the Gaulish capital of Holmgarth. What details our map lacked, Elan provided. I watched as the jarls considered the priestess. I could see in their eyes that they didn't entirely trust her. But I could see more. Elan and Angantyr loved one another. Their feelings for one another had been smothered in the presence of Hergarth, but now... Elan had saved Angantyr's life. Now, she would save us all.

"We can only hope the other kings bring us the forces we need to pull off your plan," Jarl Knud told Angantyr, his arms crossed over his chest.

"Gizer will come," Njal said affirmatively.

"Yes. He is a good king. He will come to our aid. But as for Grund and Uppsala... We have no way to know if it will be one ship or a fleet. Harald lost much of the goodwill of his allies over the years," Knud said sourly.

"As he deserved," Jarl Torel agreed. "But Uppsala would not stand if not for Harald. They owe a debt, even if they do not wish to pay it."

"My son died on the marshes before Uppsala. We paid to protect Jorund's city with our blood," Canute said.

The others nodded in agreement.

"As for Grund, Hofund is the grandfather of our prince. They will come," Jarl Torel said.

"And even if they do not, we have our prince," Halstein, one of the young warriors who rode with Angantyr, said. "With Angantyr leading us, the Gauls are not long for this world."

"May Freyr hear your words," Jarl Njal said. "Skol."

"Skol," we answered.

As I drank, I looked over my cup at my cousin. He kept his gaze low. Angantyr was modest. A lifetime of being neglected by a man who should have cared for him, he paid little attention to his own achievements. Everything Angantyr had ever done was in Harald's name—even if they had been done by Angantyr's sword. I was glad to see the jarls understood that. Even if my cousin did not see his glory, his men did. They put their faith in him. They would follow him to the end.

Freyr, I hope you see it too.

As the night drew on, the hall grew more crowded. Feeling sorer than I cared to admit, I left the great hall and made my way to my chamber. The room was dark. The sounds of the hall faded into the background. I pulled off my vest and unbelted my weapons. I was about to lie down when I heard an odd scratching sound at the door. I opened the door to find Magnus on the other side.

"Good evening," I told him with a grin.

The wolf cocked his head to the side and then trotted in. He circled the room once, then hopped up on the bed.

Chuckling, I closed the door.

Lowering myself into the seat, I sat by the fire and worked on unbraiding my hair. I had removed as much of the leaves and debris from my locks as possible, but once my hair was unbraided, I saw I still had some nature with me.

I brushed out my long, ebony locks and then shimmied out of my clothes. I had spent too many days in the saddle. Pulling on a simple tunic, I slipped into the bed with the wolf, shoving him with my backside to make room for me.

"You are worse than Dag," I told him, but as the words slipped out of my mouth, I felt a pang of guilt.

Dag.

The turn of events in the Myrkviðr had shifted my world in all new directions. I had left Skagen wondering if I had been wrong to push Dag away. And now… In the forest, I'd grown to understand myself better. I had pushed Dag away, just like I'd done to everyone else.

When I finally started letting people in, it was Ormar who was there.

It was Ormar whom I loved.

But Dag...

I closed my eyes, and pressed my cheek against the wolf's back.

"Aye, Magnus," I whispered. "The human heart is a wild thing."

CHAPTER 6

The following morning, I woke to a knock on the door. I woke with my head feeling heavy. The tonic the priestess had given me had done its job. I had slept deeply.

"Lady Ervie?" a young female voice called. "I'm Tove, attendant to Elan. She asked me to come check on you."

Apparently, Magnus had left in the middle of the night. I had no recollection of letting him out, but that didn't surprise me. I didn't even dream the night before.

Using the wall to balance, I made my way across the room to the door.

Why did everything hurt?

I opened the door to reveal a young woman with long, curly brown hair on the other side. Dressed in a slate-blue hangerok gown, she stood there with clean linens, including a new tunic, in her hand. "Elan thought you might like someone to attend you this morning."

"That was kind of her. Thank you. Please come in." I stepped aside and went to the chair to get my walking stick. I set my foot tenderly on the ground as I went, trying a bit of weight on it. It held, but it hurt. How many times had Norna, the head priestess of the dísarsalr, treated such wounds at the dísarsalr in Grund? She always told people to stay off the foot as much as possible. But from shield-maidens to farm maids, no one ever listened.

"If they walk on that foot, they will limp the rest of their lives," Norna would say with a shake of the head.

But no one listened to her.

And Norna was always right.

Now, I understood the stubborn streak I'd seen in the others. There was no time to be sick. I did not have the luxury of an injury. A bath, however...

"Is Angantyr making ready to depart?" I asked.

Tove shook her head. "Not until tomorrow."

I nodded. "Could you help me with a bath if you aren't busy? I took a tumble down a hill, and half the forest floor is still in my hair."

She chuckled. "Of course. Rest, Lady Ervie, I will see to it," she said, setting the bundle she carried aside, then departed.

Hobbling to my packs, I began pulling out herbs. I

emptied the tonic the gythia had prepared the day before, cleaned the pot, then set a fresh brew over the fire. As it steeped, I eased myself into the chair once more.

I looked around the small room. Braziers hung from the ceiling, illuminating the cozy space. Exhaling deeply, I realized I felt at ease here. Even with the Gauls threatening war and Hlod riding west, I felt safe in Angantyr's hall.

Maybe it was because I felt safe with Angantyr.

Loptr never understood me.

In Grund, I didn't feel at home.

But Angantyr was different. Our past pains bled the same. No wonder I felt at home in the world my cousin had created.

Tove returned a short while later with a bathing tub. Once the water was ready, she helped me ease myself in without banging my ankle. I was not surprised to discover numerous other black-and-blue marks on my body. I sprinkled healing herbs into the water.

"Can I help you wash your hair?" Tove asked.

"Be careful. You may find mushrooms and acorns there," I joked, trying to put my focus on anything other than my throbbing foot.

She chuckled, then said, "Lady Ervie, your back is badly scratched. Are you sure you didn't do battle with blackberry bushes?"

"If only."

I have never been one for pampering, but I was tired, achy, and just wanted a rest before I had to face whatever would come next. Closing my eyes, I let the girl work. She helped me take care of the wounds on my back and then washed out my long locks. When she was done, she looked over my clothes.

"Elan sent along the new tunic, but I think it will be easier to manage your leg in a gown."

"In my packs," I said, gesturing.

Tove nodded, then fingered through my things, setting out the red gown I'd been given in the Myrkviðr.

"I will launder the rest and have them back to you today. Do you want me to stay to help dress you?"

"No, I will rest here awhile," I said.

"Very well," Tove replied, then went to the fire and poured me a tonic. "I recognize the herbs by their smell. Morda is my mother. I grew up in the temple."

"But you don't serve there?"

Tove shrugged. "The gods do not whisper to me. I had hoped to be a good maid to Princess Hergarth, but... Prince Angantyr asked me to stay to attend the priestess Elan."

"I suspect you will be much happier looking after Elan."

"Yes, for as long as she is here. They say Angantyr

will rebuild Skagen and take the Gaulish priestess there and wed her," she said leadingly.

The truth was, I didn't know what Angantyr planned, so I said, "All things shall be as the gods will."

"Yes, Reindeer Princess, you're right. I'll return later, then. Do you need anything else?"

"No. Thank you."

"The others are in the hall when you are done. The prince is readying everything to depart in the morning."

"Thank you, Tove."

"You're welcome," she said, then departed.

I slipped down into the warm water, relishing the feeling on my tired and aching limbs.

What would Angantyr do now? I had not considered it. Skagen had never been a home for him, but it was the heart of his realm. Poised on the shore, it was strategic in every way...except when facing raiders from the east.

I exhaled deeply and slipped under the water.

Enveloped in the hot liquid and relishing the silence, my mind drifted toward Ormar again.

Ormar...

How was he feeling? Was his wound healing?

Ormar...

I sent my thoughts spiraling toward him, wanting him to feel that I was thinking of him, to send my love to him.

Ormar...

Using seidr, I sent my hugr searching. The distance was great between us, but I'd sought Loptr this way in the past, even before I'd gone to the Myrkviðr to learn.

Ormar. Ormar, can you feel me? Can you hear me?

I searched for him in the darkness, but I could feel Asa's charm separating their world and ours. Summoning up my strength, I pushed though it and continued my search.

Ormar...

I felt pulled forward. Suddenly, I sensed I was in Ormar's hall.

"Ervie?"

Ormar.

"Ervie? Are you all right? Where are you?"

"Arheimar. Ormar, are you well? Your wounds."

"I am healing."

Ormar... My thought came as a whisper. Already, I could feel the tie between us fading as my lungs burned for air. I didn't want to let go, but I was not strong enough to hold on. *Ormar...*

"Ervie... I ache for you."

"Ormar..."

Gasping, I lifted myself from the water and inhaled deeply. My lungs burned. I sat still for a long moment. "Ormar," I whispered to the absent man. "Ormar, I love you."

CHAPTER 7

After spending the morning in quiet, drinking tonic and resting my foot, I finally rose from my bath and made my way to the main room of the great hall. Jarls Njal and Torel were there with their men, but there was no sign of Angantyr and the others. Still using my walking stick, I made my way outside.

The city was bustling. Everywhere I looked, I saw warriors readying themselves to ride to do battle. The sound of hammers pounding on metal, axes being sharpened, and loud, boisterous voices filled the air. I scanned the crowd, finding Elan making her way toward me. She was wearing leather riding trousers and a tunic. Her hair had been pulled back into a bun. On her belt, I noted a slingshot. A pouch full of ammo hung there as well.

"For hares?" I asked, pointing.

She gave me a slight smile. "What kills hares can work just as well for men," she said, joining me. "How is your foot this morning?"

"Finally letting me put some weight on it."

"I don't suppose I need to caution you against using it. You know, you *could* stay in Arheimar, keep it safe in Angantyr's absence."

"I didn't know you were funny, Priestess," I replied with a wry grin, giving her a knowing look.

She merely chuckled in reply.

"I didn't have the chance to thank you for what you did for Angantyr," I told her. "My cousin has had few people he could genuinely rely on in this life. The fact that you would step between Angantyr and your princess... You have my thanks."

"I love him. It is nothing to ask."

I smiled. "I also love him, so you will get my thanks whether you want it or not."

The priestess chuckled.

Elan dug into the bag hanging on her shoulder and pulled out an apple which she handed to me. "A gift from Nantosuelta."

"Nantosuelta. The goddess who carries the bee hive?"

"You know her?"

"We've met."

Elan grinned. "From the winding stream to the sun-drenched valley."

Confused, I shook my head.

"That is the greeting the followers of Nantosuelta share when they meet."

"From the winding stream to the sun-drenched valley."

Elan nodded. "Nantosuelta is the lady of the earth, fire, bees, and...apples," she said, gesturing to the apple. "I'm not surprised Nantosuelta has appeared to you."

"And why is that?"

"I heard a story that your ancestor tasted a dragon's blood, and now you understand the song of birds. Is it so?"

"That's the story."

"Now *you're* being funny, Princess. That's not what I asked."

I smirked at her. "It is so."

"Nantosuelta transforms into a crow on the battlefield so she can help her chosen warriors. So, Reindeer Princess, I suggest you listen to her song. From the winding stream to the sun-drenched valley."

I grinned at her. "From the winding stream to the sun-drenched valley."

Behind Elan, Angantyr made his way up the road toward us. His boots and trousers were covered in mud, and he had splatters of mud on his cheeks. His weapons hung from his belt. He paused beside Elan, wrapping his arm around her waist.

The priestess took another apple from her bag and handed it to him with a wink.

He chuckled lightly, then turned to me. "Ervie... I'm glad to see you up and looking well. Last night, I stopped by your chamber to bank up your fire only to find Magnus taking up most of your bed. You spoil him."

"He's a good bed warmer."

"Magnus always leaves me for Ervie," Angantyr told Elan.

Elan chuckled.

"Things look well in hand here," I said, scanning the square.

My cousin nodded. "We will ride at first light tomorrow," he said, then paused, looking me over. "Ervie..."

"Say nothing, Cousin. We will ride at first light."

"The ankle?"

"It will hold."

Angantyr nodded once.

"She's lying, you know," Elan told him.

"I know, but I won't press her." Angantyr looked over his shoulder. "I need to go to the stables."

"I'll come with you," Elan told him.

I gestured back to the hall. "I need to prepare."

"We'll drink well tonight, Reindeer Princess,"

Angantyr said with a grin, then the pair turned and headed off.

I returned to the hall. There, I found the warriors eating, drinking, talking, and sharpening their weapons. I slipped past them, grabbing a small round of bread and a hunk of cheese, sticking them in my pocket with the apple, then retreated to my chamber.

Grabbing my quiver and fletching supplies, I sat down by the fire.

I had several unfinished arrows that needed work. As I laid out my equipment, I studied the wood and materials I had brought from the Myrkviðr.

The urge to go back tugged on my heart so hard that it surprised me.

I touched the cuff of my gown.

I had been wandering for years, drifting from place to place, never finding anywhere I belonged. Now…

In the hall, loud laughter rose up.

I closed my eyes.

Jǫrð, help me end this quickly so I can go home.

THAT NIGHT, AFTER I HAD PREPARED MY GEAR, I REJOINED the others in the hall. They were drinking and dancing until late in the night. Once the moon was high, the gothar arrived. One of the priests made his way to Angantyr.

"We are ready for you, Prince."

Angantyr nodded.

The others, noting the presence of the gothar, quieted.

"Arheimar," Angantyr called. "My brothers, my sisters, my friends. Tomorrow, we will begin our journey to Samso and then on to vengeance. Come, let us honor the gods and seek their favor."

At that, the crowd cheered, and Angantyr motioned for everyone to join him outside. Setting my walking stick aside, I limped alongside the others to the square beyond the hall. The gothar had cleared the bodies of the Gauls. In their place was a massive boar. The creature shrieked and whined, pulling at the ropes that held him.

That explained why Angantyr was covered in mud earlier.

"Come with me, Cousin," Angantyr whispered to me.

I nodded to him, and then Angantyr and I went with the priests.

An elder gothi, a tall man with long, silver hair, held a blade that shimmered in the firelight. Morda stood near him.

The warriors gathered before us. A bonfire had been lit. The boar grunted and squealed, but it had been tied to a peg and was guarded by two of Angantyr's men.

Magnus came and stood beside us. Elan stood at the front of the crowd, watching.

Angantyr stepped forward. "Friends, in the morning, we will set out to join with the other great warriors of our lands to avenge the death of King Harald. A great insult has been done to our people in the deaths of the king, his wife, his son, Lady Svafa, and all the good people of Skagen. A reckoning will fall upon the Gauls for their barbarity. We will avenge my grandfather, and when it is done, we will rebuild the great city of Skagen!"

At that, the crowd cheered.

"Our king!"

"Angantyr, you are our king!"

"King Angantyr!"

Angantyr raised his hands. "Until my kin are avenged, I will not take the title and crown of king. I will earn the honor to stand for you. I am my mother's son. When the blood of the people of Skagen has been avenged, then—and only then—if I am found worthy in the eyes of the gods, will I accept that mighty duty. But that is what comes *after*. Tonight, we must call upon the gods to grant us favor in the war ahead."

Angantyr turned and gestured to the elder gothi.

Behind the priest, three young gothar beat a drum rhythmically. Morda lifted a horn to her lips and sounded it.

"Great Freyr," the gothi called, raising his hands. "See

us here in Arheimar. We honor you, Lord. Honorable Freyr, the wealth and prosperity of your people has been wounded by the Gauls. The blood of our people has been spilled. Foreign invaders have burned and looted our lands, attacked our temple, and insulted all the gods. Freyr, your devoted servant, Prince Angantyr, will lead our people into battle. Bless him. Bless his warband. Bless the Reindeer Princess who fights at his side. Bless all our men and women. We call upon you, Lord."

Behind the gothi, the drum beat rhythmically, the priests chanting the name Freyr with each beat.

The crowd soon joined in, everyone calling the name of the Vanir god.

Freyr.

Freyr.

Freyr.

Freyr.

I closed my eyes, swaying with the rhythmic beat.

Freyr... Help me protect your people and your sacred lands. Be with us tomorrow and henceforth.

The gothi stepped toward the boar.

The creature squealed, his handlers holding him tightly.

When the gothi lifted his knife, the drums went silent.

"Lord Freyr, we make this sacrifice in your name," the gothi called, then slid the holy blade across the creature's throat.

It let out a single squeal and then dropped to its front knees.

Morda placed a large wooden bowl on the ground under the boar to collect the blood. When the bowl was full, she rose. Morda came to stand before Angantyr.

"Mark yourself as Freyr's warrior," she told him.

Dipping his fingertips into the blood, Angantyr traced blood from his brow to his chin.

The priestess turned to me.

"And you, Reindeer Princess," she said.

I nodded, then did the same, marking myself on my cheeks.

The priestess made her way through the crowd, beginning with the jarls.

Angantyr stepped before the crowd once more.

"I stand here before you with a promise. I *will* restore our honor. I pledge it to you. May all the gods hear my oath. In Freyr's name!"

"In Freyr's name!" we called in reply.

I bent my gaze toward the fire burning at the center of the square.

Freyr.

Speak.

Show them you are here.

Show them you hear their words.

Show them, Freyr. I implore you.

My head spun, and my eyes began to see in double.

My spirit felt loose, like I was half in this world and half in another. I stepped before the flames. I reminded myself that fire was simply an element of the earth. Like wind and rain, it could be summoned and controlled.

Freyr, speak to them through the flames. Use me. Together, we can show them that you are with us.

"Great Freyr," I called. "The warriors of Arheimar call upon you. Ancestors, we call upon you. Freyr, see our sacrifice made in your name. Bless our blades, our shields, our arrows, our axes. We fight in your name! Freyr, show us you are with us," I called loudly, lifting my hands into the sky.

At that, the fire at the center of the square roared upward into a towering funnel of flame. The spiral twisted into the night's sky, illuminating the crowd for a long moment before dying back once more.

The sight struck the crowd into momentary silence, then they began to cheer, a thrill of excitement washing over them.

"Lord Freyr has spoken. The gods are with us, Arheimar," I called to the crowd.

"Ready your blades. Tomorrow, we set forth for vengeance!" Angantyr added.

"An-gan-tyr, An-gan-tyr, An-gan-tyr," they called, unsheathing their weapons and lifting them into the night's sky as they screamed.

I watched as the last sparks drifted upward. The

spiral of fire, Freyr's promise, dissipated into the night sky.

A great sense of gratitude washed over me. While Freyja never answered my call, Freyr had.

Great Lord Freyr, thank you. Thank you, Freyr, for placing your faith in Angantyr.

"*Ervie.*

"*Queen of the Myrkviðr.*

"*My faith is in* you."

CHAPTER 8

The following morning, we woke before the sun and prepared to ride. Leaving my walking stick behind, I redressed for battle and made my way to the stables, doing my best not to limp too obviously. Once I got into the saddle, I would be fine. At least, that was what I told myself.

Just outside the stables, I found Utr saddled and ready to go.

"Miss me, you mischief maker?" I asked the horse. He replied by bumping me with his head in a playful manner. I stroked my hand down his face. "No excitement over deer or vætts today, please."

Securing my equipment, I mounted and joined Angantyr, who was already in his saddle.

He smiled when he saw me. "Eye looks better today," he told me. "Now you look like you painted one eye with kohl but forgot the other," he said with a playful grin.

I laughed. "And here I thought it made me look more alluring."

"You need no colors on your face to make you alluring, Cousin."

"And yet, I remain unmarried," I quipped.

"I tried it once. Can't say I recommend it."

I laughed. "Will you try again, Cousin?"

His gaze went to Elan. "Yes, when this is done. Yes."

"Good."

"And you? All the sons of Gizer love you, but I think Dag—"

"Dag. Yes. But..." I began, then paused. Of all the people in the world, there was no one I trusted more than Angantyr. "Things became *complicated* in the Myrkviðr."

"Complicated how?"

"With... With King Ormar."

"King Ormar?" Angantyr asked in surprise.

I nodded.

"Hmm," Angantyr mused. "I can't say I approve."

"He is not what you expect."

Angantyr grinned. "I jest. Ervie, if you are fond of him, then I'm sure he is a man of worth. I only say that because I was planning to ask you to take over the rule in Arheimar. If you become queen of the Myrkviðr, there is no way you will agree," he said with a laugh. "In regard to Ormar, now I am only more eager to meet him."

"You want me to rule Arheimar?"

Angantyr nodded. "It is my hope you would be willing to look after the people here, to become jarl. I know Hofund pushed you to rule Bolmsö. I won't try to guilt you into anything, Ervie. There are many good warriors here in Arheimar, and, no doubt, one of the prominent families will be glad to take on the jarldom. But Arheimar has been my home. There is no one I trust with it more than you."

"I am honored by your offer."

"Arheimar's borders lie on Ormar's," Angantyr said, then grinned. "If you are even slightly inclined, I'm sure something can be arranged...complications or not."

"Let's deal with the Gauls first."

"As you wish, Cousin."

A moment later, Halstein joined us. "The warriors are ready, Prince."

Angantyr nodded. He scanned the crowd, his gaze stopping when he looked toward the stables. There, I saw Elan mounted on an ash-gray steed.

"Sound the horn," Angantyr told Halstein.

The call of the warhorn echoed across the valley.

A moment later, horns sounded, answering the call.

"For Harald! In Freyr's name!" Angantyr called. With that, we made our way from Arheimar toward the harbor city of Keil. From there, we would sail on to Samso.

As we rode, I considered Angantyr's offer.

He was right. With Loptr eager to rule Grund upon Hofund's death, Hofund had suggested many times that I could rule in Bolmsö, the ancestral home of the first Hervor. But I never felt right about it. The people of Bolmsö ruled themselves without interference from outsiders—which I was. I had considered rebuilding my father's jarldom in Hreinnby, but the reindeer were gone. There was nothing there. I had always assumed I would just live my days in Gizer's hall. That was until I had gone to the Myrkviðr. Now, all I wanted to do was go back.

But this world also owned pieces of me as well. Angantyr most of all. The fact that he would trust me to rule the most important city in his lands upon his ascent to the throne was something I could not ignore. My cousin was dear to me. He wouldn't want me to say yes just to please him, but his offer appealed to me.

Too much was uncertain right now.

And with every mile between Arheimar and Samso, my old world drew closer.

We rode throughout the day and into the night. Our warband made camp late that night in a valley near a stream. When I stopped the horse, I hopped off, momentarily forgetting my ankle.

My body rewarded me with a sharp, painful reminder.

Suppressing a gasp, I held onto the horse's side for a moment as my head swam.

Aye, Freyr. I hope you are watching over me because this foot is a problem.

Once I collected myself, I joined the others.

Men built small campfires to warm themselves and heat their food. The fires dotted the field like a hundred flaming flowers. They sat and sang and drank. Loud voices and boisterous laughter echoed throughout the valley.

"How much farther?" Elan asked as she settled in beside Angantyr.

"We will reach the Keil by midday and arrive at the isle of Samso by nightfall," he told her.

"How are you faring, Ervie?" Elan asked me, gesturing to the foot.

"Barely hurts now."

"Ah," she said, giving me a knowing look. "You should rest all the same."

I nodded. "In a bit."

The jarls joined us, all talking about what they had seen in Skagen.

"It would be wise to rethink the city's shape," Jarl Torel told Angantyr. "It should be more heavily defended. Harald relied too much upon the goodwill of his neighbors."

"Which he did little to cultivate," Jarl Knud added, then turned to me. "They say you were at the court of King Ormar, Ervie. Is that so?"

"It is."

"You must tell us. Is he a threat? What are they hiding in the forest?"

I considered. "They are preserving their way of life, that is all. And they have no wish to be involved in the machinations of our world."

"I cannot fault them there," Angantyr said with a light laugh.

"But are they a threat?" Jarl Knud asked.

"Only to those who threaten them. They are a peaceful people but not to be trifled with."

"Some say they are elves, that their kingdom lies in Alfheim," Eluf, one of Angantyr's warriors, remarked.

"As far as I could see, none of them had pointed ears," I told Eluf with a wink.

At that, the others chuckled.

Angantyr gazed into the fire. "We shall look on King Ormar as a friend. In the future, we may need him," he said darkly.

"Why do you say that, Prince?" Jarl Njal asked.

I could see Angantyr weighing how to answer. "You

never know where enemies may hide," he said simply. "Which is why we should rest."

Jarl Torel nodded. "You are right. Let us leave you."

Eluf rose. "Shall the men prepare you a tent, Reindeer Princess?"

I shook my head. "No. I am content to sleep under the stars. But thank you."

He nodded to me, then he and the others departed.

"We *should* rest," Angantyr said.

"And here I thought you were trying to turn the conversation," Elan told him.

"I was. But we should still rest."

Moving slowly, I rose. Suddenly, I was sorry I hadn't brought my walking stick. "Come on, Magnus," I told the wolf, then pulled out my sleeping roll and shook it. "It will be cold tonight. Fleas and all, you can help me stay warm."

At that, I spread out my mat and lay down. A moment later, the wolf snuggled in beside me.

Sticking my pack under my foot to elevate it, I felt the weight of the ache I'd ignored all day. It hurt more than I cared to admit. A night's rest would help. By midday tomorrow, we would be at sea.

I looked toward the sky, my eyes growing heavy. It had been a long day in the saddle.

Overhead, the stars twinkled silver on a deep blue background.

Ormar...

I closed my eyes.

But as I drifted off to dreams, I realized that every painful step took me farther from Ormar and closer to the life, and the people, I had left behind.

Including Dag.

THE NEXT MORNING, WE SET OFF AGAIN, ARRIVING AT THE port city of Keil on the eastern coast of Jutland. A dozen boats waited to take us on to the isle of Samso. For generations, the isle of Samso was where the kings of our allied countries met during times of war. It was a small island with just a handful of inhabitants who lived in a tiny fishing village. There was nothing remarkable about Samso save one feature. Long ago, the first Hervor's father—also named Angantyr—and his brothers battled a pair of renowned warriors on the island. Angantyr and his brothers perished in the battle and were buried there. Hervor later recovered the dwarven sword Tyrfing from her father's crypt.

There was something ominous about returning to that island.

But for better or worse, we would find out what the gods were planning.

We rode to the crest of the hill overlooking Keil. In the harbor below, the ships rocked in their berths.

But something was different.

Harald's colors were gone.

The warriors of Jutland's sails were dyed green, and on them was painted the boar of Freyr, Gullinbursti.

The same sigil graced my cousin's and his warband's shields.

The message the men were sending my cousin was plain. He was their king now. His patron god was their patron god. And just like that, the people of Jutland— people of the horse for many years under Harald—were now the people of Freyr, united under Angantyr.

"Cousin," I whispered.

Angantyr was always hesitant to reach for power. Harald had undoubtedly beat the motivation to aspire for more from him. But now...

Angantyr looked over the docks. "I... I see."

"Come, Cousin. Your future is waiting."

rriving in Keil, we made ready to sail. Magnus and I boarded the lead ship. Usually, I would row, but I decided to take the time to rest my foot instead. It felt better but was not where it should be in the days leading into battle. I sat at the front of the ship, propping up my foot. Magnus roamed the boat from back to front, greeting everyone, then settled beside me.

Elan joined me.

Angantyr sounded his horn, and we pushed off.

As she stared out at the water, Elan's eyes grew glossy.

"Are you all right?" I asked her.

She gave me a weak smile. "My family history is… messy. Soon, I will face it again," she said, then shrugged. "When I joined the druids, I found solace in

my order, but I was never truly happy. When I saw
Angantyr, the gods whispered to me. I felt drawn in a
way I never had before. But there was nothing to be
done. I watched as my king passed off his daughter,
whom we all knew to be tainted, to your cousin. I could
do nothing. And now… Kjar is despicable. He deserves
what is coming for him, as did Hergarth. Even in the
eyes of our gods, their behavior was abominable. Their
whole family is a blight on our people. King Hrollaug
murdered his way into power, taking what was not his. I
feel no sympathy for that line. But our innocent people,
those who will be killed in the fighting… I only hope my
gods will forgive me."

I considered her words. "If we succeed, Kjar will be
removed from power. Those who survive will find themselves under a different ruler. And those who choose to
fight with your king are, perhaps, no more worthy than
the king himself."

"That's one way of seeing it."

"It's a better one, I think."

She smiled lightly. "Yes," she said, then turned back
and looked at the waves. "Yes."

IT WAS JUST PAST MIDDAY WHEN THE ISLAND OF SAMSO CAME into view.

"Red and white of Grund," Gunnar, one of Angantyr's warriors, said, eyeing the ships in port. "And Grund's jarls have come. There is the tree of Dalr. The silver bow of Hárclett. The twin hammers of Silfrheim. He chuckled, then added, "The Gauls will shite themselves when they face Hakon and Halger in battle."

"Whose sail is that?" Arvid, another of the men, asked, gesturing.

They muttered amongst themselves, uncertain.

"King Jorund of Uppsala," I said.

"By the gods," Arvid replied in surprise. "The king of Uppsala really came?"

"Look, there are the ships of King Gizer," Eluf said.

"They have all come for you, Angantyr," Gunnar called back to Angantyr.

"Of course they have," Eluf said. "Angantyr is our prince and, soon, our king."

My cousin merely gave them a light smile.

My eyes went to the red-and-white sailed ships of Grund, searching for the shape of Loptr. But he wasn't there.

High on the hill above the shore was a city made of tents. There, hundreds—if not thousands—of warriors had gathered.

"Kjar called up a storm over Skagen," Elan said. "But Angantyr has summoned the violence of all of nature."

"Will you not feel sorry for your people, Lady?" Eluf asked her.

Elan flicked her gaze briefly at me, then answered, "I see the gods' plans in all things. We cannot know their reasons, only trust they have them. I don't feel sorry for those whose own actions bring about their own deaths, though I would hope innocent lives will be spared."

At that, the warrior nodded.

Word must have spread that Elan had killed Princess Hergarth to save Angantyr. Otherwise, she would have received a cooler reception from the warband. While the men still eyed her warily, they knew her heart was with Angantyr, so they did not disparage her.

I was glad.

From the shore, I heard the sound of a horn. It reverberated across the coast. Soon, other horns sounded. The music echoed so loud and deep that I was sure it could be heard in Asgard. I envisioned the timbers of Odin's golden hall shaking.

Ormar... Can you see this? Ormar, this is what it means to be one of us. You belong here too.

At the top of the hill, two figures emerged from one of the tents.

His long, brown-and-silver hair blowing in the breeze, I instantly recognized the shape of King Hofund.

Along with him was another tall, thin man with long black hair.

Loptr.

"*Ervie.*"

A smile danced across my face.

"That is King Hofund," Canute told the others. "There, by the tent."

"He's come? Truly?" Eluf said, craning his neck to look.

"May the All-Father be praised," Canute said.

The men guided our ship to shore. The bottom of the ship scraped on the rocky shoreline. Once the boats were settled, we made ready to debark. Magnus jumped from the side of the vessel and ran ashore, looking back expectantly at us. I grabbed my gear and went to the side of the ship. Angantyr helped Elan down, then turned to me.

"Angantyr," I said warningly.

"No protests," he told me, grabbed me by the waist, then carried me to shore, setting me carefully on my feet.

"Angantyr," I said with false fury.

He merely laughed.

We turned toward the tents to see Hofund and Loptr making their way toward us.

Angantyr sucked in a breath, then held out his pinkie to me.

"Not Hervor," Angantyr whispered.

"Not Heidrek," I replied, linking my pinkie with his

and giving it a shake. "You know what, Cousin? I learned something in the Myrkviðr."

"What's that?"

"I will never be Hervor. But I am me, and I am worthy. As are you..."

Angantyr set his hand on my shoulder and gave me a soft smile.

"Ervie," Loptr called, rushing to join us. When he met us, he grabbed me and held me tight. "I dreamed of you."

I wasn't instantly filled with sisterly annoyance for the first time in my memory. I didn't want him to let go. I loved my brother. The pinch of pain, the emptiness, was gone. Instead, all I felt was gratitude for being there with him.

When he finally let me go, he pulled back and studied my face. "Gizer said you went to the Myrkviðr. Everyone told me you might die."

"Such little faith," I said with a grin.

"I told them that. I could feel you there. And as strange as it sounds, you felt happy, even if your face is a mess."

I laughed. "That, you can blame on an inconsiderate horse. But, happy?" I considered the word for a moment. "Yes, I am."

Loptr nodded. "Good."

"Loptr, I'm sorry I—"

"No," Loptr said, silencing me. "No. Don't." Loptr raised his eyebrows and shook his head. "*I* am sorry. I left you on your own, Ervie. I should have been there for you, and I wasn't."

"But, Brother…"

"How about this? Let's both be sorry. We'll just be two very sorry, miserable people who don't deserve anything or anyone. Agreed?"

"Loptr…" I said with a laugh.

He met my gaze. "There are a hundred people here who want to see you. Let us leave off our apologies for now. I'm glad you're here, Sister."

"I'm glad to be here."

"Good, because I will need you in the coming days."

I cocked an eyebrow at him.

"Eyfura is here. I finished her last riddle successfully. Now, I must win Gizer's approval. He loves you like a daughter. You have to convince him to let me wed her."

"How is that my job?"

Loptr laughed. "He likes you much better than me. But you are my sister, so you will be able to sway him."

I chuckled. "As you say."

"Ervie," a soft, masculine voice called.

I looked to find King Hofund there.

"Hofund," I said.

The king gave me a gentle smile and crossed the space between us, pulling me into an embrace. "Ervie…"

"I am glad to see you," I told the king.

He exhaled heavily, and I felt a weight come off him.

He let me go. "As I am to see you," he said, then studied my bruised face. "Are you all right?"

Ever the surrogate father. "Yes."

He nodded.

Hofund had aged in the years that had passed. The lines at the corners of his eyes, across his brow, and near his mouth were deeper and more numerous than they had been. His chestnut-colored hair was more silver than I remembered. Since I had left Grund, age had crept up on the king. But today, he wore his twin hammers at his sides. He had come here to do battle.

"I saw Svafa some months back. She sang for us," I told him. "They say she died bravely, defending her handmaiden so the girl could escape."

Hofund's eyes grew damp with unshed tears. "Then she is with Hervor now."

I nodded. "Yes."

"Grandfather," Angantyr said cautiously. "Loptr."

"Cousin," Loptr said happily, then pulled Angantyr into an embrace, slapping him on the back. "It is good to see you, Angantyr. We have answered your call. Grund is with you," he said, gesturing behind us. "We shall see Harald avenged and you crowned king."

"Thank you, Loptr."

Angantyr turned to Hofund. "Grandfather."

"It is good to see you, Angantyr," Hofund said. For a moment, Hofund hesitated, and then he embraced my cousin. "In blood and honor."

"In blood and honor," Angantyr replied.

After a moment, Hofund let him go.

"Shall we go to the tents? The others are waiting for you," Hofund told Angantyr, gesturing toward the rise.

Angantyr nodded, then reached for Elan's hand.

Magnus ran ahead of us.

We climbed the hill toward the tents. I winced but didn't complain when my ankle protested.

"Ervie," Loptr said in a low voice. "You're limping."

"Just a small injury. Nothing to worry about."

Loptr frowned.

We had almost reached the largest of the tents when someone called out my name from behind me. "Ervie?"

I paused, recognizing the tone.

I turned.

"Dag," I replied, my voice trembling.

Aye, Freyja. Help me.

CHAPTER 10

I stared at the blond-haired warrior. That moment when I had ridden away from Skagen flashed through my mind. Once more, I saw the forlorn look on Dag's face. He loved me. And at that moment, I questioned myself and my feelings.

Dag rushed across the space between us and pulled me into his arms.

"You're alive," he mumbled into my neck. "Thank all the gods. You are alive and back with us."

"Dag," I said gently. Pressed against him, an old familiarity rose up in me. I remembered all those nights together, our jokes and whispered words, the smell and taste of his skin. I'd forgotten how much I adored him.

Adored him.

Loved him.

I had loved him but kept him away from me...just like I'd done with everyone else.

And now...

Now, there was Ormar.

I pulled back. "I'm glad to see you too," I told him.

"If anything could tempt you back, it was this. Come, my family is inside. They will want to see you. Ervie...I missed you so," he said, lifting my hand and pressing it against his lips.

I tried not to flinch but failed. I pulled my hand away.

"Ervie?"

"Angantyr! Ervie!" Gizer called loudly, exiting the tent, his arms in the air. He laughed loudly. "By the gods, well met. And look at this beauty on Angantyr's arm. Come. All of you. Come inside."

I met Dag's gaze. "I *am* glad to see you, Dag."

Dag nodded, but I could see he was confused.

The expression on his face broke my heart.

We joined the others, entering the tent to find Gizer's family, King Jorund of Uppsala, Hofund's jarls, the shield-maiden Sigrun and her family, and so many others. Friends of my mother. Companions of the first Hervor. So many faces... everyone had come to avenge Harald.

They all cheered, calling to Angantyr.

I felt pulled in a hundred directions at once.

"Ervie," Sigrun said, pushing forward to greet me,

her daughter Gida along with her. "By the gods, I am glad to see you. Gizer told us you traveled to the Myrkviðr. We feared you dead."

I smiled at Sigrun, who had been like a second mother to me. "The gods didn't see fit to call me yet," I told her, embracing her.

"Ervie," Gida said, giving me a playful punch on the shoulder. "By Odin, it is good to see you. Ready for a fight?"

"I am. Where is that husband of yours? Has he come as well?"

Gida pointed across the room to Ásbjorn, who sat laughing with Trygve, Gida's father, the other sons of Gizer, and Jarl Leif's son Arngrimir. "He's deep in his mead, but he'll be sober and ready to fight by tomorrow."

I chuckled, then turned back to Sigrun. "I'm glad you're here."

She nodded. "I will be happy to see the Gauls punished for the loss of Svafa. All our hearts were broken to hear the news."

"Yes," I agreed.

"Who is that?" Gida asked, her gaze narrowing as she looked at Elan.

"That is the Gaulish priestess, Elan. She is the reason Angantyr is still alive. And she is a friend…"

"A Gaul *and* a friend? If you say so, Ervie."

"I do," I told her firmly.

"Reindeer Princess," Eyfura said, joining us.

"Princess of Götaland."

Eyfura embraced me. "I told them you wouldn't die. You are too quick for death. Even Hel cannot catch you."

"*You* are calling *me* slippery? You make your father's cunning look common."

Eyfura laughed, then pulled back. "He is the fox; I am only a kit. But alas, I have finally been caught," she said, her gaze going behind me. "Will you wear me as a pelt, Prince Loptr?"

"Hardly. You are an eternal rose, my princess," Loptr replied with a grin.

I looked from one to the other. Their eyes sparkled, the pair truly in love. On the other side of this battle, their future was before them. It was clear that they could hardly wait.

"Come, everyone. Come," Gizer called, waving for us to join him at the table upon which a map of the Gauls' lands had been spread.

Everyone gathered. In the crowd, I spotted Jarl Leif, his brothers Jarls Hakon and Halger, their sons, and the many young warriors I knew from Grund. In a way, it felt like a homecoming. But it was also a reminder of where I wasn't...at Ormar's side. And yet, when Dag slid in beside me at the table, a sense of ease washed over me as it always did, Dag being a steady, calming presence.

"As I look around this table, I feel Harald's absence," Gizer said. "When Grund's lands and jarls were under attack by the sea kings, Harald supported us. When great Uppsala was under attack, Harald was with us. These Gauls will pay the price for taking a great king from us. Now, my friends," Gizer said, slapping his hands together. "Let's make our plans."

With that, the discussion began.

Angantyr stepped forward and leaned against the table, looking at the map. "The Gauls will expect us to come up by the River Elbe, as we did when we avenged the insults upon Jarl Erlaug and Jarl Torsten," Angantyr said, his gaze going to the jarls.

Behind Jarl Erlaug, I saw a shield-maiden I had not noticed before—Gisla, the jarl's daughter we had saved from the Gauls. The proud girl had a fierce expression and a deadly looking sword. She listened intently as Angantyr spoke.

"Their seaboard shoreline is too far from their capital to make any sense for a landing," Loptr added, gesturing to the maps.

Angantyr nodded.

"Should we ride?" King Jorund asked. "Jutland is full of horses."

Angantyr turned and gestured to Elan to come forward.

"There is a river here," Elan said, drawing her finger across the map. "This is the Trave. The head of the river is here, at Lake Trave. It is southeast of King Kjar's capital," she said, pointing to the city's backside. "The lands between the river and the city are rural and marshy. The Elbe is the heart of our lands. They *will* expect you to travel there. They would never expect you to traverse the Trave."

"She is Gaulish. Why should we put our faith in her?" King Jorund asked.

"I am alive because of Elan. Hergarth tried to assassinate me, but Elan ended her. And when this is all done, I will take Elan as my bride," Angantyr replied simply.

"I would never trust a Gaul," Gauti hissed.

"Angantyr's choices are his own to make," I told Gauti, giving him a stern look. "The priestess *can* be trusted," I said, holding Gauti's gaze until he looked away.

"As you say, Ervie," he said, then motioned for Elan to go on.

"Why won't they expect us to come up the Trave, Elan?" Hofund asked.

"You have come to the heart of the problem with this plan, King Hofund. The area between the Trave and the capital is a swamp. Mud and muck. Efforts were made to build a canal, but the bog always swallowed the progress. Ships can journey up the river and make port here, at Lake Trave, but can go no farther inland. There are barely roads between the lake and the city."

"Then how is the river of use to us?" Jarl Hakon asked the priestess.

"I am from Lake Trave. There *is* a path to the city," she said, tracing along the map. "It is rarely used since a person must know the bog. But if you are from the village of Trave, you know it."

"It's a terrible place for an ambush," Hofund said, eyeing the map. "If they discover we are coming from that direction and pin us on the marsh, many men could die."

"Which is why we must distract Kjar's forces, make sure they stay away from the city," Angantyr said. "Jorund's and Gizer's ships will sail the Elbe. I will go with them, along with Jarl Erlaug and Jarl Torsten. They will expect us, so we will give them what they want. But Grund's ships and the rest of my jarls, along with Elan, will sail up the Trave."

"You will not sail with your men?" Gizer asked.

"Ervie will lead my forces. Along with King Hofund and Prince Loptr, she will lead the advance on the city. The rest of us will meet the Gauls on the Elbe. When the Gauls try to retreat to their capital, they will find themselves pinched."

I didn't react, not wanting the others to know that I was only now learning of Angantyr's plan that I would lead his warband. Why me?

I looked at my cousin.

He met and held my gaze.

Angantyr trusted me. That was why...

After a long moment, Gizer grinned. "Good. Good. I like it. It will be a good fight, boys!" he said, slapping Bjarki and Gauti on the backs. "Let's have meat and ale then and make ready. When are we sailing?" he asked Angantyr.

"First light. If the gods are on our side, our plan will succeed," Angantyr said, reaching out and lifting the mug a servant had set in front of him. "For Harald," he said, raising his cup. "For Harald, Aud, Halfdan, Svafa, and all the innocents of Skagen. Skol!"

"Skol!"

CHAPTER 11

With that, the men dispersed to make their plans. Eyfura pulled Elan aside, speaking in a friendly way with the priestess. Leave it to Eyfura to be shrewd enough to see that Elan would need support and friends.

I went to Angantyr's side. "Cousin, you should put one of your jarls in charge. I—"

"Ervie," Angantyr said, leveling his amber-colored eyes on me, his voice low. "There is no one here I trust more than you. No one. Everyone here has their own agenda, but you left the Myrkviðr because you knew I would need you, because you had news that you knew I needed to hear. No one here cares more for me than you."

"Elan..."

"That love is new. But my trust in you… I feel that in my spirit and have felt it all my life."

"Thank you, Cousin. I won't let you down."

Angantyr set his hand on my shoulder. "I know."

"Angantyr," King Jorund called, waving my cousin away.

Angantyr gave me a smile and then departed.

Loptr joined me, handing me a mug of ale.

"So," he said.

"So…"

"Gizer told us where you went and why. But did you find what you were looking for, Sister?"

"I think you already know the answer to that."

"I do, but I wanted to make you say it," he said with a grin as he sipped his ale.

"Stop provoking me. You have Eyfura to torture with word games."

"She's giving me a break. I thought I might sharpen my tongue against you."

"You should be sharpening your blades. I have fought the Gauls before. They are fierce warriors."

"Then I am glad to be fighting under *your* command."

I didn't miss the jealous tone in his voice. Always, Loptr wanted to be the one people noticed.

"The campaign up the Trave will take all of our efforts. You and Hofund are coming as well," I said.

"We are, but Angantyr did not ask our grandfather nor me to lead the advance, did he?"

"No, but you and Angantyr don't know one another well," I said in something of a lie. They didn't know each other well, but that was not the reason why Angantyr had not asked Loptr to lead. Loptr was many things, but the leader of a warband was not one of them. "And it's hardly surprising that Angantyr didn't ask Hofund."

At that, Loptr nodded. "Yes, I suppose you're right."

"I hope Hofund and Angantyr come to an accord. Very soon, we will all need one another."

"Why?" Loptr asked, his tone turning serious.

"Because," I said, then paused, unsure if I should say anything more, but something within me urged me to speak the truth to my brother. I turned my back to the crowd and lowered my voice. "Because Heidrek had another son who will soon come to claim his birthright."

"Bah," Loptr said, waving his hand dismissively. "Heidrek had many bastards. Everyone knows this. He even has two pretty daughters in Grund."

I frowned at Loptr. "This son is no bastard. He is a prince and a legitimate heir."

"A prince? Prince of what?"

"The Gauls are the least of our troubles, Brother. Amongst the Huns is a man named Hlod who is the lawful son of Heidrek and a Hunnish Princess."

"Ervie..." Loptr whispered, his tone indicating he

realized the gravity of the problem. "Is it true? Have you seen this Hun?"

"Yes. I have seen him and fought him. He *is* Heidrek's son."

"You're certain?"

"Those eyes..."

"You must warn Hofund. Don't let him be taken by surprise by this news."

"Yes."

"If this Hlod truly is a prince and Hofund's natural grandson..." Loptr began but left the rest unsaid. If he was Hofund's lawful, natural grandson, that made him heir to Grund and Bolmsö—over Loptr and me, who were only bound to the king by loyalty, not bloodline.

I tapped my mug against Loptr's. "Skol, Brother. Drink tonight and sharpen your blades. In the days to come, you will need them."

AFTER A TIME, THE PARTY TURNED TO DRINK AND SONG. Eyfura and my brother disappeared to a quiet corner. I, too, felt the urge to get away, but not from the crowd and noise—there was nothing unusual about that—but from Dag's lingering gaze.

My heart already hurt.

How could I tell him?

How could I hurt him?

I couldn't stand the idea of it.

So, when Hofund slipped away from the party, I followed.

Stepping out of the tent, I found the king looking across the field where the men's campfires burned.

He turned to me. "Ervie."

"Hofund."

"I was about to go for a walk. Care to join me?"

I nodded.

With that, the two of us turned and made our way away from the party. I tried my best to hide my limp, but failed.

"Your leg," Hofund said.

"I was thrown. It's nothing. Just a little tender."

"Hmm," Hofund mused. I could tell from his tone that he knew I was understating it, but he asked me nothing more. We walked for a time in silence, then Hofund said, "Gizer told us you traveled to the Myrkviðr."

"I did."

"Gizer's sons were lamenting over it, all of them thinking you'd ridden off to your death. But Loptr wasn't worried. Nor was I."

"No?"

Hofund gave me a light smile. "You have always been very determined, even as a child. You would worry your mother, but she knew well enough that your resolve was tempered by level-headedness. She was right. What did you do in the Myrkviðr?"

"I met with King Ormar. He and his people trained me to wield my father's sword...and his magic."

Hofund was silent a moment as he considered, but then he asked, "Did you learn what you wanted to know?"

"I had a start, but the gods saw fit to send me back to my family."

"Will you return to the Myrkviðr when this is done?" This time, I heard a catch in Hofund's voice.

"Yes, but not to run away from something. At least, not this time. This time I am running toward."

"Toward what?"

"King Ormar."

At that, Hofund paused, then laughed. "The gods have their own ways. I am glad for you, Ervie."

I gave him a gentle smile. "Thank you, Grandfather."

At that, Hofund smiled.

We rounded a bend in the island, then hiked up a rise. There, sitting shadowed in the moonlight, was a burial mound. As we approached, flames sprang to life at the entrance to the mound, barring our way. The sight of it was amazing to behold, but even more so because the fire burned blue.

"Of the gods," I whispered.

Hofund stood there, the light of the blue flames reflected on his face. I knew the look on his features. He was thinking of her. "She dared the flames to speak to her father's spirit. From here, she reclaimed the sword Tyrfing."

"What happened to the sword?"

"No one knows but your mother. Blomma took the sword, and it was never seen again."

I looked back at the mound, imagining Hervor braving the flames. Before, I would have felt envious and resentful. Now, I merely felt impressed.

"Did you know her when she came to Samso?" I asked.

"We had met. And I was already in love with her." Hofund laughed.

I stared at the fire. "She was fearless."

"Yes. Reminds me of someone else I know," he said, giving me a wink. "I will honor her father," Hofund said, then left me, making his way to the mound.

I watched as Hofund approached the burial site. He knelt on one knee when he reached it and bowed his head. The blue flames illuminated his face. I could not make out his words, but I heard him speak.

The blue flames danced and then grew quiet, burning down to a slow flicker.

When he was done, Hofund rose.

The fires went dark.

We were alone once more, with only the moon and stars above us.

Hofund rejoined me.

We stood in silence for a long moment. I weighed whether or not to tell Hofund what I had learned of Hlod. We were mere hours before battle. The news would unsettle him, and it had been years since Hofund fought. The idea that something I said could shake him, make him less ready on the battlefield, made me stay silent. There would be time to tell him later. He was dear to me. I would not risk him.

"You want to tell me something," Hofund said, reading my disquiet.

"Yes, but not now."

I could feel him smile in the darkness. "Are you certain?"

"No, but I will stay silent, at least for the moment."

Hofund took my hand and placed a kiss thereon. "Your parents' child... Come, then, Reindeer Princess. Let's rejoin the others before they think the dwarves have stolen us away."

"Have you ever seen a dwarf?" I asked the king as we returned to the tents.

He chuckled lightly. "No."

"Nor I. Nor elves either, although King Ormar claims his father was one."

"Do you believe him?"

"Yes."

"Why?"

"Because I love him."

Hofund chuckled lightly. "I can think of no better reason."

CHAPTER 12

When we finally arrived at the camp, Dag was waiting for me outside the tents. Hofund gave me a knowing glance, then disappeared within.

I went to Dag.

"I looked for you on the tent roof, but no luck," he told me with a grin.

I chuckled. "I went with Hofund."

Dag nodded, then shifted. "Your leg. And Ervie, your face? What happened?"

"Of all things, I got thrown. I banged up my ankle a bit, but it's mending."

"You will need to watch it tomorrow."

I nodded.

We stood in silence for a long moment.

I struggled to find the right words, but Dag spoke first.

"Ervie, I..." he said, then stepped close to me, meeting my gaze. He took my hand. "I've been thinking of you every day since you rode away. I should have stopped you. I wanted to. Whatever you were looking for out there, you didn't need it. Everything you needed was right here. Ah, gods. Ervie, I love you. I missed you so," he said, then pulled me close.

My heart ached. All those old feelings swelled inside me like a river in the springtime. Despite my belief that my feelings for Dag had simply faded in the wake of what had bloomed between Ormar and me, they hadn't. They were still there. I held a deep affection for Dag, a love I never really let myself feel. There had been something blocking me.

Whatever that block was, now...

Now...

Gods, no.

Jǫrð, no.

Freyja, no.

"Dag," I whispered, then stepped back, overcome with a sense of guilt. My loyalty to Ormar swelled within me. I would not disrespect the king I loved.

Dag met my gaze and held it. "I see another man in your eyes. Before you left, we weren't tied to one another, not really. Just jokes and play. But your leaving made me realize how much I love you. I cannot live without you, Ervie. I want you for my wife, Reindeer Princess. You love me. I know you do. Whoever he is, he doesn't know you like I do. I know *everything* about you. I know what every smirk means. I know what you like to eat and what you don't. I know which songs make your foot tap. I know which stories make you laugh. I know that you like to sleep on your left side. I know how you like to be kissed—everywhere. I know what wounds your heart and what moves you. Whoever he is, he doesn't know you like I do."

"Dag…"

"You don't have to say anything. Whoever he is, he doesn't matter to me. He doesn't know you as I do, and in the days to come, you will see I am right. You are different now. I see it in your eyes. You went to the Myrkviðr to reclaim something of your family. You found what you were looking for. That lostness… it's gone. But whoever he was, it wasn't because of him. It's because of *you*. You are home now. That is what is important. You are with your family again. And, soon, you will find your way home to me. I never stopped loving you. And one day, you will ask me to marry you," he said, then gently set his hand on my face, his thumb stroking my cheek.

I closed my eyes and exhaled deeply, relishing the familiar touch.

Yes, this felt like home.

And yet...

Ormar.

Aye, Jǫrð, please help me.

The goddess must have heard my plea because someone emerged from the tent a moment later.

Angantyr cleared his throat. "I'm sorry for the interruption. Ervie, I wanted to discuss the launch plans."

Dag lowered his hand and then clasped my fingers, setting a kiss thereon. "Go on with you, then," he told me with a smile. He turned to Angantyr. "Prince Angantyr," he said, giving him a short bow.

"Prince Dag."

With that, Dag disappeared back into the tents.

Clearing my throat, I tried to master my emotions. Apparently, I was doing an abysmal job.

"All right?" Angantyr whispered to me.

"No."

He laughed lightly. "Aye, Cousin. I would do anything for you, but that is a mess even I can't help you sort out."

"Let's hope the Norns feel differently," I replied.

Angantyr merely chuckled.

I exhaled deeply.

I had left Skagen an empty person. Now, I returned to find love and acceptance waiting for me everywhere I turned.

Or had it been there all along, and I'd been too miserable and blind to see it?

No more of this.

Tomorrow, I would lead the warband into battle. There was no time for any of this.

But then, an unfamiliar feminine voice whispered...

"Ervie, to love is part of life."

Freyja?

I spent the rest of the night alongside Angantyr and the others, preparing for the coming morning's battle. When the plans were settled, we rejoined the warriors gathered outside. At the fires nearby, Loptr was singing a rousing ballad. He had everyone clapping, dancing, and drinking.

Eyfura beamed lovingly at my brother from the sidelines, clapping as he sang. When his lines were done, and the music spun into a reel, my brother hopped down from the stump he'd been standing on and grabbed Eyfura's hands, turning her in circles as the pair laughed.

He dipped her low, making her chuckle, then lifted her once more, planting a kiss on her lips.

The crowd cheered.

"It's hard to believe he is the brother of the woman they call the Reindeer Princess," Elan said, stepping in beside me. "If you were not the mirror of one another in looks, I would call the others liars."

"My brother and I wear our shared life experiences differently."

"So I see," Elan said. "Princess Eyfura is very kind. She is the daughter of the shrewd king with all the handsome sons?"

I nodded. "She is."

"I remember that king...from before. Your King Harald did not impress me much, but that man," she said, her gaze going to Gizer, "is not one to be trifled with."

"You have read him well."

"So, your brother will wed the princess."

I nodded. "Yes."

"And he will become king of that man's lands?" she asked, gesturing to Hofund.

"King Hofund is our foster grandfather. He raised our mother as his own."

"Your brother will become king, but you will not be queen?"

"I have no interest in ruling Grund."

Rather than chide me, Elan said nothing, merely watched the others. I could see her eyes following them, observing the little exchanges. "A different fate awaits you, Reindeer Princess. I see the shadow of its shape on the other side of this battle," she said, then shook her head. "Let's hope it is a good one."

"May the gods hear your prayers."

"Indeed. Good night, Reindeer Princess."

"Good night, Priestess."

At that, Elan drifted back to Angantyr, and I took a moment to slip away from the others. Limping as I went, I made my way back toward the shoreline. I was not surprised when I found Magnus trotting alongside me. I was nearly halfway to the ships when I spotted a flash of light out of the corner of my eye. There was a flicker of purple light. And then another. And then another, like balls of flames shooting toward the skyline.

Confused, I stopped to look.

Magnus whined, but not in fear. His tail wagged.

The light was coming from the direction of the mound.

Curious, I turned in that direction.

On the one hand, I had no business going toward the mysterious purple light.

On the other hand, how could I ignore the call?

Retracing the steps I had taken with Hofund, I went to the burial mound of Hervor's father. There, the blue fire burned at the entrance to the mound. But before it, in shimming light, was a figure I would recognize anywhere...

"Blomma," I whispered, rushing toward her.

"Ervie," she said gently.

"Mother... How are you... Why?"

Blomma gave me a patient smile and said, *"The gods are moving on the eve of this battle. The Norns weave and make things new. A window opened for me to speak... Ervie, your battle is not with the Gauls. Caution. Caution with Hlod. You must not believe a word he speaks."*

"Mother."

Blomma began to fade.

"Aye, Mother, don't go." Never in my life would I have thought I'd need my mother's advice on matters of the heart, but now... "I need you, Mother," I said, hearing the desperation in my voice.

My mother smiled gently at me. *"Love fiercely, for the Norns always weave,"* she said, reaching out to touch my face.

"Mother."

"Ervie," Blomma said, her tone and expression turning serious. *"Watch over Loptr,"* she told me, then faded.

I stood staring at the place where my mother had been. Her words had been ominous. But she also spoke a truth I already knew. The Gauls presented a physical threat to our world, but Hlod...the threat he carried in his blood was more profound. He could undo the very fabric of our world.

My gaze went to the mound where a blue fire burned.

If the other Hervor had been brave enough to push through those flames and enter the mound, I had courage enough to face whatever came next.

Including the trials of my own heart.

CHAPTER 13

I walked away from the mound. On the rise was a wide oak tree. I limped over to it and settled into a crook in the trunk, sitting between the massive roots. Exhaling deeply, I stared at the ships in the harbor below. They rocked on the black water, the wave caps colored silver in the moonlight.

I closed my eyes and pressed my fingertips against my eyelids.

My mother had come.

While I had felt her presence before, even sometimes hearing her voice, she had never shown herself until now.

Why now?

Watch over Loptr.

Part of me rebelled at the idea. My brother would be king of Grund. He didn't need me to watch over him.

But if that was true, my mother wouldn't have warned me.

Aye, Mother. What are the Norns weaving? "You could have stayed a little longer," I whispered into the wind. But as I thought over my mother's words, I realized she *had* guided me. She'd told me to love fiercely.

But love whom?

With Ormar, I was whole.

With him, I felt something I'd never expected to feel in this life.

I'd never expected any feelings for Dag to remain.

But they did.

I sighed heavily. Gizer would sail down the Elbe, and I wouldn't be there to keep an eye on Dag. I hated the thought that Dag would go into battle unsettled—that was my fault.

But my own challenges awaited me.

I would lead Angantyr's forces into battle. Injured.

But my cousin trusted me, and I wouldn't let him down.

Yet, Hofund was right. If we got pinched in the swamps, everything could go wrong. And it was up to me to make sure it didn't.

I turned, adjusting my pack into the crook of the roots to make a pillow, then propped up my foot on one of the tree roots. Wiggling, I got comfortable. Magnus lay down beside me, setting his head on my stomach. He exhaled deeply, then closed his eyes.

I did the same.

Tomorrow, we would engage the Gauls.

Jǫrð.

Lady of the earth.

Watch over me tomorrow in the swamp and mists.

Freyr, give me strength.

And, Blomma, guide me to see all the things I must see…

A SOUND OF A BIRD CALLING FROM THE TREE OVERHEAD woke me. It was early in the morning; the sun had not yet risen. The sky was a deep purple color, the stars retreating as a ribbon of grayish-gold appeared on the horizon. From the shoreline, I heard voices as the warriors woke.

I sat up slowly, taking in some slow, deep breaths. I closed my eyes and listened to the bird singing overhead.

Awake. I'm awake. Let's all be awake.

Exhaling deeply, I reached for that place deep within myself where my power lived, and then I spun it outward toward the bird.

Let me see what you see. Let me be what you are.

My body shuddered, and soon, I found myself sitting on a tree branch. I shook, feeling my feathered body, then launched myself from the tree. Taking to the sky, I swooped down toward the ships. There, I saw the first of the men rising. Several gathered by the fires on the shoreline to eat a morning meal before setting off for war. I turned, my course diverting to the tents. There, too, I found many waking. Bjarki and Wigluf were outside Gizer's tent, sharpening their weapons. I turned and spun, spotting a familiar bright pair at the edge of the forest—Loptr and Eyfura. Apparently, they had spent the night in one another's company, away from prying eyes.

At the end of all of this madness, Angantyr would be king, and my brother and a dear friend would be wed.

There was something to be happy about.

I trilled a note toward them.

Loptr looked up, his brow scrunching. He sensed… something. Our parents' child, he couldn't help but do so, even if their power had passed him by.

I turned once more.

On the peak of the hill above the camps, I spotted one last figure.

Swooping, I found Elan there. The priestess was on her knees, her entwined hands pressed against her forehead in prayer.

May her gods and ours hear her prayers.

I called to her, swooping low to circle around the

priestess, who opened her eyes to watch me. Her gaze narrowed, and then she smiled.

Leaving her, I fluttered back over the camp toward the trees again.

As I went, however, I spotted Dag standing outside the tents. He was looking down toward the boats, scanning them.

"Have you seen Ervie?" he asked Bjarki.

"Slipped you, did she?" Wigluf asked, making him and Bjarki chuckle.

Dag merely frowned but said nothing. Instead, he made his way toward the ships.

I fluttered onto a branch.

"Thank you, sweet winged one," I told the bird. *"Now, on to your bugs…"*

I let go, opening my eyes once more.

I sat still for a long moment, looking out at the water as I centered myself in my body once more.

I was surrounded by friends and family. When I'd left Grund, I'd fled to Gizer to escape the crush of memory and pain of loss. There, I found family and love. But in search of more, I'd gone to the Myrkviðr, where I had found myself.

Now, I felt like I sat between two worlds—my past and my future.

What are you doing here? my mind kept repeating.

The answer was obvious. I was here to protect my

family, be there for Angantyr in his time of need, keep my world safe, and warn them of the dangers on the horizon. But in the end, where did I really want to be?

I wanted to go back to the forest, to my king.

I wanted to be with Jǫrð's people.

The pull in two directions was so palpable that I could barely stand it.

But today was not the day to be concerned with such things.

Today, we would fight. And when the battle was done, we would see what happened next.

Putting my weight on my good foot, I rose and picked up my pack, strapping Riddell over my shoulder and adjusting Hrotti. I turned to make my way to the boats, feeling a sharper pinch in my ankle than I wanted to be there.

It made no difference—aching or not, I was on my way to war.

CHAPTER 14

By the time I arrived at the beach, many of the others had also gathered. Angantyr was there, talking to his men who were sharpening their blades and mending their gear. Gunnar and Halstein were teasing Eluf about something, the younger warrior's ears and cheeks turning red from the conversation.

The warriors, still laughing, nodded to me when I joined them.

"Good morning, Reindeer Princess," Gunnar told me, wiping a tear from his eye.

I cocked an eyebrow at him, then turned to Eluf. "Feeling all right this morning?" I asked him. "You look like you might have a fever."

At that, the others howled with laughter.

Eluf's cheeks reddened further. "All is well, Princess. I was just receiving some unsolicited advice."

I didn't need to ask the nature of that advice. "Ah," I said simply. "Well, whenever you get advice, always consider the source," I told Eluf, then winked at Gunnar, making the man laugh.

Angantyr chuckled lightly, then shook his head. "They are always on about something. And Gunnar has no shortage of counsel to give."

"Thank you for the warning," I said with a grin.

Angantyr laughed. "We will leave within the hour. The others are coming now," Angantyr told me, looking over my shoulder.

I turned back to see that Gizer and his warband had assembled. How often had I fought with them? In a way, I was sorry not to be joining them once more. Dag, however, was not there. I scanned the shore, spotting him talking with my relation, Jarl Eir. He and the red-headed jarl were joking and laughing. I was surprised by the flash of jealousy the sight evoked in me.

Smothering it, I looked toward King Gizer. Behind him were Jarls Hakon and Halger of Silfrheim. Both hulking men, the twin brothers were known to be a terror in battle. Behind them came their slew of sons and the warriors of Silfrheim. The twins' elder brother, Jarl Leif, came with his son Arngrimir and the warriors of

Dalr. Hofund, Sigrun and her family, and the others from Grund were already aboard their ships.

Everyone was here to avenge Harald.

Loptr, neatly redressed, his hair pulled back in braids from his temples, joined us, Eyfura alongside him.

"In blood and honor," Loptr told Angantyr.

"In blood and honor," Angantyr replied.

Eyfura joined me, handing me a jar of salve. "You won't need it, but just in case."

"I was grateful for the last jar. I used it to save a dear friend."

"In the Myrkviðr?"

I nodded.

"And who were you battling in the Myrkviðr?" she asked.

"Everyone has enemies."

"Do they? Are you telling me that somewhere out there, someone hates the Reindeer Princess? Impossible."

"Possible. Let me assure you," I said, thoughts of Hlod threatening to take Hrotti coming to my mind.

"Hmm," Eyfura mused. "I wonder who hates me?"

"No one could hate you, Eyfura."

"But you just said *everyone* has enemies."

"Everyone but Eyfura."

"I suppose there are a few spurned men out there who might be angry at my refusal."

"They hate themselves for not being good enough to win you."

"When has that man ever blamed himself because a woman didn't love him? Fortunately, I won't have to face such worries anymore."

"And why is that?"

Eyfura paused. "Loptr?"

My brother turned from his conversation with Angantyr to us.

"Do you want to tell her, or shall I?" Eyfura asked.

Loptr grinned. "I won't deny you the pleasure."

Eyfura smiled at me. "Loptr asked for my hand last night, and my parents have granted us permission to wed. If the gods agree, we will see to it when the battle is done."

"How can they not?" I asked, embracing Eyfura. "I am glad for you," I said, then turned to Loptr. Smiling, I said, "You don't deserve her. You know that, of course."

"Of course," Loptr said with a laugh.

I smiled at him. "I am glad for you, Brother."

"May Frigga shine upon you both," Angantyr told them.

"Thank you, Angantyr," Eyfura replied.

Gizer and his sons joined us. "Come, Angantyr," Gizer said, slapping him on the shoulder. "We have a city to burn."

My cousin nodded, then stepped aside and pulled

out his horn. He put it to his lips, sounding the piece. The call echoed across the island. Soon, others trumpeted in reply. The sound of warhorns filled the air.

"From your lips to Odin's great hall. May our ancestors watch over you all," Eyfura told us.

"Are you sailing with your father?" I asked Eyfura.

She shook her head. "My mother and I will go on to Skagen with a group of warriors. We will prepare the city for your return."

"Skagen is underdefended," I said, frowning hard. "You must be careful."

Eyfura laughed. "You and Loptr made the same face at my news. Uncanny how similar you look when you do that. I have my knives, Reindeer Princess. You need not worry."

"Ervie never worries," Dag told her, joining us. "She knows the gods watch over her."

"Ervie never worries about herself. It is the rest of us she frets about," Eyfura replied.

"Come, boys," Gizer said, waving for them to go to the ships. "Let's make ready."

Gizer and the others departed, but Dag lingered.

"Ervie," Dag said, taking my hand.

The feel of his hand on mine evoked an unbidden smile.

He motioned for me to step aside with him.

"Daggers sharp?" he asked, tightening a lace on my jerkin.

"Of course. Yours?" I asked, adjusting a buckle on his sleeve.

He nodded as he made a tweak to my quiver strap. "May the gods go with you. I will see you again in the burning ruins of Holmgarth."

"You just told Eyfura the gods watch over me," I told him with a wry grin. "I'm safe, remember? So, may the gods protect *you*."

Dag chuckled, then turned serious. "Ervie, bravado aside, you're injured. Be careful."

"Bravado? Who, me?"

"Ervie…"

I took hold of his chin. "Don't worry about me. I mean it. Keep your mind on the battle, or the next time we see one another, it will be in Valhalla," I said, giving his chin a soft shake before I let him go.

He grinned. "I always fight well. Better than you, shield-maiden."

I laughed. "I need to tell Eyfura to check you for fever. You're lost in a fit of imagination."

At that, Dag chuckled. Giving me one long, last, lingering smile, he turned and joined his father and brothers.

I went to Angantyr's men. "By Freyr, you are a fierce

warband. The Gauls will quake in their boots and call upon their gods in fear. Let's make ship," I told them.

With that, they cheered.

I turned to Angantyr. "I will see you in Holmgarth, Cousin. May Freyr keep you safe."

"And you."

Elan joined me.

"Ready, Priestess?"

"The gods whisper. The time is right."

"Then let's set sail," I told her.

With that, Elan and I boarded Angantyr's lead ship and made ready.

Soon, the entire fleet departed Samso. I watched as dozens upon dozens of ships launched. It was Gizer who led the first of them out. Angantyr and Jorund followed, their vessels making their way back to sea. They would travel to the Elbe and begin their trek.

Our path, however, took us in a different direction.

Grabbing the horn, I set it to my lips and blew.

Angantyr was trusting me with his men. He charged me—and Elan—to lead them to victory. May Freyr, Freyja, Jǫrð, and all the gods be with me.

On another ship, a horn sounded in reply.

I looked to see Loptr standing at the prow.

And down from him, yet another horn answered: Hofund.

The red-and-white sails of Grund fluttered in the breeze.

"Hervor," I whispered into the breeze. "I know you watch over the king of Grund. Guide us to victory or meet us in Odin's hall."

"Ervie.

"Granddaughter.

"I watch over you all."

CHAPTER 15

We sailed throughout the day, nearing the entrance to the Trave by midafternoon. We passed several small homesteads along the way. When we reached the mouth of the Trave, we could just make out a village in the distance.

I crossed the deck of the ship, joining Elan. "Should we be concerned?"

"This is the village of Trave where I grew up. My family lives here."

"Your family?" I asked, unable to hide the surprise in my voice. "Will they send a rider to Kjar?"

"Before Hrollaug's father took the throne, my great-grandfather was king. He was murdered by Hrollaug's father, and my family was ousted from power. Those of our line who survived retreated here, to the village of Trave. Our line is all but broken. No,

Ervie, they will not send a rider. None in our lands hate Kjar and his family more than the people of the Trave."

"Yourself included."

"Yes."

Suddenly, Elan's indifference toward her rulers made more sense. She had no loyalty to Hergarth, not just because of Angantyr, but because of an old grudge seething within her. Elan was taking vengeance for her family.

"Does Angantyr know all of this?"

Elan nodded. "Yes. It was how I assured him I would be able to get us up the Trave unimpeded."

In the village, someone rang a warning bell. Voices rose up in the village, and the people scurried back to their houses. Soon, I saw warriors rushing toward the dock. Their leader, an older man with fading red hair, called to his archers to make ready. He and two young warriors made their way to the end of the dock.

Elan went to the ship's prow and called out in a dialect I didn't know.

The older man stepped away from the others to the end of the pier. "Elan?" he called.

She replied to him, speaking in her native tongue once more.

I turned back to warriors. "Slow," I called.

Halstein sounded his horn. It reverberated across the

water to the other ships, who answered in kind. Our ships slowed as they approached the village.

Elan and the man called to one another.

After the exchange, the man bowed to Elan and then lifted his hands in respect.

Elan answered in kind.

With that, the man and the warriors turned and made their way off the dock, walking with purpose back into the village.

"The men of Trave will rally and fight with us. They will gather their warband and meet us on the shores of Lake Trave. Chieftain Hrothgar will see to it."

"Can the chieftain be trusted?" I asked.

Elan smiled lightly. "I hope so. He is my uncle."

At that, I laughed. "You are full of surprises, Priestess —or is it Princess?"

She winked at me. "Aren't you glad you kept me alive?"

"I credit the gods for inspiring me."

"Mine or yours?"

"Both?"

Elan grinned.

I turned back to the others. "We'll make our way upriver. Oars," I called.

A man at the back of the ship called to the others. Behind me, I saw Loptr, Hofund, and the other vessels prepare for their upriver journey.

Elan sat once more at the prow of the ship.

I took a spot on the front bench, lowering myself carefully, then grabbed an oar handle.

"Do you trust them, Ervie?" Eluf asked in a low voice.

I considered for a moment, then said, "I do. It will serve Angantyr well to leave the Gauls in the hands of people he can ally with."

Gripping the oar, I started to row.

The Norns were weaving.

I *was* glad I had spared Elan. If I had not, none of this would have been possible. Not this plan, not their love, not our friendship...

With each row, I honored the ladies of fate. Over and over again, I whispered their names.

Thank you, Skuld.

Thank you, Urd.

Thank you, Verdandi.

Thank you, Skuld.

Thank you, Urd.

Thank you, Verdandi.

Thank you, Skuld.

Thank you, Urd.

Thank you, Verdandi.

Thank you, Skuld.

Thank you, Urd.

Thank you, Verdandi.

Weave us all a better future.

I T WAS LATE IN THE AFTERNOON WHEN WE FINALLY REACHED the lake. There, we anchored our ships and came ashore. When I went to slide off the side of the ship, Canute was waiting for me.

"Ervie," he said, reaching for my waist. "If you hit the rocks too hard on that foot… Don't argue, Reindeer Princess. We need you and that bow—not to mention that sword—intact for the fight ahead."

I let him help me down, then we made our way to shore. The cold water felt strangely relieving on my ankle. But I would not be sorry when the soreness wore off, and I didn't have to think about it anymore. As it was, I was trying not to think of the trek ahead of us.

Loptr, Hofund, Jarl Leif, Jarls Hakon and Halger, Jarl Eir and her sister Dissa, and all the others met us ashore. Elan went ahead into the reeds to look for the men from the village. As we waited, I explained to the others what Elan had shared with me.

"Her family used to rule?" Loptr asked.

"Yes."

"Can we trust them, Ervie?" Jarl Hakon asked me.

"It is in their best interest for us to succeed. They want to restore their line."

"The Gaulish priestess handed her family an army," Jarl Leif said, not hiding the suspicion in his voice.

"You're not wrong," I told him. "But Angantyr already knew of Elan's plan—and her family history. If the people of Trave take the Gaulish throne, Angantyr will have an ally he can trust." And the Norns knew he would soon need all the allies he could get.

"It's a match of hnefatafl," Loptr said. "For now, all our pieces are moving in the same direction."

"For now," Jarl Halger said. "That's the problem. And when we retreat to find our boats burned?"

"We outnumber them by a great force," Jarl Eir told Halger. "They wouldn't be so stupid."

Halger grinned at her. "Yes, Eir. As you say, Eir."

She rolled her eyes at him.

"Look, she is coming," Jarl Hakon said, gesturing.

Elan appeared then with a group of six warriors, including the man she had spoken to on the dock.

"Ervie, King Hofund, honorable jarls," she said, "this is Chieftain Hrothgar of Trave, my uncle," she said, gesturing to the man.

"Elan has explained what is happening. We want you to know that we did not join in the fighting against your King Harald. We are happy to join your warband in the taking of Holmgarth," the chieftain said.

"And the removal of Kjal's head," a younger warrior with reddish hair added.

"My cousin, Wulf," Elan introduced.

The young warrior bowed to us.

"We're glad to have you fighting with us," I told the chieftain.

"We will lead your warband through the bog. We must leave now if we are to make it before nightfall," Chieftain Hrothgar said.

I nodded, then turned to the others.

"We will make ready," Hofund said, gesturing to his men. As he and Jarl Leif departed, the pair talked in low tones. I could sense that Jarl Leif was still hesitant, but Hofund would convince him.

Following the Gaulish chieftain through the tall reeds, we made our way to join his party. Soon, we found ourselves in a clearing. Several dozen Gaulish warriors waited. Many had painted their faces with swirling blue designs. And all of them were outfitted for war.

"Princess," Chieftain Hrothgar said, gesturing to a horse for me. "There are horses for King Hofund and Prince Loptr as well."

"Thank you, Chieftain," I told him then slipped onto the pale gray beast while Elan slid onto a deep chestnut-colored stallion. I reined in beside her. "Your uncle and cousin are here. Your parents?"

"I had a mother," Elan said. "She died when I was very young. My father was… I was born of a coupling at a fertility festival. We say I was begotten by the gods. I didn't know my father. Only my uncle and cousins are left. Our family was much decimated in Kjar's family's ascent to the throne."

"I'm sorry for it."

"We all have our burdens, Reindeer Princess."

Elan, Loptr, Hofund, and I joined the chieftain at the front of the party, then headed out with the Gaulish warband.

There was a cart path around the lake, but it soon narrowed to a slim path that snaked through the reeds and marsh. As we went, sea birds called through the mist.

People in the reeds. People scaring fish and frogs. Go away. Go away.

Behind us, the men fell quiet as we worked through the unfamiliar terrain.

"Ervie," Loptr whispered to me. I could tell by the tremor in his voice that he had grown uncertain.

But I trusted Elan.

"It will be fine, Brother," I told him over my shoulder.

We rode throughout the afternoon, rounding the lake. It was nearing dusk when we took a path away from the water and started making our way inland. We rode into a thick grove. There, the Gauls came to a stop.

"The city is not far from here," Hrothgar told us. "We must go the rest of the way on foot."

"We must be certain Gizer has launched his attack before we push in," I said.

"Our people know the terrain well. We can send scouts."

I shook my head. "No. We should not risk discovery. I will look to it."

"Ervie," Loptr began, looking confused.

"I learned much in the Myrkviðr, Brother. I can see what is happening in the city without being seen," I told him, then turned to Elan. "I will need a moment."

She nodded. "I understand."

Once more, she turned to her uncle and said something in an unfamiliar dialect.

The man let out a low "hmm," looked me over once more, then nodded. He motioned to me to go on.

Favoring my good leg, I slid from the horse and moved ahead of the party. I went around the trees and away from the rest of the group. Finally finding a wide oak, I pressed my back against it and closed my eyes. I inhaled deeply, smelling the aromas of ferns, loam, wild-flowers, and the scents of the forest around me. Thoughts of Ormar came to my mind, but I silenced them. Instead, I listened to the sound of the wind rustling the leaves overhead. I heard the calls of the birds.

Sun. The sun is sinking. The sun is going away.

Refocusing, I ignored the birds and made ready.

Inhale.

Exhale.

Jǫrð, help me find a way.

Be with me.

Help me fall into myself.

And then, I let go. I fell deep into the well of myself, letting myself be sucked into the fathomless depths of my spirit. From within the place, I heard the beating thump of my own power.

"*Reindeer Princess.*

"*Child of Jǫrð.*

"*Rise.*

"*Rise.*"

Feeling the full force of my power, I lifted into the sky in the form of a hawk.

I flew upward, dodging the branches, then burst above the canopy. Below, I saw the shapes of the warband hidden by the leaves. I called to them, letting out one shrill note, then turned and made my way toward the city.

Feeling my body grow accustomed to this form, I moved quickly toward the city, following the spirals of smoke lifting into the air. I could smell the scent of men. I flew fast toward the city. It was a massive walled edifice. A wooden fence surrounded the town, which was filled with roundhouses. A deep ditch surrounded the turreted wall. Within the village, I spotted a large roundhouse. It, too, was walled.

But what I did not see were warriors.

Common people made their way quickly down the streets, hurrying their livestock and children inside, but otherwise, the place was quiet, deserted.

I spiraled higher, away from the city, to the river. In the distance, I saw fire and heard the sound of rough voices carried by the wind. Angantyr and Gizer had engaged the enemy.

They needed us.

Now.

Turning, I flew back to the glade where our warband was hiding.

Slipping through a gap in the trees, I followed a beam of sunlight toward the forest floor. When I was close, I reached within myself once more and let go...the feeling like pulling a cork from a jug, and walked into my human form.

The effect must have startled the others.

Several of the Gauls jumped back, their hands on the hilts.

Loptr gasped.

I turned to Hofund.

"The attack has begun. The city is undefended. We must bring the reinforcements now," I told him urgently, then turned to Elan and Hrothgar. "We must go."

The chieftain stared at me for a long moment then said, "My people will get them to open the gates. Stay back. Give us time to get in. We will ensure the gates stay open. Watch for our signal."

I nodded.

With that, the Gauls spoke to one another, many of them giving me sidelong glances, then headed off.

I could feel eyes on me. Everyone was staring at me, but now was not the time. The others needed us.

"We should summon the others to make ready," Loptr said, grabbing the horn on his belt.

I stayed his hand. "By the time we get to the gate, it will be dark. We will use darkness and silence to aid in our task," I told him, then turned to Hofund.

The king nodded in agreement.

"We go forward," I called to the warband. "Silently. The Gauls will signal, and then we will attack." With that, we turned and headed out.

Behind me, I heard Jarl Leif say, "I'm beginning to feel old, Hofund. That walk made my feet ache."

Hofund chuckled. "We are not old."

"You aren't feeling it because the Gauls gave you a horse."

"Don't complain. Eydis will fix you a hot bath full of herbs and rub your feet when you get home."

"And chide me for going in the first place. 'War is a

young man's game.' That is what she told me, trying to shame me into staying home."

"Out of love."

"She armored Arngrimir like Thor. But for me, she sent extra blankets and rations."

Hofund laughed, then said, "*I* am glad you are here, old friend."

"In blood and honor."

"In blood and honor."

I smiled as I listened to the warriors. Once, the two men were feared throughout the land. Jarl Leif's wife spoke some truth. War was brutal on the body, but a warrior's heart also thundered to the sound of Thor's hammer. There was no stopping that, no matter the age.

We wove silently through the forest.

I knew it was taking everything within the men following me not to blast their horns and call Odin, running headlong into war. But this was a gambit of shadows. We would win by playing things smart.

We followed the road to the edge of the forest. Once there, I gestured for the others to stay back.

The gate was still closed.

"They've already gone in," I told Elan, who stood beside me.

"Yes."

Behind me, I heard worried murmurs.

I met and held Elan's gaze. "From the winding stream to the sun-drenched valley."

She gave me a grateful smile. "From the winding stream to the sun-drenched valley."

In silence, we waited as it grew increasingly dark. The sky faded to deep blue.

Then, a man appeared on the rampart near the gate. He held a torch aloft, waving it from side to side.

The gate swung open.

I turned back to the others. "Jarl Leif, you and your men make a path to the king's roundhouse. Secure the building."

Leif nodded. "I'll see to it."

I turned to Hofund. "The rest of us will reinforce Angantyr and Gizer."

He nodded.

"Go silently," I told the others, then we all moved quickly and quietly toward the city.

Rushing through the field, I glanced briefly to the side where I spotted an old, rotting stump.

Sitting on it was a gray fox.

When I met its gaze, it barked at me, then turned and jumped from the log, disappearing into the tall grass.

I smiled, then pulled my bow and nocked an arrow.

The gods were with us.

CHAPTER 16

We slipped into the city to find that Elan's uncle and his warriors had subdued the men at the back gate. Elan briefly shared the plan for Leif to take the king's house with the others.

"Wulf will go with you," the chieftain told Leif, then turned to me. "The rest of us are with you."

Taking the warriors of Dalr with him, Leif headed off with Elan's cousin.

The rest of us made our way toward the city's front gate.

Weaving through the shadows, we snuck up on guards stationed throughout the city, subduing them silently.

Hoisting my bow, I took down two men on the ramparts before they spotted us.

Quick and quiet, we made our way toward the front of the city.

When I approached a corner, however, I discovered a large force on the other side.

I signaled to the archers. Moving into shadows, they got into position then waited for my signal.

I turned to Hofund who nodded to me.

I lifted my hand, giving the signal.

Several warriors at the back of the party fell, alerting the others.

"Warriors! Warriors in the city! Sound the alarm!" one of the Gauls called, but I silenced his cries with one of my arrows.

A bell began to clang loudly, and a chorus of voices rose up from somewhere ahead of us.

"You can only stay in the shadows for so long," Loptr told me and, with a grin, pulled his twin blades.

My mother's warning came to mind. Truth be told, I had never fought alongside Loptr before. We had trained together, and he was a good fighter, but he hadn't seen much battle. My brother had never raided, although Hakon and Halger had often encouraged Loptr to join them. Loptr involved himself in Grund's defenses, but he was not in charge of that either, the task falling to the shield-maidens Thora and Thordis.

I frowned.

Despite being our parents' child, Loptr was not like

them—or me. He would have made a very good skald. He liked to drink, sing, and dance. My brother was smart, but his sword arm...

A band of warriors raced toward us. Hakon and Halger led their men forward, running to engage. Scanning around, I spotted an auctioneer's platform. I moved quickly toward the rise, my ankle reminding me as I went that *quickly* was not a good idea. Regardless, I made my way there and nocked an arrow.

Aiming down the lane, I took my first shot, my arrow piercing the throat of a massive warrior who had been lumbering, sword in hand, toward Hakon.

The giant paused mid-step, his eyes rolling back, then fell to the ground.

Hakon looked over his shoulder, gave me a wink, then carried forward.

My gaze went from the Hakon to Loptr.

He rushed toward a spry warrior wielding a staff. The Gaul and my brother were equally quick, the pair fighting fiercely. In fact, they were moving so quickly that I couldn't get a shot in. But I did spy a female Gaulish warrior making her way toward my brother. She hoisted her sword and screamed as she rushed Loptr. I blinked, realizing the woman looked much like the man Loptr was battling.

"From the winding stream to the sun-drenched valley," I whispered, then let my arrow fly.

The arrow hit its mark, piercing the woman's chest, stopping her. She let out an odd, strangled scream and then fell.

Her death distracted the young warrior who fought Loptr, giving my brother an opening.

Loptr's blades found their mark.

An odd feeling washed over me. I realized I had just ended the Gaulish versions of my brother and myself. It left me with an unsettled feeling.

Turning, I rushed from the platform and hurried to rejoin the group. King Kjar had left a small band of warriors to protect the city, but they hadn't expected us. By the time I joined the others, the Gaulish warriors had already been defeated, and Hakon and Halger were working with Elan's kin to open the front gate.

We burst through the gate and made our way down the road toward the war going on downriver. Something big was on fire...a ship? A building?

My thoughts went to Dag, worry washing through me.

I immediately pushed the thoughts aside.

Fear had no place here.

Loptr joined me.

Meeting my gaze, he nodded to me.

We fell in line beside Hofund, who had blood splattered across his face and chest.

"We should rush them," he told me. "Take them by

surprise and confuse them. Don't give them time to adjust."

I nodded. "Who can argue with the king of Grund?"

At that, Hofund laughed. "For Odin! For Valhalla!" Hofund screamed, hoisting his hammer into the air. He then rushed into the fray, the rest of us following behind him.

Overhead, I heard a squawk.

I looked up to see a crow flying above us.

I scanned the battle, first spotting Angantyr and Magnus battling against a Gaul on a knoll not far away. My cousin was faring well, Magnus biting the leg of the attacker.

Gida and Ásbjorn rushed past, the couple fighting in tandem.

My eyes darting quickly across the battlefield, I found Dag fighting two warriors at once. The blond-haired son of Gizer was struggling.

"By Hel," I cursed, looking around for higher ground. Seeing a pile of dead men, I quickly rushed to the top. I nocked an arrow and sent it flying, catching one of the two men fighting Dag in the shoulder. The warrior turned to see from where the arrow had come—just in time for me to nock another and send it speeding directly into the man's eye.

The warrior fell, leaving the other man for Dag to battle alone.

Still, I didn't like what I saw.

The man was much bigger than Dag and knew how to use his weight to his advantage. Dag was in trouble. Too many battling pairs were between us. I couldn't get a clear line of sight on the Gaul.

Slipping Riddell on my back, I pulled my axe and rushed across the field.

As I hurried, I tried to push away the pain in my ankle and my fears. What if I didn't get there in time? What if something happened to Dag?

Somewhere in the distance, the Gauls sounded a long, wooden trumpet. The instrument's sorrowful echo floated across the valley.

I turned to look.

King Kjar and his men were fighting their way toward Angantyr.

But they weren't going to get far.

Gizer, Bjarki, and Wigluf were on a path to intercept him.

The Gaulish king would not live to see the stars come out that night.

I was nearly to the other side of the fray when a man hurled a spear at me. I saw it out of the corner of my eye and lifted my shield just in time, sending the spear bouncing off. The silver-haired Gaul who'd thrown the spear rushed me.

Auðr's words came back to me, reminding me of all

the reasons—no, excuses—I had made that kept me from fighting with my father's sword.

No.

Not *my father's* sword.

My sword.

Slipping my axe back into my belt, I reached for Hrotti.

When I pulled the dwarven blade, lightning cracked. The earth rumbled. The wind rushed around me, causing my hair to fly up. I hoisted my sword and then met the grizzled warrior's attack. Dwarven steel or not, this man would try to kill me. As evidenced by the scars on his face, he'd seen many battles. Seeing me—a small woman —he'd thought me an easy kill. He was wrong.

When our swords met, he realized that truth.

But I had no time to dally with him.

I had to get to Dag.

Remembering what Auðr had taught me, I repressed the instinct that told me to hack and slash the way Gizer had shown me. The urge to fight like a berserker was strong, but it would not serve me here.

Pulling back, I waited for the Gaul to launch his attack once more, and then the dance began. Dodging and parrying his blows, Hrotti sliced through the air with a silvery whine that unnerved the man. I spun around him, getting behind the warrior.

Sweating and breathing hard, he tried to stab me.

I blocked the move and then met his eyes.

He growled something at me in a language I didn't know.

I stared at him—seeing the lines on his face, the color of his eyes, the curl of his silver hair lying in wet ringlets on his head, the scar on his cheek.

And then, as I did with birds and animals, I changed my appearance. Shifting my features, I took on the man's form, reflecting his own face back to him. My skin felt warm as magic filled me, my body tingling.

The Gaul gasped, then stepped back.

The moment was enough.

I spun Hrotti, then stabbed the man in the gut.

With a groan, the Gaul fell.

Yanking the sword back, I pushed toward Dag.

Hrotti had an interesting effect on the Gaulish warriors around me.

Suddenly, I found the path between Dag and myself clear.

When I finally got to him, I found Dag fighting hard and bleeding from a wound across his cheek. The massive Gaul had Dag pinned under his shield.

I scanned around us. There were none of our warriors here in this strange little corner of the city. The Gaul pulled a dagger from his belt.

"Jǫrð, be with me," I said, then swung my arms behind me. Calling up my magic, summoning all the strength of air, I waved my arms toward the Gaul. The force of the gust of air was so strong that the Gaulish warrior stumbled. The momentary distraction allowed Dag to roll away.

Sword in one hand, dagger in the other, the man turned toward me. But the Gaul was no fool. He had seen me coming, and seidr or not, dwarven blade or not, he had seen me limp. The Gaul rushed me quickly. Using his full force, he kicked the shin of my injured leg hard.

I couldn't suppress my scream.

My ankle buckled, and I went down on one knee.

Holding Hrotti above me, I barely blocked the man's killing blow.

Dag appeared in time before the Gaul could end me. He engaged the warrior once more. I rose, my leg throbbing, then went after the man. Dag and I wove around him like snakes, baiting and striking. The man was soon red-faced and sweating.

Hrotti, lend me your strength. Lend me your strength, I pleaded with the sword, gripping my hand around the pommel.

Then, I swung.

The blade sang as it slid through the air. It landed on the man's wrist, cutting through the bone.

He screamed in agony.

Dag took the opportunity, plunging his blade into the man's chest.

The Gaul's eyes rolled back into his head, then he fell to the ground.

Dag and I stood, both of us breathing hard, and stared at the dead man.

That had been far too close.

I lifted my gaze, looking at Dag. He had a terrible cut on his face, the wound stretching from his ear to the corner of his mouth.

"You're hurt," I said, then grabbed his arm. Limping badly, I pulled him away from the fray, but I couldn't put weight on my leg. Aye, gods. Was it broken?

"The others…" Dag said, gripping his face in pain as blood oozed from between his fingers. Fear flashed in his eyes when he realized the severity of his wound. I had never seen such a look in Dag's expression. At that moment, I, too, felt scared.

"The others don't want you to bleed to death on this battlefield any more than I do," I said tersely, dipping into my vest for a cloth. I pressed it against his bleeding face.

Across the field from us, I heard the call of Gizer's horn.

Dag and I turned to look.

The king was regrouping his warband to make a final push against the Gaulish warriors who were fleeing.

My gaze darted quickly back to Angantyr.

King Kjar lay dead at my cousin's feet.

Elan stood beside him, her slingshot in her hand, her hair unbound.

"Don't let them escape," Gizer screamed. "Slay them all."

The Gauls fled in terror.

In their haste to get away, three Gaulish warriors turned our way.

I could see in their eyes that they thought us easy kills.

I stepped between them and Dag, holding Hrotti before me. Suppressing the intense pain radiating from my leg, I summoned all the magic within me and channeled it into the sword. The blade glowed blue. Hrotti in one hand, I reached with the other toward the sky.

Thor, I whispered in my mind. *Thor! Show them what it means to be a child of Jǫrð. Thor, Brother, hear me. Help me, Thor!*

The sky cracked with lightning.

The men's eyes went wide, and they turned and rushed off in another direction.

I looked back at Dag.

"Ervie," he whispered. "Your eyes...like lightning."

"Don't try to talk," I said, then turned back.

I scanned the crowd for Loptr, cursing myself for losing him in the fray.

A great sense of relief washed over me when I finally spotted him. Mud and blood splattered on his face, he stood beside Hofund. The king of Grund's twin hammers were wet with blood. Loptr was breathing hard, his neatly braided hair undone and sticking to his face.

Loptr and Hofund regrouped Grund's warriors and headed off toward the king's hall to reinforce Leif.

I bent to the ground, snatching the sword of the Gaulish warrior from the dead man's hand. The blade's guard been beautifully worked with a swirling knot symbol, the pommel shaped like a crescent moon. On each side was a pale, blueish-white stone. The blade itself had been etched in woven designs that featured a dragon.

I handed the sword to the Dag. "Whoever he was, he was a fierce warrior and a man of importance. Don't let that dimple in your cheek be the only reminder of your battle with him."

Dag shook his head. "We earned it together."

I grinned at Dag, then said, "Very well. You carry it for the next thirty years. I'll carry it the thirty after that."

Dag tried to laugh, but he had gone pale as snow. "Ervie," he whispered, clutching his abdomen, then crumpled to the ground.

CHAPTER 17

I t was my good fortune that Bjarki saw us then because mere moments after Dag fainted, the burly warrior appeared at my side.

"Ervie," Bjarki said, bending to look at Dag.

"He took a terrible injury to his face. He may be hurt elsewhere. I don't know. We need to lay him down somewhere," I said.

Bjarki nodded. "Dag?" he said, shaking Dag's shoulder, but Dag didn't move.

"Your father has the Gauls on the run. Let's take him back to the ship," I said.

Bjarki nodded, then hoisted his brother over his shoulder.

Snatching up the Gaul's sword, I slipped it into my belt and limped behind Bjarki.

Bjarki and I made our way through the crowd back to

the ships. The pain in my leg was searing, but I pushed it aside. There was no time for that now.

A small band of men watched over the boats. When we arrived at the docks, I saw that one of King Jorund's ships was on fire. The men had cut it loose, and the burning ship was floating back down the river toward the sea—away from the port, city, and other vessels.

The men who'd been protecting the ships now helped the wounded back on board.

Many warriors had been injured in the battle.

Part of me felt a pang of guilt that I had left Angantyr to sort out the mess, but Dag was all that mattered.

Bjarki found a spot on the ship for Dag, laying him down. Moving quickly, I opened the medicine bag hanging from my belt and pulled out what supplies I carried.

"Water," Bjarki said, handing me a skin.

I cleaned my hands and then went to inspect Dag's wounds. Moving gently, I tipped his head to the side to see the cut thereon more clearly, but when I did, I noticed blood seeping through his vest.

"By Hel," I swore, then quickly undid the laces on his jerkin and lifted his tunic to find a stab wound. The cut had been made by a dagger. From the look of it, the injury was deep.

"By Odin," Bjarki swore. "Dag got separated from us. I don't know how it happened. One moment he was there with us, and the next, he was in a fracas with the Gauls. It's not like him to be so distracted."

I clenched my teeth hard, knowing full well what had distracted Dag. The mixed emotions and confusion between us had nearly gotten him killed. I refocused. All of my training at the dísarsalr returned to me in an instant. Norna had taught us what to watch for, the signs to seek to determine if a puncture was lethal. Working quickly, I examined the wound to the abdomen. I studied the blood and its flow. The damage *was* deep, but nothing vital had been injured. I quickly flushed the wound with water and then applied some of the astringents I carried, cleaning the cut. Once that was done, I used the healing salve Eyfura had given me.

"Here," Bjarki said, digging out his own jar. "Use mine as well."

Behind me, they were bringing in more wounded, but I focused on the task at hand. I took Bjarki's jar and tended the wound. Once it was treated, I pulled out my supplies and began stitching the gash closed. When I finished the stitching, I wrapped his abdomen with a length of clean linen I carried. It would hold well enough for the moment, but Dag needed to see the gothar.

With the abdomen wound mended, I turned to care for his face.

The laceration was deep. The sword had penetrated

into the mouth at the corner of his lips. Thankfully, however, it had not cut through the skin beyond that.

I washed the wound, forcing my emotions to be quiet as my hands worked.

Tears threatened.

If either of these wounds soured...

No.

I couldn't—wouldn't—let that happen.

I would fix this as best I could.

But as I tended to the wound on his face, I realized the wound was disfiguring. He would carry the scar on his handsome features for the rest of his life.

Just as he carried the scar on his heart.

And I was responsible for both.

For what?

Why?

I had pushed Dag away all these years because I hated part of myself. That wasn't his fault. It never had been. And now... Now that I was healed, I could see the truth.

I loved Dag.

Aye, gods.

Once his cut was cleaned, it was time to sew the wound shut.

I paused a moment, willing my hands to be still.

"Bjarki," I whispered, poised above Dag's face with

the needle, but scared to make a move, knowing Dag would wear each stitch on his face.

"There is no one he trusts more than you, Ervie. Go on with it," the warrior said softly.

I thrust my feelings aside and began my task. I focused all my concentration on the work.

Jǫrð, be with me.

My mind went to the Valkyrie Eir, to whom the Norns had granted the gift of healing.

Eir, sister of the starlight steeds, I hope to ride alongside you one day. Today, guide my hands. Shed your magic on me.

Concentrating on the task, I didn't sit back until the work was done.

When I did, I was surprised to find others crowded behind me.

There, I found Elan, Angantyr, and Gizer.

"Elan," I said, rising.

When my leg protested, Angantyr held my hand and helped me up.

"Elan, have I done all right? Maybe you should—"

Elan shook her head. "We watched you work, Reindeer Princess. There is nothing I would have done differently. He was in good hands."

I turned to Gizer. "Oh, Gizer," I said, my words coming out in a broken half-sob. My emotions startled me.

But they didn't surprise the king.

Gizer pulled me into a tight embrace. "He will be all right. You worked quickly. He will heal."

I nodded, my head on his chest. My tears coming unbidden, I wept. My body shook as I let the emotions loose. If Dag died, I would never forgive myself. I stayed there for a long moment, soaking in the fatherly warmth and comfort I felt from Gizer, then, I let him go. Dashing away my tears, I turned and looked back at the others who had been brought to the boat.

"There are others wounded here. I can help," I said, refocusing. I turned to Angantyr. "We have won the day?"

"We have won the day," he said with a soft smile.

"Praise Freyr."

"And hail King Angantyr," Gizer said, slapping my cousin on his back. "You should rejoin the others in the king's hall."

Angantyr nodded. "Soon enough. I will see to the warriors first," he said, gesturing to the wounded men.

"You're letting Jorund get all the plunder," Gizer told him.

"So are you."

Gizer huffed a laugh, but his eyes drifted to his son. "I will take my share from my boys," he said absently, but I could see his thoughts were not on the pillage.

"Loptr?" I asked Angantyr.

"He is with Hofund and the others in the king's hall. He's well enough. Spitting fire and drinking mead."

I shook my head.

"I will check on the others," Elan told Angantyr.

"I'll join you," my cousin said, then paused, setting his hand on my shoulder. "You did well, Cousin. Thank you for all you have done for me. Now, rest. You will not admit it, but that leg is not right. Sit and rest."

With that, Angantyr and Elan departed.

Bjarki and Gizer shared a few low words. Bjarki nodded, then turned to go, giving me a soft smile before he left.

With a sigh, Gizer sat down beside Dag. "Your mother is going to scold me, boy. Best wake before we get to Skagen."

Suddenly feeling all my aches and pains, I moved to sit down beside the pair, but my leg protested. I bit my lip.

"You better look at it," Gizer told me, pointing to my leg.

I nodded. Lowering myself once more, I pulled up the leg of my trousers. My shin had already turned purple, the injury melding down into my still swollen and colored ankle.

Gizer rose and wet some cloths, then handed them to me.

"Wrap it," he told me, watching me as I gingerly touched the bone. "Is it broken?"

"I don't know."

"Once the battle fever wears off, you'll know one way or the other. Whoever he was, he must have spotted that bad ankle."

"He did and tried to use it to his advantage."

"You used your father's sword."

I nodded.

"I heard it clap like thunder. Here," Gizer said, then touched his chest. He chuckled lightly. "It is a mighty thing to see dwarven steel come to life on the battlefield. But for the first time, I felt something other than excitement."

"And that was?"

"Worry," Gizer said with a laugh. "Because I know you won't pull that blade unless you're in trouble."

"Are you getting sentimental, King Gizer?"

"You're entirely to blame."

I laughed. "You will hear Hrotti more often now. Don't let it alarm you. It's time for me to wield the sword I was given."

Gizer nodded slowly as he considered. "Good," he said, then eyed me over. "I think you found what you were looking for in the Myrkviðr."

"I did."

"At the court of King Ormar, nonetheless. The Norns weave in mysterious ways."

Hearing Ormar's name struck me hard. I felt like a knot had formed in the pit of my stomach, and then a wave of nausea rolled over me. It was so violent that I turned and gripped the ship's rail. Leaning over the side, I retched again and again. When I was done, I turned back slowly, this time feeling the terrible pain in my leg.

Gizer handed me his water skin. "Now the pain will come," he told me. "And it will be bad. You should rest."

"And you should join the others."

"Bah," he said dismissively. "I'm tired myself," he said, then propped his back on the side of the ship, and wiggled in until he was comfortable.

I narrowed my gaze at him but said nothing more.

Dag was hurt.

I was hurt.

That was why Gizer wasn't leaving.

Settling in beside Dag, I set my head on his shoulder.

"Ervie," he said in a whisper.

"Don't talk," I told him. "I've stitched your wound. Don't move your mouth."

He didn't say anything for a long moment, but then I heard him quietly whisper.

"I love you."

"I love you too," I replied, tears slipping from my eyes as I drifted off to sleep.

CHAPTER 18

I woke sometime after dark, awakened by the feeling of someone settling in beside me.

I opened my eyes a crack to find Loptr there. "Brother?"

Loptr lifted a finger to his lips, then gestured beside me where Dag and Gizer slept.

"Elan said your leg was injured," Loptr whispered. The scent of strong spirits wafted from him.

"It will mend."

Loptr frowned. His gaze told me he already knew I was downplaying the truth. The injury was bad. It would mend, but how long and at what price, I still didn't know. "Dag?"

Shifting, my leg from my hip to my toes protesting when I did, I set my hand on Dag's forehead. No fever, but he was sleeping deeply.

"We need to get him to Skagen. He will need care and rest," I said.

Loptr nodded. "Angantyr is making arrangements to depart. Elan's Gaulish relatives were very helpful. The city is quiet tonight. Despite the conflict, the people are not rebelling. In fact, they seem glad. Apparently, the priestess was not wrong in her assessment of her people's feelings toward their king. Hofund and I will return with the Gauls to Lake Trave, then make our way back to Skagen."

I scanned the ship where the other wounded lay sleeping.

"The others…"

"Many good warriors were lost. Jarl Leif took an arrow to the shoulder, but he is well enough and is resting in the king's hall. We will leave at first light."

I nodded.

"Thank you, Ervie."

"Thank me for what?"

"I saw what you did when the battle began. You watched over me. Thank you."

I simply nodded.

"No one told me the fun I was missing," he said, pulling his dagger and twirling it.

My gaze drifted down to Dag. "It's not all fun."

"No, but there is glory enough," he said, then slipped the blade back into its sheathe. "Hofund and I will leave soon. I just wanted to check on you and let you know. Angantyr said you will sail with the others."

I merely nodded. I was in no condition to ride back to the Trave. And I wouldn't leave Dag.

Loptr rose and then bent to kiss me on the top of my head. "Be well, Sister. I will see you again in Skagen. And may the gods watch over Dag," he said, then drifted away.

After he'd gone, Gizer opened one eye and said, "I'd hoped he'd get a good beating from the Gauls."

"Why?"

"Because he needs to be reminded the world is not easy. Your parents' deaths taught you, but Loptr missed the lesson."

"Yet you said yes to him marrying Eyfura."

Gizer nodded.

"Why?"

"I will not make Harald's mistakes. And…"

"And?"

"And he is your brother. Your twin. Whatever the Norns wove you out of, he is made of the same cloth. Something will awaken it, eventually. And when it does… Well, then I know my daughter will be safe."

I smiled at the king. "May the gods curse anyone who dares do harm to Eyfura. And may all our world rain down upon them like fire."

"May the Norns hear your words and hold us all to them."

I CLOSED MY EYES, NOT WAKING AGAIN UNTIL I FELT THE boat moving. Gizer and Angantyr were standing at the prow talking. Magnus had curled up beside me, his head on my lap. Someone had covered Dag and me.

Dag stirred in his sleep.

"We're leaving for Skagen. Rest," I whispered, then curled beside him, my head on his chest. Closing my eyes, I fell asleep again.

It was not until we heard the horn sounding in the great harbor of Skagen that I opened my eyes again.

The sun had risen.

And the pain in my leg had awakened. Shooting pain seared up my leg to the top of my head.

Noticing I was awake, Angantyr joined me.

"Cousin," he said, a worried expression on his face.

Shifting carefully away from Dag, I reached up for Angantyr. "Help me up."

"Rest until we make berth."

"I just need to go slow. I'll be fine. Help me up."

Angantyr frowned but did as I asked. My body

complained loudly, but I leaned against Angantyr as we approached what was left of the port of Skagen.

The city had burned to ashes. The great hall on the hill was nothing but a charred shell. The wooden horses that had sat before it were scorched down to mere skeletons. So, too, had the great temple of Skagen been destroyed. Once, the shining temple had been a beacon to all who visited the city. Now... So many houses and buildings were gone. On the west side of the city, however, some buildings remained. Hearth smoke spiraled up from the small houses. Our ship made its way toward the small fishing dock. The fleet would not be able to come in all at once. Many ships would have to sit at anchor in the harbor.

It was a strange feeling approaching Skagen, knowing that Harald, Aud, Halfdan, and Svafa were gone.

Our world had shifted underneath us.

Everything was different now.

Angantyr's gaze surveyed the horizon.

"You return a king," I said.

"I was glad to see the light go out of Kjar's eyes," Angantyr said. "In his death, I have restored my family's honor."

"Do you trust the Gauls to keep the peace now?"

Angantyr nodded slowly. "Yes. I spoke at length with

Elan's uncle. He will see that peace is enforced. I believe my alliance with him will hold."

I huffed a light laugh, then said, "And marrying Elan won't hurt anything."

"No. It won't. How the Norns weave."

"That they do, Cousin."

"Now, my attention must turn elsewhere. To rebuilding Skagen and preparing for Hlod."

"Yes."

"But for now…" he said, his gaze returning to the others. "I will see to those who were wounded." He looked toward Dag. "Will he be all right?"

"He hasn't taken fever."

"Gizer sent his gothar to Skagen along with Kára and Eyfura. They will see to him."

"Good."

"Ervie… Your leg. Don't push your limits."

"I have limits?"

Angantyr gave me a look.

"Yes, Cousin."

As the ship made port, I spotted Eyfura in the crowd. Her red hair made her stick out like a rose in a field of daisies. She waited with several others, including her mother Kára, for the first of the ships to arrive.

As soon as we came to the dock, the ship was tied up, and a crew of people got to work unloading the wounded men from the boat. Gizer debarked to speak with his wife and daughter.

Soon, all three of them hurried onto the ship.

"Ervie, Dag," Eyfura said, rushing to join Dag and me.

"The pain is keeping him asleep. I cleaned and treated his wounds. The injury to his face is bad. He will need tonics for the pain, and the wounds should be cleaned again."

Kára, who was usually jovial and laughing, looked pale. "Thank you, Ervie."

"Let's get him up," Gizer told Angantyr, then the pair went to Dag. "Well, boy. I let you sleep cozy curled up beside Ervie the whole ride home—much to Magnus's annoyance. Time to get to the tents and let your sister prod at you."

"Ervie," Dag called weakly as he opened his eyes.

"I'm here," I said. "Try not to talk."

He looked around in confusion. "I'm so thirsty," he whispered.

"Come on, Son," Kára told him. "The gothar are here. Let's have them see to you."

Gizer turned to his daughter. "Ervie's leg is half broken. She's pretending it doesn't hurt. Get her off the ship and see that it's examined by someone other than her."

"Ervie," Eyfura said in annoyance, turning her attention to me.

I shrugged, then bent to grab a pole used for pushing ships from the dock. Steadying myself with it, I said, "Let's go."

Eyfura assisting me, I made my way to the side of the ship. But as I went, I began to feel the injury's extent. Had the bone been broken? I wasn't sure now. My entire leg felt numb.

"Ervie," Eyfura chided me. "What happened?"

"The bastard who got Dag went for my wounded leg."

"It is fortunate the two of you are still alive."

She wasn't wrong.

"Let's get you to the tent," Eyfura said.

I nodded.

Eyfura walked alongside me, going slowly, holding me as she went. I could sense her mind was busy. Loptr.

"He's fine," I finally said. "He and Hofund will return with the ships from Grund. He wasn't injured."

"It's not nice of you to read my mind, Reindeer Princess."

"Then I guess there was no use in traveling to the Myrkviðr to learn seidr after all."

"So, you *did* learn to read minds?" Eyfura asked probingly.

"No. It is only I know *your* mind, Princess. It's on my brother."

At that, Eyfura laughed. But I also heard the sigh of relief in her voice.

"Your other brothers are fine as well," I told her teasingly.

Eyfura grinned. "I assumed."

I shook my head.

We made our way down the dock to a tent erected not far from where the market used to be. There, the gothar from both Gizer's hall and the hall of Skagen worked quickly, seeing to the wounded.

"There are many here who need attention more than me. Leave me there," I said, pointing to a bench, "and see to Dag."

"Are you sure?" Eyfura asked.

"Gizer is exaggerating. Dag needs you."

Eyfura helped me sit and then met my gaze. "I'll be back for you."

"Bring some mead."

Eyfura rolled her eyes and then went to her brother.

I sat slowly. When I moved my leg, tears came to my eyes, and for a moment, I saw a swarm of black dots. Pushing the pain away, I sat. I watched as the gothar worked. There were people here with injuries far more severe than my own. I had no business waiting for the gothar when others needed their attention far more. Besides, Angantyr surely needed my help.

I was about to rise when a young gythia approached me.

"Reindeer Princess, where are you going?" she asked.

"I was…" I began, but the girl met my gaze and gave me a scolding look.

Aside from her dark eyes, something about her appearance was arresting. She must have been one of the gythia from Skagen. I didn't recognize her from Gizer's people. She was, perhaps, fourteen years of age with a heavy brow, a firm gaze, and long, thick dark hair she'd pulled into a braid.

"Let's have you sit there," she told me, pointing to a cot. "I will see to your leg."

Leaning on the girl, I hobbled to the cot and lowered myself. She knelt beside me and began to undo the laces on my boot. As soon as she eased the boot off, I felt a throbbing in my foot. A wave of nausea washed over me. I barely kept myself from vomiting. The priestess rolled up the leg of my trousers and removed the binding there to reveal the purple-and-yellow bruise radiating from my shin up and down my leg. Touching the wound gently, she considered the injury.

I fought back the urge to scream when she touched the most tender part of the wound.

"Hmm," she mused, then opened her kit. "It isn't

fully broken, but the bone is fractured. Stay here," she said, then disappeared. The priestess returned a few moments later with a steaming mug in her hand. "This will help you with the pain. And it will heal you from within."

Drinking the tonic, I tasted many familiar herbs and roots. But there were also mushroom and berry flavors I didn't recognize.

"What's in this?" I asked.

"You trained in the dísarsalr, Reindeer Princess. Do you need me to explain it to you?"

I looked into the cup again, trying to figure out what she had put in the concoction, but my head felt woozy.

"Be still now, Princess. I will bind the leg so that it will heal quicker, but you must not put any weight on this leg for seven nights. You *must* rest. Seven turns of the wheel, day to night to day once more. Do you understand?"

"Seven nights."

"Yes, seven nights," she said with a nod. "I will wrap the ankle as well. They will both heal if you do as I say," she told me, then got to work. "But you *must* do as I say, or all will be undone."

As she worked, the room around me grew dizzy. The tent seemed to spin, but I couldn't feel the pain in my leg anymore. I felt wave upon wave of nausea.

"I might be sick," I told her, trying to sit up.

"No, you won't be," she told me, waving her hand over my face. "You will be at ease. Now, no riding or fighting for seven nights. Do you understand?"

"Yes."

"If you do not heed me, you will wear the pain of these injuries all your life. One wound for leaving the shadows and the man the Norns have given you, and another for protecting the man you love. But more—worse—if you do not listen to my words."

"What?" I asked. Her voice sounded far away.

"Seven nights, Hervor, Daughter of Mjord and Blomma," she said, leaning over my face and looking down at me. Her voice grew distant, echoing hollowly. "Seven nights to make you whole again. But if you do not wait and give the Norns time to do their spinning, your world will be torn apart and rewoven, and the worst injuries will live in your spirit forever. Do you understand?"

"I... What do you mean? The Norns?"

But the girl simply rose and disappeared into the crowd. When I looked for her again, I didn't see her anywhere. Then, my vision grew blurry, and sleep claimed me.

CHAPTER 19

I woke the following day with a pounding headache, a rumbling stomach, and the strange sense that the gods had—for reasons I didn't understand—intervened in my life again.

Sitting up slowly, I looked around the tent for any sign of the young gythia who had mended my leg.

She was not there.

Why was I not surprised?

Who I did find, however, was Dag. He was lying on the cot next to me, sleeping soundly. Fresh bandages had been applied to his face. Someone had removed his tunic to treat his stab wound, redressing him in a clean shirt. Reaching over, I set my hand on his forehead. No fever.

He stirred in his sleep. "Ervie?" he whispered.

"I'm here," I said, turning on my side to look at him.

He opened his eyes just a crack and looked at me. "Are you hurt? Your leg?"

"Mending. Don't try to talk."

"Always shushing me," he whispered with a light laugh.

"Ah, I see my favorite patients are awake," a light voice called.

I looked to see Eyfura coming our way. She smiled at me and then went to her brother.

"Sister," Dag said, reaching for her.

"You are on the mend, Brother. But don't task yourself. I will bring you something for the pain."

"And something to eat," he whispered.

"I'm afraid it's broth for you for a few days," she told him, then turned to me. "How is the leg?"

"It's fine. I need to go see Angantyr."

Eyfura laughed. "You're funny, Reindeer Princess. It's almost like you think I'd let you go somewhere. Besides, Angantyr has more help than he needs. They're building a new hall. New temple. I'm not sure there isn't anything they aren't building. There were sacrifices to Freyr last night. My father urged him to go ahead and wed, but he wouldn't do it without you present. So, you must rest."

"He waited? For me?"

"Mm-hmm," Eyfura replied. "I think Loptr is jealous of Angantyr's love for you. He complained there was no wedding feast just because you were still sleeping."

"I'm not sure that means he's jealous."

"Then you don't know him as well as you think, shield-maiden."

"Perhaps," I said, then laughed. "Although, I suspect it was the lack of ale that wounded him more. What will you do with a skald for a husband?"

Eyfura grinned. "Laugh the whole day long. What else can a woman ask for?"

My gaze drifted to Dag. He held back the smile on his lips, but I could see it in his eyes. He winked at me.

I grinned at him.

"All right, then," Eyfura said, coming to my bedside. "Drink," she said, handing me a small tonic.

"What's this?"

"For the pain."

"I feel no pain."

"I know. I've been giving you this brew every few hours since you got here. Trust me, you don't want me to stop. Drink."

Frowning, I swallowed the potion. I recognized the taste. Soon, my head would grow heavy, and I would sleep again. "Eyfura..."

"I will wake you when I must. But for now, rest, Ervie. Mend."

I sighed and then lay back.

"As for you," she told Dag. "Broth, then a tonic of your own. And no complaining or trying to get up, or

Kára will chide us," Eyfura said with a laugh, then left us.

On the cot beside me, Dag reached out for my hand.

I took it and held his gaze, my eyes on his until sleep took me again.

SOMEHOW, THE DAY AND THEN NIGHT PASSED. WHEN I woke again, it was morning.

Eyfura was pulling up a coverlet on Dag when she spotted me looking at her. She gestured for me to be silent, then came to me.

"How is he?"

"Sleeping. Healing is taking all of his strength. Your fast work saved him. Others have not been so lucky. Sigrun and Gida of Grund came to see you, but you were sleeping. As did Jarl Eir and her sister."

"That was good of them."

"I think we can get you outside for some fresh air now," she told me, then went to a table nearby to grab a crutch. Eyfura returned with it then bent to help me up. Holding on to me, she helped me rise. "Do everything you can not to put any weight on that leg," she told me.

"For seven nights," I said under my breath.

Eyfura raised an eyebrow at me.

"It's nothing," I said. "Just…a dream, maybe."

"You are the daughter of Mjord and Blomma. You understand better than most the importance of dreams. Listen to whatever warnings you were given."

"Yes, Princess."

Eyfura laughed. "There is a difference between you and Loptr. He knows when to listen and isn't stubborn."

"Partners should be balanced in all things," I told her with a wink.

With that, Eyfura laughed, then we made our way to the exit. As I went, I saw many warriors being treated for horrible injuries. The Gauls had been fierce in battle. A scratch here or there was expected, but these warriors had been horribly maimed and wounded.

"The price of vengeance on Harald's behalf was high," I said.

"My mother said the same. But in Angantyr's hands, Jutland will be reshaped. Harald was a failing king. His people are safer now under Angantyr."

"Yes. He will bring the jarls together in a way Harald never could."

"People are drawn to his sincerity. Harald may have raised him, but he is the blood of Hofund and Hervor. I see that earnestness in all those raised under King Hofund's watchful gaze."

"First, you tell me that my brother *isn't* stubborn. Now you are saying he's earnest?" I asked with a laugh.

"It will surprise you to hear, Reindeer Princess, that he is the most earnest man I've ever met."

Seeing Loptr through Eyfura's eyes was enlightening. I had never thought of my brother as an earnest man. But in things that mattered…yes, he was. He was mirthful, yes, but he was faithful to the families and jarls of Grund. And since he'd decided he would wed Eyfura, he had never strayed. My brother might dance with or smile at other women, but his heart belonged to the daughter of Gizer. He was earnest in his love for her.

I looked over my shoulder at Dag.

I, on the other hand, was a disaster.

Eyfura followed my gaze. "Every time he woke, he asked about you. All of my brothers have been in love with you at some point, but there is something to be said for *earnest* love."

I couldn't bring myself to look at her. My feelings were a torrent. Everything had happened so quickly. When I'd ridden away from Ormar, I knew I belonged with him in the Myrkviðr.

But the truth was, I had emerged from that place a different woman.

And that woman had room in her heart to love Dag the way he deserved.

And I did.

I loved him.

I loved them both.

"I sense…obstacles," Eyfura finally said.

"Yes."

"Hmm," Eyfura said. "We all know and love you, Ervie. You will do what is right," she said affirmatively, then pushed open the tent flap. "Though I can't say I would mind being your sister twice-over."

I gave her a soft smile.

"Angantyr will be at the hall. Can I trust you to at least go slowly?"

"Yes."

"I'll hold you to that."

"Thank you, Eyfura. For everything."

"It is nothing…Sister."

CHAPTER 20

I left the convalescence tent and made my way, slowly, toward the hill where the great hall of Skagen formerly sat. The skeletal structure I'd seen upon my arrival had already been cleared. Fresh timbers were being brought in from the surrounding woodlands. Men were working, sawing, and chopping everywhere I looked.

Not far from the remains of the hall, workers were busy clearing the ruins of the temple. It was there that I spotted Angantyr.

Turning slowly, I made my way toward him.

Magnus saw me first. Barking, he rushed my way.

"Easy, Magnus. Easy," I called, shaking my hand toward the wolf to keep him from jumping up.

Angantyr turned. Seeing us, he whistled to Magnus, slowing the wolf's steps.

Jogging behind the wolf, Angantyr joined me. "Ervie," he said, eyeing me over. "May Freyr be thanked. I am glad to see you up and about."

"It will be slow-going, but I am grateful to the gods. I guess they don't want me in Valhalla yet."

"I'm glad of that. I'll see you in my own hall first," Angantyr said.

"I was told I'd find you there," I said, gesturing toward the hall.

"Freyr will have his house before I have mine."

"As you wish, King Angantyr."

At that, my cousin laughed.

"There was nothing left of the old temple, so we removed the charred timbers yesterday and made sacrifices last night. Hofund and Loptr have been busy plotting and sketching. Soon, it will be all new and more grand than ever before."

"I'm happy for you, Cousin."

"Ervie," someone called.

I turned to find Elan coming with baskets heaped with herbs. Sigrit, the young girl who attended Svafa, was beside her.

"From the winding stream to the sun-drenched valley," I told her.

"From the winding stream to the sun-drenched valley," Elan answered.

I looked at the girl. "Sigrit... I am glad to see you again.

"Thank you, Princess. And you."

"When Sigrit learned I'd returned to Skagen with my future wife, she came to see if she could help Elan. Sigrit was so good to Svafa," Angantyr said, pausing to clear his throat. "We are glad to have her with us."

"I'm glad to be of help," Sigrit said, then smiled. "Lady Elan and I have been collecting healing herbs."

I looked into the baskets, identifying many herbs good for clearing poisons from the body.

"We should take these to Eyfura," Elan told us, then turned to Angantyr. "Unless you need me otherwise."

He shook his head. "No. Go where you are most needed. We are grateful for your healing hands."

Elan kissed him on the cheek and then set her hand on Sigrit's shoulder. "Come. I'll show you how to make a poultice."

"I think you are a gythia, Lady Elan," Sigrit said with a laugh.

"Something like that," Elan said, then the pair made their way back to the tent.

"What can I do to help?" I asked.

Angantyr looked me over. I could see he was considering telling me to sit and do nothing but thought better of it.

"Some of the men from Arheimar are working there," he said, gesturing to a smithy nearby. "I'm sure they can use your help with fletching."

"They're prepping arms?"

"I haven't forgotten what you've told me. This war with Kjar weakened us. I won't have Hlod take me unaware."

"Wise."

"I'm glad you think so," he said gravely. "Very soon, I must share the news of this threat with the others. Ervie, you must tell Hofund about Hlod. I wouldn't have him be the last to know."

"Yes. I will."

"And Ervie…" he said, smiling lightly. "My warband from Arheimar said you led them well, as I knew you would. While you fletch, think on my offer again. Please."

"Yes, Cousin."

Angantyr held out his pinkie. I latched mine around it and gave it a shake.

Turning, I made my way to the fletcher's bower, which sat beside the smithy where the men were working.

"Lady Ervie," Gunnar called. "Take this spot by the fire," he called, gesturing.

I scanned the space, spotting the fletcher's supplies

on a different table. "I think I'm of best use there," I said. "But my thanks."

"We lost you in the fray, Reindeer Princess," Halstein said. "But it wasn't hard to find you once you pulled that dwarven blade."

"Did you see when she pulled lightning from the sky?" Eluf asked. "Like Thor himself."

"That will teach those Gauls," Gunnar said with a laugh which the others joined.

"It was a fierce battle," Halstein said. "I was working my way to you and Prince Dag when I got swamped. Lady Elan said the man you and Prince Dag killed was King Hrollaug's brother."

"King Hrollaug's brother?" I asked as I slowly lowered myself onto a bench. I told myself not to wince, but I couldn't keep that promise. My leg protested loudly. I barely kept myself from crying out. Apparently, Eyfura's tonic was wearing off.

"That's what she said. The sword you won from him has a name: Moon-something. You will have to ask Lady Elan."

"Will you ride back to Arheimar with us when it is done?" Eluf asked.

All of the men turned toward me.

"I…"

"Maybe she will return with King Gizer," Halstein said as he tried to read my face.

"Or go back to Grund with her brother," Gunnar offered.

"Or stay here in Skagen," Arvid added.

"But we heard a rumor," Eluf said. "It would be good to have you in Arheimar, Lady Ervie."

"Princess," Halstein corrected him, slapping the young warrior across the back of the head.

"*Princess* Ervie," Eluf corrected himself.

I smiled gratefully at them. "I cannot say what my plans are yet. But for now, I know that I will sit and make arrows."

At that, the men chuckled.

"It's as good a task as any," Halstein agreed.

Smiling, I dipped into my satchel and pulled out my fletching kit. When I did so, I found several tools therein I had brought with me from Torkell's old workshop in the Myrkviðr. My mind was instantly flung backward in time to the fletcher's hut where Ormar would stop to— albeit indirectly—check on me. All that time, Ormar kept himself from feeling something for me. He was pretending he felt nothing for me, just as I was pretending to feel nothing for him.

The truth, however, was much different.

"Lucky the leg wasn't broken," Halstein said. "All the same, you won't be able to dance at Angantyr's wedding."

"Something tells me Princess Ervie is not the dancing type," Arvid chimed in.

"Get enough ale in me, only the gods know what I might do. I am the granddaughter of Loki, after all," I replied jokingly.

"Are you, Princess Ervie? They whisper it, but is it true?" Eluf asked.

I laughed. "No. But it makes for a good story," I said, then lifted a piece of wood and began whittling.

"Just the thing a granddaughter of Loki would say," Halstein said with a laugh.

"I say, did you see Princess Ervie's brother in battle? Prince Loptr spun his twin knives like a whirlwind. He was like a scythe come alive," Eluf said.

"That he was. He fought well," Halstein said.

"And I've heard people say he is no warrior, just a creature of the mead hall, but that's not true at all," Eluf said.

At that, Gunnar coughed lightly, then nudged Eluf to silence him.

"What? That is what they say. Many men whispered that Gizer would not give Eyfura to Loptr because he was no warrior, but he proved his worth against the Gauls."

"Eluf," Halstein chided the young warrior. "You've no sense at all. Hold your tongue in front of Princess Ervie."

Considering his words, I paused a moment and blew the dust from the arrow I was crafting. "Don't chide him, Halstein. Eluf is only saying what many think. I am glad my brother has proven us *all* wrong," I said, giving Halstein a knowing look.

Getting my meaning, he nodded to me.

"No, Princess Ervie won't return with us to Arheimar," Eluf said sadly. "They say you will marry Prince Dag. Is that true?"

"I might. Or, I might not. He hasn't asked me yet."

"She will," Gunnar said. "She almost died saving his life. I saw it with my own eyes."

"Of course I did," I replied.

"Because you love him?" Eluf asked.

"Prince Dag owes me a lot of silver. Can't let a man like that die," I replied with a wink.

At that, the men laughed.

"Come back to Arheimar with us, Ervie. Be our jarl," Eluf said.

Sliding my knife down the length of the wood, I replied, "It's for the Norns to decide, not me. My job is to sit on my arse, make arrows, and eat meat pies."

"Meat pies?" Eluf asked.

I nodded. "Yes. They are making them in the tent there," I said, pointing. "I saw them working as I passed. Pity, though, it's so far away."

"Boy," Halstein called to a teenage boy sitting not far

away from the others. I recognized him from Arheimar. He was a shy, quiet boy, but he had fought well. "What are you waiting for? Go get the Reindeer Princess a pie."

"I… Of course," the boy said, setting down the shield he'd been mending. "Of course. I'll be right back," he told me.

"And some for the rest of us too," Halstein said. "A whole basket."

At that, the others laughed.

Giving me a brief, shy glance, the boy hurried off.

"Half in love with you, that one is," Halstein told me.

"Only half?" Gunnar joked.

"What is his name?" I asked.

"Sithric."

I nodded. "You abuse his weakness for your own gain," I told Halstein with a playful smile.

"Of course we do. But you will not complain when you have a meat pie in your hand, will you, Reindeer Princess?"

At that, I laughed. "No, I will not."

And with that, the men turned back to their work, me along with them. But as I whittled, my mind wandered.

To the Myrkviðr.

To Ormar, whom I had left in his own sickbed.

Ormar…

I sent my mind searching for the king, feeling for him in the space between us.

And like lightning striking, I felt him reach back for me. And within that connection, I felt an overwhelming wave of love.

"Ervie..."

Aye, Norns, how you weave.

CHAPTER 21

I spent the rest of the day working on arrows and turning myself inside out about Angantyr's offer to rule Arheimar, about Ormar and Dag, about Hlod. Luckily, one of those problems found an opportunity to sort itself out when Hofund appeared with a round of bread and a mug of ale. He set them on my workbench.

"I passed by three times today, and you never looked up. Your forehead was scrunched up, just like your mother's used to when something was troubling her. I thought some food and ale might help."

I blinked hard, refocusing, then gave him a soft smile. "Thank you."

He sat on the bench beside me. Lifting an arrow, he inspected it. "Well made."

"I have Sigrun to thank."

Hofund nodded, then smiled. "She and Trygve are at the hall working on the construction and teasing poor Ásbjorn mercilessly."

"As a son-in-law deserves."

Hofund chuckled.

"Is all well in Grund?" I asked.

"Yes. It is quiet."

"And at the dísarsalr?"

Hofund smiled lightly. "Norna often asks for news of you. As does Eylin. I share it when I have it."

I felt a pang of guilt in my heart. But it was nothing compared to the sorrow I knew Hofund would soon feel.

"There is something I must tell you," I said, turning to the king.

"The thing that was troubling you on Samso."

I nodded. "In the Myrkviðr, King Ormar's people were attacked. I joined them to fight off those attackers. They were Huns."

Hofund stroked his beard. "I have heard of these people. Nomads, are they not? Horse people?"

I nodded. "They have a great empire to the east. And they keep pushing west. I… I fear they do so with renewed purpose."

"Into King Ormar's lands?"

"I'm sure they mean to acquire them on their way through…to here."

"Here? To our people?"

I nodded.

Hofund stared at me. "There is something you are not saying."

"There is a prince amongst them...Hlod. He is the grandson of the king of the Huns. His mother's name was Sifka."

Hofund held my gaze.

"And... his father, by his account, was Heidrek."

Hofund went rigid. After a long moment, he asked, "Is he telling the truth?"

"He has *her* eyes, the same as Angantyr."

Hofund inhaled a shuddering breath, then looked away.

"He is coming for us. And he has his father's violence in him."

After a long pause, Hofund asked, "Does Angantyr know?"

I nodded. "We didn't want to tell you until after the battle. I knew you would be...troubled."

"He is dead more than twenty years, and that boy still finds a way to bring misery to those I love. I have often asked Thor what I did to displease the gods that they took away my wife and sons. Not to forget the misery Mjord's death caused your family. Now..." Hofund shook his head. After a long moment, he rose. "Thank you, Ervie. I will speak with Angantyr of this.

Soon," he said, then rose. Unnerved, he turned toward the shore.

"Hofund," I called after him.

He paused.

"We are with you, Grandfather. You're not alone in this."

At that, Hofund gave me a grateful smile. His eyes glossy with unshed tears, he nodded to me, then turned and went on his way.

My heart ached for him. As broken as I was over losing my mother and the father I never knew, Hofund suffered the same heartaches. Yet he was a king. People depended on him. He had to go on, no matter the losses he faced.

Perhaps Hofund understood my pain better than I thought.

Sitting back, I ate half the loaf of bread, sipped the ale, and then slipped the rest of the bread into my satchel. When I rose, I accidentally put the tiniest amount of weight on my foot. I was met with a sharp reminder that it was not healed. Packing up my things, I grabbed my crutch and then slowly made my way back toward the convalescence tent.

When I entered, I found Eyfura sitting on the floor with five small children and two very energetic kittens. Eyfura was handing the children honey biscuits while the children took turns playfully teasing the kittens with an old bootlace.

"What do we have here?" I asked.

"Mischief incarnate," Eyfura said. "And some kittens," she added.

I chuckled. "I see."

"The children heard I'd prepared some honey-herbed biscuits for the wounded. They suddenly all had very sore everything. And two kittens."

The children looked up at me, uncertain of what I was going to say.

"You will make excellent warriors one day," I told them. "Already, you know how to employ the tactic of distraction."

At that, the children laughed.

"But we truly are ill," one of the little girls said with a giggle, her mouth full of biscuit, crumbs dropping from her lips. "I have a…broken stomach."

"Me too," a second little girl added with a giggle.

"Yes, you are all so very ill," Eyfura agreed, nodding. "I best give you all another biscuit. What do you think?" she asked the little boy beside her.

His eyes wide, he nodded.

I chuckled.

One of the wild kittens spotted me then. She arched her back menacingly at me, then attacked, climbing my leg like a tree. Barely managing to balance myself, I removed the wild fluff ball from my leg and gave it a pat. I was rewarded with my hand being viciously attacked.

"You must be careful of that one. She is one of Frigga's kittens. She's fierce," a little boy said, taking the kitten from me.

I laughed. "I shall be mindful," I told him, then ruffled his hair.

I gestured to Eyfura that I was on my way to check on Dag.

She smiled and nodded to me, then turned back to the children. "Now, I lost count. Who has already had a biscuit?" Eyfura asked the children.

"No one!" one of the little girls lied. "You didn't pass them out yet."

"Are you sure?" Eyfura asked suspiciously.

"Yes, Princess," another girl replied, nodding eagerly as she quickly wiped the crumbs from her mouth.

Chuckling, I left Eyfura and stopped at the small cooking station where I ladled out a pot of broth. Fingering through the herbs on the table, I selected a few healing herbs and added them to the crock. Taking what was left of my bread, I broke small pieces into the liquid and left them to soak until they were soft.

Grabbing a wooden spoon, I awkwardly crossed the room with the hot crock in one hand. When I got to Dag, I set the bowl aside and sat down slowly on his cot.

It was not lost on me that I had left Ormar in precisely the same condition.

Once more, I found myself at the bedside of a man I cared about.

When I quizzed myself, I acknowledged that I wouldn't have shown the same attention to Gizer's other sons. I loved them well but not enough to tend them.

They were not Dag.

Dag opened his eyes and looked at me.

"Ervie," he said.

"I brought you something to eat," I said. "It's just broth and soft bread, but better than mushroom tonics," I said, then moved to help him sit a little so he could eat. When I did so, however, I winced and let out a little "ahh," in pain.

Dag laughed.

I couldn't help but join him. "We're broken. Both of us, but no talking. Here, let me move the bedroll to prop you a little," I said, adjusting him as best I could, being careful not to bump his wound. Finally, I got him upright enough to eat then settled him in with the crock and spoon.

"Small bites only, and favor the good side of your mouth," I said.

He nodded.

"The warriors of Arheimar told me a tale about the man we battled. He was the brother of King Hrollaug."

"He was fierce," Dag whispered.

"He was protecting his throne. If Kjar died, perhaps he would have been king. It is a fine sword," I said, gesturing to the blade which sat propped in the corner by his bed. "Have you seen it? It has a name, but I don't know it. We must ask Elan."

Dag turned to look, but I could tell he was not much interested. He was in pain and, from the look of his drooping eyelids, dazed from the tonics. But that was not all that was bothering him. I could see it in his eyes.

He ate in silence for a long time, then asked, "Where did you go?"

"The smithy. There was fletching that needed doing. I lent a hand."

Dag looked at my hands. "They are red from work."

A ripple of laughter erupted from the children. Dag and I both looked to see Eyfura chasing them, the wild kitten in her hands, as she mock-attacked the children.

Dag huffed a laugh as he watched his sister. He finished what was in his bowl and then set it aside. His eyes suddenly grew wet with unshed tears. "I always dreamed we would one day have a brood of children like that. But in the Myrkviðr..." he began but didn't finish.

He didn't have to.

He looked at me.

I held his gaze, then swallowed hard. "I...I left you one person and came back another. Something within me was healed in the Myrkviðr. It's hard to explain. I'm not afraid of some things anymore, feelings I tried to deny, but now…" I swallowed, feeling tears well in my eyes.

"There is someone else."

I nodded.

Dag looked forward for a long time, then nodded. In a whisper, he said, "There were no promises made between us, Ervie. There was only ever love. And there still is," he said, then turned to me. "And one day, you will ask me to marry you, Reindeer Princess."

"Dag," I said with a sorrowful laugh, feeling a stray tear trailing down my cheek.

He reached out and wiped it away. "I love you, Ervie. And you love me. I can see it in your eyes. Now, you *know* you love me in a way you never knew. I've waited this long. I can wait a little longer."

"But Dag…"

"I don't care about whoever is in the Myrkviðr. He means nothing to me. You will work out what is right, like you always do."

I swallowed hard, moved by Dag's words. I'd planned to return to my people only for a time. I'd intended to return to the Myrkviðr and be at Ormar's side.

Now…

"To that end, Ervie, find me an ale. Don't let Eyfura

see. She'll chide me," he whispered, forcing himself not to laugh.

I chuckled, then winked at him. I scanned around the room, spotting Sigrit working at the herb sorting table. The girl must have felt eyes on her, because she looked my way. I gestured for her to come to me.

She scampered across the room quickly.

"Lady Ervie?" she asked.

"I am sorry to ask it, but I am poor at hobbling with one hand. Would you mind fetching a tankard of ale for me?"

"Of course!" she said brightly then set off.

"You see," Dag whispered to me. "This is why I don't doubt you, Reindeer Princess. Not now. Not ever."

My stomach twisted, and I swallowed hard.

Aye, Norns, how do I get out of this tangle?

CHAPTER 22

Our plan was a success; I slipped Dag an ale under the auspices that it was my own brew. He barely finished half of it before he slept. Taking care of the other half of the tankard, I made my way to the bench where Sigrit was working.

"Elan has gone to help Angantyr," she told me. "And Princess Eyfura has gone to have her evening meal with Prince Loptr and the others in the tent. Won't you go with them?" she asked.

"I'm fine where I am. But what about you?"

"I told Elan I would finish with the nettles and then go for the evening meal. She tried to talk me into going, but I wanted to complete my task here first. I like working with the herbs."

"Perhaps you should study with the gothar."

Sigrit shrugged. "No. I can learn well enough in the

hall. I will be glad to help Elan when she is queen. Svafa taught me much about being a good ruler," she said, then paused, a shadow crossing her face. "Did you hear what happened?"

I nodded. "Svafa loved you, and she is in Valhalla now. I'm certain she is glad to see you using your life in ways that make you happy."

At that, the girl blinked back her tears and then nodded.

"I tell you what, if you promise to bring me back something to eat, I can finish these nettles for you."

"You're sure you won't join the others?"

"Not tonight."

"Is your leg hurting? Do you need one of the gothar?"

"No. My leg is fine." *My heart is another matter entirely.* "I will stay with Prince Dag."

"Oh. Oh!" she said, then smiled brightly at me. "All right. I can do that. I will bring you back a huge platter."

"*After* you eat."

"*After* I eat."

I nodded. "Off with you then," I said, waving.

The girl smiled at me and then departed.

I settled in at the bench and got to work. The smell of the herbs took me back to my days at the dísarsalr. The work there had been peaceful, but the temple was not for me. Many times, I found it dull. While I was not Loptr, I liked the laughter and joy of the hall, even if I watched more than I participated.

Nonetheless, I hadn't forgotten what Norna had taught me.

Slipping on a pair of gloves, I began plucking the sharp leaves. Every time they poked through the material of my gloves, I let it serve as a reminder of the pain my actions would cause Dag and Ormar.

How had it come to this?

SIGRIT WAS FAITHFUL TO HER WORD, RETURNING WITH A massive platter of meat, cheese, bread, and vegetables. I set some bread aside for Dag, but he didn't wake again.

When the moon grew high, I heard the sounds of revelry coming from the tent where the others rejoiced over the defeat of the Gauls. Amongst the music and laughter, I heard Loptr's voice rising in song.

I rolled my eyes and shook my head.

I returned to Dag. I pulled a blanket over the warrior, gently touching his head to check for a fever— there was none—before lowering myself onto the cot beside him. I shifted slowly, moving my sore leg onto the bed. Struggling to get comfortable, I finally lay down and then turned to face Dag, whose eyes fluttered open briefly.

"It is night," I whispered to him. "Sleep."

"My Reindeer Princess," he whispered, then drifted back off into dreams.

I closed my eyes and bid my mind be quiet. In the end, all would be as the Norns willed. It was, as Loptr said, hnefatafl. There was nothing to be done.

"If only it were that easy, Reindeer Princess," a young female voice I recognized as that of the gythia who'd attended me whispered back to me.

THE NEXT SEVERAL DAYS PLAYED OUT THE SAME WAY. IN THE morning, I would leave to help with what little jobs I could, returning to check on Dag throughout the day and to tend to him at night. For his part, he slept most of the time, but I was glad of it. A wound to the abdomen would take time to heal, but he was coming along well. The pallor of his skin was improving, and he could sit up easier as the days passed.

As I tended Dag, I was continually reminded that I had left Ormar behind in a similar condition.

Who was there to watch over him?

On the morning before the seventh night since our return to Skagen, I woke to Queen Kára's booming laughter. I opened my eyes to find Dag standing, supported by Bjarki, nearby.

Wigluf was joking with Dag. "Bah, think nothing of it. It will give you a fierce grimace. Warriors will shite themselves when they see you in battle."

I sat up slowly, giving the others a soft smile.

"Ah, Ervie is awake too. Loptr was looking for you," Queen Kára told me.

"Must not have been looking very hard," I said, rubbing my temples.

At that, the others chuckled.

"We were about to wake you," Kára told me. "The gothar have read the runes, and the signs are good. Angantyr will take his bride and crown tonight. They are preparing the temple now."

"I should go help," I said.

Kára laughed. "That's what Dag said. We can all go together."

"I best hurry. I hear Loptr can't find me anywhere," I said, making the others laugh. I looked to Dag. "Did the gothar say you are well enough?"

He nodded.

"He must go slowly," Kára told her son, giving him a knowing look. "And not for long."

"Yes, Mother," he whispered, giving her a playful look.

Kára opened her mouth to chide him but, in the end, said nothing.

"Very well," I said, rising slowly.

Wigluf held my arm until I got my crutch under me.

We left the tent and began our way toward the temple. Much progress had been made in the passing days, the people working overnight by firelight to complete the work. The frames were in place at the great hall, and construction on the walls and roof was underway.

Everywhere I looked, I saw people working to rebuild Skagen.

At the temple, more progress had been made. Angantyr had planned the new temple to be much larger than the old. It occupied twice its former space.

There, we found Loptr, Hofund, and Angantyr gathered at a table, looking over a sketch. Loptr was explaining something to Angantyr, gesturing to the drawing, while my cousin stroked his beard as he considered. Standing next to Angantyr was Hofund, who stood in the same stance. Not for the first time, I wondered how things might have gone differently if Angantyr had been raised at Hofund's side rather than in Skagen. But it didn't matter. It was done. Now, Angantyr would be king here.

The three of them looked up as we approached.

Angantyr smiled, looking us over. "Ervie. Dag," he said, joining us. He gripped Dag lightly on the shoulder, then eyed him over. "Elan tells me you are healing well. I am glad to see you on your feet, my friend."

Dag tried to smile, but it pained him. "Thank you."

"Ah, Bjarki," Loptr said happily. "The men were looking for you at the hall. They want to raise the internal supporting beams but are waiting for your help. They need your muscle."

"I will see to it. I suppose it won't hurt to take Wigluf as well. Every little bit of muscle is useful. Come on," Bjarki told Wigluf, slapping him on the shoulder.

The two men departed, Wigluf reproving Bjarki as they went.

"It is coming along so quickly," I told Angantyr, gesturing to the temple.

"I'm not sure any of us have slept more than a few hours here or there, but I will waste no time seeing Freyr honored here."

"I'm told to expect a wedding and a crowning tonight."

Angantyr grinned. "Gizer is to blame. He goaded me into speaking with the gothar. He threatened to wed Elan to one of his sons if I didn't marry her first."

I chuckled. "Will the temple be ready?" I asked, looking from Angantyr to Hofund and Loptr.

Hofund nodded. "The hall will take longer, but the temple will be ready enough by nightfall."

"And the docks and city longer than that, but Hofund and Loptr have shared some good ideas on improving things and making better use of the land. I will take my time and see it done right," Angantyr said.

"We've missed you in the feasting tent these nights, Ervie. There has been great celebrating, song, and ale. Last night, Jorund's skald sang of our father. I was sorry you weren't there to hear it," Loptr told me.

He realizes I'm nursing a nearly broken leg, doesn't he?

"I had other things to attend to. But I'm glad to know Mjord was remembered."

"It was you wielding Hrotti on the battlefield that inspired him," Loptr told me.

"It *was* a sight to see," Hofund agreed. "Your father would be proud of you, Ervie."

I smiled lightly but didn't miss the quick flash of jealousy on Loptr's face.

"Thank you," I told the king, then turned to Dag. "We poor invalids are going to be of no use when it comes to hard labor," I told him, then turned to Angantyr. "Is there anything we can do to help?"

"If you can continue to lend your hands at the fletcher's workshop, I can't ask for anything more."

I looked to Dag, who nodded.

"We can do that."

"Good," Angantyr said. "Let me walk with you to the bower, then return after that," he told me, then gestured to Loptr and Hofund that he would be back.

Dag and his mother exchanged a brief word, then Queen Kára headed up the hill toward the great hall, following Bjarki and Wigluf.

Dag, Angantyr, and I made our way to the tradesman's row, Dag and I settling in at the workbench at the fletcher's hut.

Angantyr sat beside me. "Ervie," he whispered, looking over his shoulder to make sure no others could hear us. "There was a rider. A small party of Huns was seen at the edge of Ormar's borders between my lands and the Myrkviðr."

"Hlod?"

"I don't know."

I frowned.

"Your expression matches my feelings. I sent men from Arheimar to see what they could discover. I don't know if they are a scouting party, simply lost, or worse. Have you spoken to Hofund?"

"I have."

"Then I will gather the other kings as soon as I can. And we should get word to King Ormar. You cannot— must not—ride, but no one can get through the Myrkviðr to Ormar except you. Would Ormar trust someone if they were sent by you? *Your* messenger?"

"Perhaps," I said, my gaze quickly flashing to Dag, who listened carefully to us. "There is another way to warn him, but my strength may not be enough. Let's see what we learn then choose from there. And if I cannot accomplish it, we can send a rider."

Angantyr nodded. "We must be prepared if they are planning an attack."

"Cousin," I said, taking his hand. "Give yourself this day, just this day, to be at peace. Don't think about this anymore. Look at the new life cropping up around you. You will wed tonight and become king. Take a moment to accept the honor you deserve and the woman you love. War can wait."

Angantyr frowned.

I laughed. "Don't be stubborn. I know what threats you face, but allow yourself, for once, to enjoy what you have earned. *You. Angantyr.* What *you* have earned."

"You're right," he said, then set his hand on my shoulder. "And hopefully, *you* will not be too stubborn to take what I have offered. But I suspect I will have to get past Ormar to get you to accept," he said with a chuckle, then rose and went on his way.

I turned back to the workbench, considering Angantyr's words.

"What did Angantyr offer you?" Dag asked, his voice little more than a whisper as he struggled not to use his lips.

"Arheimar. He wants me to rule as jarl there."

"Will you?"

"It is a fine jarldom, and they are good people. But things are…complicated."

After a long pause, Dag asked, "Ormar. Because of King Ormar?"

I stared before me for a long moment, then said, "Not just because of Ormar."

"But it is *him*."

I nodded, then turned to look at Dag. "Please forgive me for things becoming so confusing. It was never my intention to hurt you or anyone else."

"Do you love him?"

I nodded.

"And you love me."

Again, I nodded.

Dag paused, then pulled his knife from his belt. He picked up a length of wood and began working. "You love me more. I'm not worried. You will see, Reindeer Princess. In the end, you will see."

CHAPTER 23

Dag and I worked the rest of the morning at the fletcher's workshop, not speaking of Ormar again. Instead, we went back to our old ways of poking fun at Dag's brothers or rehashing the details of the battle. We fell into a natural rhythm.

One that felt good.

Comfortable.

Much to my relief.

When the midday meal was prepared, a horn sounded outside the massive tent.

Dag and I made our way slowly, joining the others.

"Ah, here you both are," Gizer said, crossing the tent to join us. The king must have been laboring hard all morning. His tunic hung loose and untied, revealing the tapestry of tattoos on his chest. "Ervie, you are still supported by sturdy oak. What do the gothar say? How long until you will walk with ease?"

"I was told I must rest seven nights for the mending to set."

"Seven nights. Just long enough to keep you from doing any of the hard labor, but good enough for you to be ready to sail home with us," he said with a grin.

"Ervie will become jarl of Arheimar," Dag told his father.

"Is that so?" Gizer asked.

"It is not decided nor widely known, if you understand me."

"I do," Gizer said, then turned serious. "It is a generous offer, Ervie. And not so different from Hofund's offer of Bolmsö, but I suspect you are more inclined to accept the proposal from your cousin."

"Bolmsö was Hervor's island, and her people rule themselves in peace. I will not disrupt their world. I don't belong there."

"But you belong in Arheimar?" Gizer asked, raising a playful eyebrow at me.

"I..." The king knew well that I warred with the sense that I didn't really belong anywhere. Now, I felt differently. When I rode from the Myrkviðr, I thought I belonged *there*. And I was eager to get back. Now, I wasn't sure. The truth was, part of me wanted to rule Arheimar. I liked the idea of leading a jarldom sitting on the borders of the Myrkviðr. I would be close to the man I loved.

Except I also loved the man beside me.

Gizer, sensing my hesitation, laughed. "Aye, Ervie. Let the Norns sort it out. Come on. Let's get some ale. You aren't drinking enough these days. Drink like Thor. It will help you forget the pain in your leg," he said, then turned to the crowd. "Thorir, bring Ervie and your brother horns of ale," the king called to his youngest son. Gizer turned to Dag. "Arheimar is a fine city, Son," he said, then winked.

Dag chuckled lightly. "I know, Father."

Queen Kára joined us. "Aye, gods, you smell bad, Gizer," she said, taking his chin and giving it a shake.

"You'll have to find a rain barrel to dunk me in, Wife," he said, slapping her playfully on the backside.

Dag rolled his eyes.

Kára laughed, then gave her husband a sly look. "You didn't say how long to hold you under."

Gizer grinned. "Careful, woman, or I'll pull you in with me, and we'll both drown."

"Not a chance," Kára replied. "I will live longer than you, Gizer. That way, I can enjoy your wealth on my own."

"And a new, young husband?" Gizer asked her playfully.

"Maybe."

"Do that, Queen Kára, and I will come from Valhalla and haunt you until you die."

They both laughed.

Thorir arrived with ale horns for Dag and myself.

"Thank you, Brother," Dag told him.

Thorir looked over his brother's wounds. "Are you... are you all right? Is the healing coming along?"

Gizer's sons were an interesting lot. They teased one another mercilessly, but in the end, they loved one another dearly. They were a close family. Many times, I envied them. At the moment, I had no idea where Loptr was, and he had only passingly noticed that I might have a limp for the rest of my life. Perhaps that was why I felt better at Gizer's court. They had made me feel like one of the family.

"I will mend."

"Winter is coming," Gizer said. "You should sit on your arse in Arheimar and get fat," Gizer told Dag.

Dag merely chuckled.

"Arheimar?" Thorir asked, confused.

"Will you let your mother and me go parched?" Gizer asked Thorir. "Give those horns to Dag and Ervie, then fetch us drinks, boy," Gizer told his son.

Thorir passed me the drink—to which I mouthed the words "thank you"—then the warrior made his way to get another round.

Gizer chuckled.

"How is the hall coming?" I asked.

"We will have it done by month's end and be home before winter," Gizer said. "Jorund is already looking anxious to return to Uppsala. We need to keep him drinking so he stays in Skagen. Come, Wife, let's get to it," Gizer said, taking Kára's arm and crossing the room to meet Thorir who was coming with the drinks.

I motioned to Dag, and we joined the others at the table.

We spent the midday meal chatting with family and friends. When the others were ready to get back to work, I eyed Dag closely. He was looking pale, and there were dark rings under his eyes.

"You need rest," I told him. "You've done too much today. You should get some sleep if you don't want to miss the crowning and wedding."

"I won't argue," Dag said. "What about you?"

"Somewhere around here, there is an anxious bride short on friends. I need to find Elan."

"Then, I will see you tonight, Reindeer Princess."

"Can I help you back to the tent?"

Dag shook his head. I saw a sad expression play across his features, but he buried it. "Go find Elan. She will need you. I'm just going to snore and drool on my cot," he said, then laughed quietly.

"As always."

"As always," he said, a slight smile lighting up his face.

"Make sure Eyfura looks over those dressings later."

"Yes, Ervie."

"No complaining."

"Of course not, Ervie."

With that, Dag headed off.

Leaving the feasting tent, I hobbled to the main road and gazed around. I spotted Angantyr at the temple. The walls had gone up on four sides, and work was underway on the roof. While it would not be ready in all of its glory, it would be ready enough by nightfall. I didn't see Elan in the crowd or on the hill at the construction of the great hall.

Suddenly, everything felt too far to walk—or hobble, as it were—to check for her.

A sparrow landed in a tree nearby.

Noise. Noise. The humans are making so much noise.

Sitting down on a nearby barrel, I closed my eyes and felt for the sparrow's life force, drifting gently toward the creature.

Let me borrow your eyes.

Let me borrow your wings.

Shifting my spirit, I slid into that of the sparrow. As always, it took me a moment to get my bearings. But once I did, I lifted off, taking to the sky in search of the priestess. I swooped across the city, feeling my heart pattering quickly in my chest. I flapped my small wings. It was different inhabiting the body of such a small bird compared to that of an owl or eagle. The effort it took for the sparrow to fly gave me a renewed respect for the creature.

I spun over the city, looking for any sign of Elan. Finally, I spotted a shimmer of light not far from a wooded glen.

A colorful spiral of rainbow-colored light rose from the forest. I made my way toward it, slipping down into the leafy canopy of trees. In a small glade, I found Elan on her knees, her eyes closed in prayer. She knelt before a stone on which was an apple, a bit of honeycomb, some flowers, and a goblet of milk.

I could hear her soft words as she prayed to her gods.

She was speaking in a dialect—or perhaps the language of her gods—I didn't understand.

Suddenly, I felt very sorry for the priestess.

She was far from home.

No mother.

No family.

It was only her and her gods.

I alighted on the branch, then gently let the sparrow go.

When I opened my eyes, I found Loptr standing before me, staring at me wide-eyed.

"Ervie," he whispered. "What were you doing? Your eyes were rolled back. You wouldn't answer me."

"In the Myrkviðr, I learned to control a fylgia. I was... not here."

"Where were you?"

"I borrowed the eyes of a bird to search for Elan. She's in the woods there," I said, pointing.

"Through the eyes of a bird?"

"Yes, I used it as my fylgia."

"You learned how to do that in the Myrkviðr?"

I nodded.

I watched Loptr's brow furrow as he considered, jealously contorting his features.

"Brother," I said. "Our parents' talents with seidr never appealed to you before. Don't let petty jealousies come to your mind now. You will wed Eyfura and become King of Grund. You have a happy life before you, one you always wanted."

"Don't presume to read my mind, Ervie. You don't know what I want," Loptr replied waspishly.

My empathy for my twin evaporated in an instant. "Yes, I do. You want whatever you think makes people like you. And right now, you think that having Hrotti and being able to use seidr will earn you favor. Even though you never once considered it nor cared about it in the past. You're jealous, Loptr."

"Jealous? Of you?"

"Not of me, precisely. Only of what I have and can do."

Loptr blew air through his lips. "What is there to be jealous of? You're like some nomad, not stopping anywhere long enough to be of any good to anyone, just living off the kindness of Gizer and others. No one can rely on you for anything. Who can be jealous of that?" he replied angrily, then turned and walked away.

I opened my mouth to hurl an insult in reply but closed it before the words left my lips. The truth was, Loptr had plucked at the one string he knew would hurt me. The one string that was, in a way, true.

I had wounded Loptr with the truth.

He had paid me back in kind.

Rising, I steadied my crutch and headed toward the glade where I had seen Elan.

With every step, Loptr's words rang in my heart. He wasn't wrong. I wasn't reliable. Ormar was wrong to put his faith in me. And so was Dag. I had managed to prove fickle to both. I hadn't meant to act capriciously. I was just...wounded. I'd run from Grund wounded. I'd run to the Myrkviðr wounded. I wasn't trying to be changeable. I was just hurt. I didn't want to live like that anymore.

In that single moment, I made up my mind.

I would take the jarldom in Arheimar.

There, I could be of use to Angantyr and his people.

At least I would be some good to someone.

But even as determination swelled up in me, I also realized my reaction was one of overreaction.

Nothing was ever going to be that easy.

In the running to Arheimar, I was running *away* from Dag *and* Ormar.

"Let Frigga bind your tongue, Loptr," I cursed my brother, knowing fully that he had been right.

CHAPTER 24

By the time I made it to the forest's edge, Elan had appeared. Her eyes looked red and puffy. She wiped the back of her hand across her cheeks as she tromped over the ferns toward the road. So lost in her thoughts, she looked up in surprise and gasped when she saw me.

"Oh! Ervie. Sorry."

"Not so easy to sneak up on a priestess, or so I thought."

"Easy enough to sneak up on a bride, however."

I chuckled. "I'm guessing you may need some help in that department."

"Help?"

I nodded. "Come with me."

At that, Elan and I made our way to the healers' tent.

"And what are we doing here?" Elan asked.

I scanned the space, spotting Sigrit. I called to the girl, then turned to Elan. "Enlisting help."

A smile on her face, Sigrit joined Elan and me.

"Lady Elan, Lady Ervie. Did you need something?"

I nodded. "Elan will wed tonight. Presumably, in a sweaty tunic, stained apron, and trousers—"

"Hey—" Elan began in protest, but I silenced her with a look.

"Unless we help her," I continued. "Who can we see in the village? In the market? Is there anyone who survived the fire who might be able to assist the next queen of Jutland?"

Sigrit considered the question. "Yes, I do know who to ask. Come with me," the girl said, pulling off her apron and setting it aside.

Sigrit led us down the lane away from the heart of the city to a small cottage at the edge of town not far from the woods where the men were working. She went to the door and knocked. A few moments later, an ancient woman appeared. She was a bent thing with white hair pulled back in braids from her temples, her face deeply lined.

"Sigrit? Little Sigrit? Is that you, sweet?"

"Mother Ama, I've come with visitors."

The old woman looked back at us. "Oh! Visitors!" she said, then clapped her hands together. "It's been strange days. No visitors since they took poor Svafa from us, but

I thank the gods every day I open my eyes and see the sun once more. Come in. Come in," she said, then stepped back.

Sigrit gestured for us to follow her inside.

"I say," the ancient woman told me, looking at my crutch. "Did you get that fighting the Gauls, shield-maiden?"

"I did, but the Valkyries were with me. That Gaul is a feast for the worms now."

At that, the woman laughed. "That is the way of battle."

"Mother Ama, this is Lady Ervie, cousin to Prince Angantyr," Sigrit said, introducing me.

"Oh, indeed? Svafa spoke of you many times. Little Blomma's daughter."

"Yes," I said.

"And this is Lady Elan, who will wed Prince Angantyr."

At that, the old woman studied Elan closely. "Ah, so you are the Gaul who stole the prince's heart. They tell me you are some sort of priestess for your gods."

"Yes. We are called druids, Mother. Our work is similar to that of your gothar."

"Hmmm," the old woman said as she considered. "Did you bewitch our prince?"

"Mother Ama," Sigrit protested.

Elan raised her hand, gesturing to Sigrit that it was

okay. "It is a fair question and one I would ask too. I am glad to know Angantyr is so well loved. No, Mother. From the moment I saw Angantyr, I loved him. I have traded much for that love, but he is worth it."

The old woman nodded as she considered Elan's words, then said, "Then it is the will of the Norns. We will not judge their choices. Now, little Sigrit, tell me why you have come."

"The Prince and Lady Elan will marry in the new temple tonight."

"So I have heard. They have called throughout the village to invite us all to come. A new temple. A new king. A new queen. Ah, but I shall miss Aud. Harald... well...but Queen Aud was one of us. And, of course, Svafa."

"Mother Ama, Svafa asked you to make her a new dress before the Gauls attacked. I was wondering... Lady Elan has nothing to wear for her wedding. I was think-ing, maybe, if you finished the gown intended for Svafa... Well, I don't think Svafa would mind seeing Elan have it."

At that, the woman let out an excited breath and then clapped her hands together. "Dear girl, what an excellent idea. Svafa was taller than our future queen, so I will need to fix the hem, but yes, the gown is done. Come and see, come and see," she said, then led us all across the room to a trunk. "The Gauls paid me no mind, thinking I had nothing of value. All they saw was an old woman in a hut," Mother Ama said, opening the trunk. "They did not see value in thread and cloth."

The old woman pulled a deep purple gown from the chest. The dress was trimmed at the neckline and sleeves with embroidery depicting vibrant red poppies and deep green leaves. It was a beautiful work of art.

"Did you make this yourself? All of this embroidery?" Elan asked, lifting the sleeve.

"I did," the old woman replied.

"Lady Svafa called her the most talented dressmaker in all of Scandinavia. And Svafa loved fine dresses," Sigrit said with a laugh.

The old woman joined in the laughter. "That she did. Come, Lady Elan. Let's get you into the gown so I can hem it in time. We won't have you tripping over your wedding dress."

"But," Elan said, then paused. She looked at me. "Are you sure this is all right?"

"Svafa was like a mother to Angantyr. I'm sure."

And with that, I let Mother Ama take over. I settled into a chair by the fire. The woman's old dog lifted his head to greet me, wagging his tail, then went back to sleep again. I hated to admit it, but my whole body was aching. I felt better, but still. Even the slightest twitch in the wrong direction made my leg feel like it was on fire. And my ankle still hurt. When I saw Narfi again...

Feeling the weight of my injuries, I closed my eyes for only a moment...

Just a moment...

A little rest...

Some point later, Sigrit shook my shoulder. "Lady Ervie? Reindeer Princess?"

"Hmm?"

At that, the other women laughed.

I opened my eyes to find Elan standing in a freshly hemmed gown, her hair fixed in pretty braids.

"Awake, Reindeer Princess? I'm not sure who was snoring louder, you or Dub the dog," Elan said, gesturing to the ancient hound.

"I...sorry," I told Elan, moving to rise.

"It's good you rested. You are on that leg too much," Elan told me.

"If you need anything else, Lady Elan, I'm always here. A queen will need her finery, and I have a few more gowns left in these old hands," Mother Ama told Elan.

"You have my eternal thanks," Elan said, giving the old woman a kiss on the cheek. "Be sure you come to the feast tonight. There will be much merriment."

She chuckled and patted Elan's arm. "Thank you, my queen."

"The sun is going down," Sigrit said. "I sent one of the neighbor's children to tell Angantyr where Lady Elan was, but I am sure they will be ready for you soon, Lady."

Elan nodded. "Yes, you're right."

Grinning, I made my way to the door.

"You, too, Reindeer Princess. I'm here if you need me," Mother Ama called.

"Thank you, Mother Ama. We are grateful for your kindness. May the weavers bless your hands," I told her.

At that, the old woman gave me a toothy smile.

I must have slept longer than I realized. Sigrit was right. The sun *was* already setting. The sky was streaked with bright orange and vibrant pink, the horizon trimmed in violet.

"Will you look at that?" Mother Ama said. "Ah, Frigga is working her magic tonight for you, Lady Elan. The gods bless your marriage. You will see. I look forward to seeing your many sons and daughters racing up and down the streets of our renewed Skagen."

At that, Elan smiled as she looked at the sky.

"Frigga or Nantosuelta?" I asked the priestess.

"Or both? Why not both, Reindeer Princess?"

"Indeed, why not both?"

CHAPTER 25

The three of us made our way to the temple.

"I'll be right back," Sigrit said, running ahead.

As we went, many of the townspeople called to Elan.

"Blessings to you, Lady Elan."

"May Frigga bless you, Lady!"

"May Freyja and Freyr offer you their good tidings, Lady Elan," they called.

Elan's eyes grew wet with unshed tears.

"I...I cannot believe they are accepting of me," she whispered. "Not after everything that has happened."

"Everyone has heard the tale of what you have done. They know your loyalty lies with Angantyr. That has won their respect. And mine."

Elan gave me a soft smile. "Thank you. For everything. From the first moment until this one. You've quite upended my life, Reindeer Princess."

"I'm glad I intervened."

At that, she chuckled. "Me too."

When we turned the corner where the road led from the docks to the temple, a breathless Sigrit met us again. This time, she had a bouquet of wildflowers—red poppies, purple asters, and daisies.

"I remembered there were some growing near the water's edge," she said. "I saw them when Eyfura sent me for meadowsweet. Now, you are truly a bride."

Elan hugged the girl and then kissed her on the top of the head. "Thank you, Sigrit."

I snatched one of the poppies, sticking the blossom behind my ear. "Settled."

At that, they laughed.

We made our way down the street toward the temple. A large crowd had gathered.

Torches burned within the temple. Nearby, the large tent had been reorganized to host the festivities. Bonfires dotted the field behind the tent. I smelled roasting meat and baking bread in the air. All of Skagen had worked to prepare things for the new king and his bride.

The crowd parted before us, leaving us a path to make our way to the temple.

The black-robed gothar waited by the unfinished

door of the temple. Inside, the temple was full of people. At the front, I saw Angantyr and Magnus.

One of the gothar sounded a horn.

Another began to beat a drum.

We made our way toward the temple.

The people called their blessings to Elan as we went, asking Frigga to bless the priestess.

When we reached the entrance to the hall, one of the gothar signaled for us to wait.

"Great Freyr," a gythia called, reaching toward the sky. "Our future queen shall take her first steps into your sacred hall. Bless her, Freyr. Shed your abundance upon her. Bless her with fertility and health. May she ever be a servant to you and all the gods in this sacred space. As Skagen begins anew, bless Elan who will wed Angantyr and be our queen."

At that, one of the gothar sounded the horn.

The gythia then gestured for Sigrit and me to enter the temple. I smiled at Angantyr and made my way to him, Sigrit alongside me. Angantyr had redressed. From the looks of his tunic, neat braids, and silver pieces in his hair, I suspected Loptr's involvement. When I reached my cousin, I gently set my hand on his shoulder and then stepped to the side of him, not far from where Hofund and Loptr waited. Sigrit gave Angantyr a quick hug and then joined me.

The horn blew once more.

We all turned back and waited for Elan's approach.

When I did so, I caught Dag's gaze.

The irony was not lost on me.

It was at Angantyr's last—doomed—wedding that my mind had started to come to terms with the idea that maybe there was something real between Dag and me.

Now…

I gave him a soft smile.

He winked at me.

Then, with drummers and pipers following her, Elan entered the hall.

Svafa, I hope you can see this from Odin's great hall. Look what's become of the dress you commissioned.

The gothar led Elan to the front of the temple.

A makeshift altar had been set at the front. A slab of wood supported by two tree trunks served as the holy altar. The whole room smelled of freshly cut lumber. The floor had not yet been laid with flagstones. Straw covered the ground. No effigies or carvings of Freyr or other gods adorned the place. Everything—even the smell of the place—was new.

But it was fitting.

Angantyr would usher in a new era for the people of Jutland.

A gothi stood before Angantyr and Elan.

"Honorable Frigga, today Angantyr and Elan come before you to be wed. Frigga, wife of Odin, offer your blessings to this couple. With their marriage and crowning, Skagen is born anew. Freyr, to whom this holy temple has been dedicated, bless your son Angantyr. Bless his endeavor to restore our city in your name. Odin, All-Father, we honor you, Lord, in this great hall. May you and all the Æsir and Vanir bless Elan and Angantyr. We shall begin this day with an exchange of swords," the gothi said, then turned to Angantyr.

For a moment, I panicked. Had anyone prepared Elan? Did she have something to offer?

I studied her quickly. She had a knife on her belt, and her expression was steady.

If the moment came to confusion, I would step forward.

"Elan," Angantyr said, reaching to Hofund for a sword. "To you, I gift the sword of King Hofund of Grund, my grandfather. We offer this to you in keeping for our children. May the sword of King Hofund protect our family and serve as a reminder of my loyalty."

I flicked my gaze toward Hofund. The king always wore the sword on his belt but preferred his hammers in battle. Yet, how often had I seen Hofund use the blade in training and when dealing with ruffians? It was his sword, commissioned by him as a young man. That he would give it to Angantyr moved me. Not only was it a show of loyalty to Angantyr's new bride, but it was also

a show of love and loyalty from Hofund to Angantyr—
one very late in coming.

I turned back to Elan, but the priestess did not hesi-
tate. She removed the dagger from her belt and handed it
to her husband. "This silver knife was given to me by the
order of druids when I completed my training as a
priestess. I am a child of my gods. Angantyr, keep this
sacred blade for our children so they may know they are
twice blessed—by your gods and mine."

Angantyr took the dagger.

The two of them sheathed their weapons and then
turned to the gothi once more.

The priest held a wooden bowl full of soil. Lying on
the dirt were two rings.

"Love is born from a place deep within us, like roots
within the soil. As you become husband and wife, you
also become king and queen. May the very land bless
your marriage. Let these rings bind you to one another
and the people of Jutland who you will serve," the gothi
said. He took a small handful of dirt and then passed the
bowl to a gythia. With his dirt-covered fingers, he drew
runes on Angantyr's and Elan's brows, binding them to
one another and the land.

The gothi then lifted one ring and handed it to
Angantyr. He gestured for Angantyr to place the ring on
Elan's finger.

"With this ring, I take you as my wife," Angantyr told her, slipping the ring on her finger.

The gothi handed the other ring to Elan.

"With this ring, I take you as my husband," she said, placing the ring on Angantyr's finger.

"Let Frigga, Freyja, and Freyr bless this couple," the gothi called. "Not only have they been united in marriage, but we doubly bless them as our king and queen," he said, gesturing for a gythia to come forward.

The priestess held a basket in her hands. Within it were two crowns made of tree branches.

"The crowns I present to Angantyr and Elan have been taken from a young oak. The tree's woven branches serve as a symbol. Skagen will grow again and become the pillar of strength it once was. But it will also grow into something new, something full of hope and promise. With these crowns, you become our new king and queen," the gothi said, then took one of the crowns from the basket and placed it on Elan's head. "Elan, I crown you Queen of Jutland." Taking the second crown, he placed it on Angantyr's head. "Angantyr, I crown you King of Jutland. May your ancestors bless you. May the gods give you strength and guide you. King Angantyr, kiss your queen. In so doing, claim both queen and crown as your own. Queen Elan, kiss your king. In so doing, claim both king and crown as your own."

At that, the gothi stepped back. Angantyr met Elan's

gaze, then set a gentle hand on her cheek. He then leaned in and placed a kiss on her lips.

At that, we all erupted in cheer.

Outside, and across all Skagen, horns sounded, and we heard calls of joy.

"Now, shall we have a running of the bride? Who can reach the entrance of the great hall first?" the gothi asked.

At that, the crowd cheered, but I paused.

"Who will run for Angantyr?" the gothi called, eliciting many volunteers.

Laughing, Angantyr pointed to Eluf. "Eluf of Arheimar will run."

The crowd whistled and called out.

I knew my people were keen to keep their tradition, but the reality was that there was no one there for Elan. Had things been different, I would run. But now... Afraid no one would speak up for her, I turned and gave Loptr a desperate look.

"And for Queen Elan—"

"I will run for the queen, if she will have me," Loptr shouted, eliciting a cheer.

Elan inclined her head to him. "I am honored, Prince Loptr."

Loptr gave me a wink, then went to the gothi.

"Come, then," the gothi called, motioning for Eluf and Loptr to follow him to the temple door. Angantyr and Elan trailed behind the priest, the rest of us following.

Magnus bounced around excitedly, sensing something fun was about to take place.

"The first to reach the door frame of the new hall wins," the gothi told Loptr and Eluf.

"Are you ready, Prince of Grund?" Eluf asked Loptr teasingly as he pushed his hair back over his shoulders.

"Are you, warrior of Arheimar?"

"More ready than you. Your boots are too new, Prince Loptr. They will hurt your feet before you make it to the hill."

"Hardly," Loptr said with a laugh. "You should be more worried about your ale paunch slowing you down."

"On the count of three," the gothi began. "One, two, three!"

And off they went, the pair racing down the street toward the great hall.

Magnus rushed behind them.

Elan turned toward me and reached for my hand.

She gave it a soft squeeze and then let me go as we turned to see who would reach the top of the hill first.

Eluf was a fierce warrior, but I knew my brother. There was no way he would lose, especially not in front of Gizer. Eluf was not racing Loptr, he was racing Loptr's hubris. But for all my brother's pride, I was eternally grateful for what he had done for Elan—and me. Loptr and I lived worlds apart, in both distance and in the mind, but we were still twins.

When Loptr reached the top of the hill before Eluf, I was not surprised. Touching the beam, he let out a cheer of victory.

"Well done, Prince Loptr. Well done!"

"Come now, friends," Angantyr called. "Let us feast and praise the gods."

At that, the crowd cheered.

"Come, Loptr," Angantyr yelled. "I owe you a drink! You too, Eluf!"

Loptr waved to Angantyr. Laughing, he threw his arm around Eluf's shoulder, and the two men made their way back down the hill to join us.

Hand in hand, Elan and Angantyr led us to the festival tent.

And at that moment, all felt right with the world.

CHAPTER 26

The night began with great cheer, dancing, and music. As the evening rolled on, the drunken revelry did not let up. Even I found myself pulled in, imbibing in a way I had not done since I'd left Gizer's hall. Musicians gathered, playing reel after reel. Angantyr—who was rather drunk—and Elan spun to the music, their eyes only on one another. Everyone danced, including Loptr and Eyfura, who looked at one another with such love, I felt jealous.

What a mess I'd made of things.

My thoughts went to Ormar and the words we had shared.

I had promised to come back.

And I had meant it.

Now?

My gaze flicked to Dag.

He had spent most of the night drinking with his brothers. While his physical wounds still pained him, I could see in his eyes that he was haunted by his heart. And that was my fault. The fact that he hadn't joined me and would not meet my gaze again told me everything I needed to know. The wedding had evoked strong, painful emotions in him.

I hated this.

I hated it for all of us.

As much as I didn't want to hurt Dag, when I thought about hurting Ormar, I felt like I'd rather die.

Feeling frustrated with myself, I tried to refocus my attention on the joyful crowd.

My cousins, Jarl Eir and Dissa, and their shield-maidens had found many handsome partners to share in their merriment. Jarls Hakon and Halger tested anyone who would dare to feats of strength when they were not too busy laughing and drinking. King Hofund, Jarl Leif, and King Jorund sat with King Gizer and Queen Kára at one table, all rehashing the glory of their past achievements. Sigrun and her family were with them. Jarl Leif looked a bit haggard, his shoulder still bandaged from the arrow he had taken, his arm in a sling.

Everywhere I looked, people looked happy.

Once more, that odd sense that I didn't belong gnawed at me.

Perhaps it was the misery lingering in my heart, or

maybe I just missed the Myrkviðr, but I was suddenly struck with the urge to walk. Feeling pulled outside, I left the tent and slowly walked down the road away from the festivities.

All across Skagen, fires burned, and people cheered their new king.

The moon hung in a crescent overhead.

This night would make six nights.

Whatever the Norns were weaving, I was about to slip away from their tangle. The warning had hung over me these last days like a dark shadow. I was glad to know that I would soon be free.

One night to go.

I wasn't surprised when a shadow appeared beside me, a warm nose poking into my hand.

"Magnus," I said, patting the wolf on his head. "Too much excitement for you too?"

The wolf whined at me in agreement.

"I don't know where I'm going," I told him, then continued on my way. "Ever feel the urge to just go?"

Magnus trotted ahead of me.

I took that as a yes.

I ambled down the lane until I reached a crossroads.

The road trailed onward toward the docks. Another went toward the hall. Behind me was the temple. But on the long road before me was the way back to Arheimar... and it would also begin a journey back to the Myrkviðr.

I stood still, staring down the road.

I could just leave.

I could just get on my horse and go.

But if I did that, why had I come all this way?

Angantyr was king now.

The most immediate threat was settled.

I could return to Ormar and be done with all of this. Be happy. Not worry about any of this anymore.

I *should* just go.

But the moment I thought it, a horn sounded from the gatepost at the end of the road. I watched as torches came to life. There was a commotion amongst the guards. Whoever had come, it had created confusion.

A boy came racing down the road, jumping fences and cutting across gardens toward the festival tent.

A moment later, the gates swung open, and riders appeared.

I could not make them out clearly in the darkness.

They trotted down the road toward me.

Magnus stood before me, the wolf stiffening as he watched. As the riders drew near, the hackles on Magnus's back rose, and a low growl emanated from him.

A wind blew across the city, drifting up the lane, blowing my hair back.

"Ervie...the past has come again."

My skin rose in gooseflesh.

And then, I saw.

At the front of the party were Halstein and Canute. But behind them...

Gasping, I pulled Hrotti.

The sword made an angry crack as it left its scabbard. Overheard, the sky rumbled with thunder, and a bolt of lightning blasted between the clouds.

"Ervie," Halstein said, gesturing for the party to halt. "Are you..."

"Well met, Reindeer Princess," Hlod called to me, tapping his reins to coax his horse forward.

Magnus growled low and mean.

"Hlod, what are you doing here?" I hissed.

"Peace, Princess. I am here to make amends. Let me begin with you. Princess Ervie, I ask for your forgiveness. In my haste, I acted unwisely. You and King Ormar's people suffered the price for my impatience. You have my sincerest apologies."

Nothing in me believed him. "You didn't answer me. Why are you here?" I asked again, shifting my stance.

As I did so, Hrotti sang—the sword let out a piercing whine that echoed across Skagen. The men flinched as it made their ears hurt.

But not Hlod.

Hlod looked from the blade to me. "To make peace, Princess. To make peace."

A moment later, Angantyr appeared behind me, the warriors of Arheimar with him.

"Princ—King Angantyr," Halstein said. "We went out as you asked and encountered this party on the road. They asked us to escort them here. Their leader, Hlod, asked to meet with you."

Angantyr stared at Hlod.

At that moment, I realized the similarity in their looks. Hlod may have had his mother's long, black hair, but the cut of their chins, the shape of their noses, the color of their eyes...Hlod and Angantyr *were* of the same blood.

"King Angantyr," I said. "This is Hlod of the Huns."

"*Prince* Hlod," Hlod corrected me, then turned to Angantyr. With a smile, he added, "And I am here to meet my brother."

CHAPTER 27

A ngantyr paused for a moment, then inclined his head to Hlod. "You are welcome, Prince Hlod. In the name of the gods, I invite you as my guest. Come and drink with us. A feast is underway. Tonight, I have become king of Jutland and a new groom. Let my men see to your horses. Join us."

At that, Hlod smiled and then said, "I have come for different purposes, but I will not offend our father's gods by rejecting your invitation. We will join you." With that, Hlod and his Hunnish warriors began to dismount.

I turned my back to their party.

"Cousin," I said softly to Angantyr in protest.

"I hear you, but to turn away a guest is an affront to the gods," he whispered back to me. "I will not test them on this night."

Understanding, I nodded, but I still didn't like it.

I'd left Ormar wounded in his bed because of Hlod. I would never forget what he had done to the king. I'd rather spit in Hlod's eye than drink with him. Whatever change of heart he now professed, I didn't believe him. Hlod wanted something.

Sheathing my sword, I waited for Hlod to join us.

Magnus growled as the man approached.

"Easy," Angantyr told him, but the wolf merely grew silent. The hackles on his back remained upright, and he eyed Hlod carefully.

"A wolf of Bolmsö?" Hlod asked.

Angantyr nodded. "He is."

"I will see our grandmother's island one day. Perhaps we can go there together."

"Perhaps," Angantyr said.

"You do not seem surprised by my presence, Brother," Hlod told Angantyr.

"I was surprised when I first heard of you, but Heidrek had many bastards."

At that, Hlod prickled. "I am no bastard. Our father wed my mother, Princess Sifka, daughter of King Humli, when he visited our people. Their time together was brief, but I was born nine moons after their wedding night. We may have many bastard brothers, but I am not one of them."

"Brothers and sisters," Angantyr said. "Many of them here in Skagen."

Hlod laughed. "I, too, have many sons and daughters. So many I have lost count. It is a rare maiden who says no when I ask her to lift her skirt. And even if she does say no, it makes no difference anyway. I have her all the same," he said, then laughed, slapping Angantyr on the back.

I wanted to stab him in the throat.

Angantyr gave Hlod a stony stare. "We do not behave so in Skagen. But come," Angantyr said, leading us down the road back to the tents.

"So, they say that mighty King Harald came to his end at the hand of the Gauls," Hlod said, looking toward the hall on the hill. "It is a fine new hall you are building. Once, our father ruled as king in Harald's stead here in Skagen."

"Yes, when the king was ill. Skagen is the heart of our people's land."

"That it is. As his sons, we must be proud of all Heidrek did to build the wealth of Skagen while Harald sat to rot like a gourd in the sun. Tell me, did he die with his wits about him?"

"He did," Angantyr said, tension in his voice.

"And Harald... He had a son, but they tell me the boy perished."

"Yes."

"Hmm," Hlod mused. "I am glad to see my brother as king. I will drink a toast to you, King Heidrek."

"I am called Angantyr amongst our people."

"I have heard this rumor. Why don't you keep our father's name?"

"Because our father's name and memory are cursed here," Angantyr said as we approached the tent. "We do not speak of him in honor. He died a coward, murdering his own mother, brother, and other noble men in acts of shameful betrayal."

"Other noble men... Yes, like the Reindeer Princess's father," Hlod said, needling me once more.

I really, really wanted to stab him in the throat.

"Yes," Angantyr replied tersely.

"Hmm," Hlod mused, then looked back toward the harbor. "There are many ships, many kings in Skagen for your crowning."

"Yes."

"And our grandfather, King Hofund, is he here?"

My irritation getting the better of me, I said, "You should not pester King Angantyr with questions. It is not proper to do so on his wedding day."

At that, Hlod turned to me once more. "As you say, Reindeer Princess. You must tell me, how is King Ormar faring? I have much regret for nearly killing the burned king. They say he is the son of Freyr. I will ride to him next with my apologies."

"Ormar has no interest in your apologies."

"I guess you would know," he said with a light laugh.

"Did you take a wound in battle, Princess?" he asked, gesturing to my leg.

I simply smiled at him but didn't answer.

When we reached the tent, Angantyr turned to Hlod and said, "Come, I will announce you to the crowd." With that, he gestured for the Huns to follow him inside.

I paused to let them pass, then turned to Halstein.

"Halstein, their party... There were no other men with them?" I asked.

Halstein shook his head. "Not that we saw, Princess. Only Hlod and his two men. They asked for an escort to meet with the king."

I frowned. "I don't like it. I fear this is a prelude to something more. They may have men encamped somewhere not far from our borders. Send riders. Check along the boundaries of the Myrkviðr."

"Yes, Jarl," Halstein told me. "I'll see to it."

I paused at his use of the title, but there was no time. I turned to Canute. "We must rally Skagen's guard. Put the men on alert. Quickly and quietly."

Canute nodded to me, then both men turned and went on their way.

Feeling ill at ease, I turned and followed the others inside.

The tent had fallen into a hush as the others looked on. Gizer's sons had come forward, as had Hofund and Loptr. People whispered and stared.

The look on Loptr's face told me he knew who had come.

As did Hofund's…and the reflection thereon broke my heart.

But of everyone there, Gizer's reaction most surprised me. His eyes shifted from Hlod to the ground. His brow furrowed as he shook his head.

He knew.

He knew!

Of course he knew. Heidrek had traveled with Gizer for many years, Heidrek living with Gizer, who was his foster father for a time. They had traveled and raided together before Heidrek wed Princess Helga, Harald's daughter and Angantyr's mother. Was that when Gizer and Heidrek met the Huns? Did Gizer know that Heidrek had wed Princess Sifka?

I stared at Gizer for a long time. Finally, the king met my gaze. In it, I saw his admission of guilt. All this time, he knew.

So, Heidrek had wed Princess Sifka before marrying Princess Helga. That meant Hlod was Heidrek's eldest son, heir to everything that had belonged to his father.

Everything Angantyr had worked hard to take for himself.

Everything Loptr cherished.

By right of blood, Hlod could lay claim to our world.

Because even from his grave, Heidrek was still hurting the people he should have loved.

"Friends," Angantyr began carefully. "Let us have music and drink. Tonight, the gods have brought us a special guest. May I introduce Prince Hlod, grandson of Hunnish King Humli, son of Princess Sifka and...my father, Prince Heidrek. May I introduce you to my brother."

CHAPTER 28

There was a stunned silence in the tent.

Elan, sensing the shift, turned to the musicians. "Let's have music," she called. "As the king requested."

At that, the men began playing once more, and the crowd started whispering to one another.

My gaze shifted back to Gizer, but he and his wife had disappeared into the crowd.

Instead, I found Dag, whose brow had furrowed as he stared at Hlod. Without another moment's hesitation, he crossed the room to join me.

But he was not the only one.

Loptr and Eyfura spoke in low tones, then Loptr turned to Hofund, who looked like he'd seen a spirit rise from the grave. Loptr whispered to Hofund, then took the king by the arm, and the trio made their way to us.

"Prince Hlod," Loptr called cheerfully. "We are pleased to meet another son of Heidrek."

Hlod eyed Loptr up and down. "Are you?"

Servants appeared, offering ale horns to Hlod and his men.

Hlod drank then looked over Loptr. "I see your sister in your face. You are Loptr, son of Mjord and Blomma."

Loptr nodded to him. "Indeed, Prince Loptr of Grund."

"Prince? What was your father king of?"

Loptr shifted, quick to hide a flash of emotion, then laughed lightly and set his hand on Hlod's massive shoulder. "My father was the Reindeer King, Prince Hlod. If you know my sister, then you know that."

Hlod shifted to move Loptr's hand away. "Yes, your sister and I have met," he said, smirking back at me. "She wields your father's sword. Why do you, his son, not carry the dwarven blade?"

"You must be unfamiliar with the ways of your father's people," Eyfura told Hlod. "Amongst our people, a woman is equal in value to a man as a warrior."

When Hlod set eyes on Eyfura, he stared at her for longer than comfortable. After a moment, he laughed. "I thought maybe it was because he was too ergi," he said, chuckling, his men joining him. Hlod turned to my brother once more. "Is she your woman?" Hlod asked, gesturing to Eyfura.

Loptr smiled then said, "She is her own woman, but kind enough to give her heart to me."

Hlod rolled his eyes. "I did not ask for poetry," he said, then turned to Eyfura. "What is your name?"

"I am Eyfura, daughter of King Gizer and Queen Kára."

"King Gizer?" Hlod said, then turned to his companions. They shared a look. "My grandfather will be very pleased to hear Gizer is in Skagen," he said, then turned back to Eyfura. "The fancy-dressed brother of the Reindeer Princess did not answer my question. Are you wed to Loptr of Hreinnby, Princess Eyfura?"

"I will be."

"Then, you are not," Hlod said affirmatively, then scanned the rest of us. When his gaze settled on Hofund, Hlod smiled. "You look as if you have seen a spirit rise from the mound. You must be my grandfather, King Hofund of Grund."

Hofund nodded once.

Then Hlod did something I did not expect. He stepped toward Hofund and then dropped on his knee. His companions followed suit.

Hofund merely stared.

"In blood and honor, Grandfather. I thank your gods and mine for bringing us together at last. Your son

Heidrek was a great warrior but lacked honor. You will find that I have the warrior spirit of your son but not his madness. I am honored to meet you at last."

Hofund looked pale. "Her eyes..." he whispered.

Jarl Leif appeared beside Hofund, a worried expression on his face as he looked from Hlod to Hofund.

"King Hofund is at a loss for words. As are many in this place," I told Hlod. "Your existence is a surprise to many here."

Hlod looked over his shoulder at me, a sly smile on his lips. He rose and turned to Eyfura once more. "Where is your father, Princess Eyfura? I want to meet the renowned King Gizer who made such a lasting impression on my father."

A flicker of anger shot through me.

"Gizer," I called to the crowd, unable to hide the irritation in my voice.

How could he have kept such a secret from everyone? Why?

There was a murmur in the crowd, and a moment later, Gizer appeared with Kára at his side. There was a glow in Kára's eyes that I recognized. It was usually reserved for her boys when they had done something horrible. Now, that glare was trained on her husband.

"King Gizer," I said as Gizer approached. "Prince Hlod of the Huns wishes to make your acquaintance."

Gizer wouldn't meet my gaze. Instead, he pulled on a

false smile. "Prince Hlod. Well met. We have heard many stories of your prowess."

"Which I take from my father, whom you raised as your own son, did you not? King Humli remembers when you and Prince Heidrek visited us many years ago. You will remember my mother, Princess Sifka. She told me that you complimented her hair, saying her raven tresses shone with all the blues and purples of a night's sky. Another poet," he said with a laugh. "It was a fine compliment for a princess."

"Umm. Yes. Of course. I remember her," Gizer said.

"My mother is a beautiful woman," Hlod told Hofund. "That is, no doubt, why your son married her. But she is a widow in love. King Gizer and Prince Heidrek were with us only long enough to eat my grandfather's food, drink his ale, get a child upon his daughter, and slaughter his warriors in their leaving, never to be seen nor heard from again."

Hofund looked at Gizer.

"Slaughter is an exaggeration," Gizer said with an awkward laugh. "There was a misunderstanding, that's all. It was best that Heidrek and I left. All this happened, of course, when Heidrek and I raided in the old days, before the tragedies."

Hofund's expression was flat.

"Come, Grandfather. Say something. They did not tell me that the king of Grund was mute. You and I will sit with my brother, and we shall speak of the future," Hlod said, motioning to Angantyr. But then Hlod paused and turned to Eyfura. "Suddenly, I understand my father better. Heidrek lost his mind and heart to Sifka, the most beautiful woman of her age. Now, I stand before an even greater beauty. Will you sit beside me, Princess Eyfura?"

Eyfura paused.

It wasn't like her to be uncertain.

She quickly looked toward Loptr, then smiled her best, most polite—and fake—smile at Hlod. "Very well," she told him.

With that, Angantyr, Hofund, Hlod, and Eyfura went to a quiet part of the hall.

Elan, struggling to catch up with the turn of events, gestured to one of the servants to take food and drink to the table. "Gentlemen, this way," she said politely to Hlod's warriors, motioning for them to join her at the table.

"Ervie," Dag whispered. "Did you know my father's part in this?"

"Not until I saw the look in his eyes."

Dag's brow furrowed, then the two of us turned and joined Gizer and the others.

When we got to the king, I found Jarl Leif had beat me to the questions. His foul mood matched my own.

"Why didn't you tell anyone?" Leif asked, a waspish tone in his voice. It was unlike the jarl to be venomous.

He was a kind-hearted and jovial man, but this was no light matter. "Hervor's grandson... Hofund should have known."

"What was there to know? Heidrek was rash. He wedded and bedded the princess before I could even intervene. You know how he was. Our entire world is shaped by the rashness I could not wring from him."

"And this Hlod, Sifka and Heidrek's son? The child was just left behind?" Kára asked. The queen sounded uncharacteristically aggravated.

"We were with the Huns no more than a month. There was no time for Heidrek to know his wife was pregnant. Heidrek got bored and caused some *trouble* with King Humli. We had to leave in a hurry."

"I love you like my own father, Gizer, but you are not being honest with us. Did you know about Hlod?" I asked.

Gizer frowned. I could see the pain and guilt in his expression. "There were...rumors. I placed no value in them. They are *Huns*," he said by way of explanation, giving a half-laugh. "For all I knew, the girl was pregnant before Heidrek wed her."

"But she wasn't. That is Heidrek's child," Leif said.

"Look around you, Leif. There are three of Heidrek's bastards in this tent! Harald spent a lot of silver to keep that boy's indiscretions quiet," Gizer replied.

"But none of them were the sons of a princess," Leif

replied angrily. "Nor were they Heidrek's firstborn. This man puts Grund in danger."

"Not just Grund," Loptr said. "Bolmsö too."

"He will argue for Jutland as well," I warned. "You will see."

"He has no claim here," Gizer said dismissively.

"Hlod is Angantyr's elder brother. With Harald and Halfdan dead, the rule goes to Heidrek's line."

"This Hlod is nothing," Gizer said indifferently. "There is no saying he is even Heidrek's son."

"Didn't you see those eyes?" Sigrun asked. "He carries the wolf-blood of Bolmsö. Those are Hervor's eyes. You have not forgotten them, Gizer."

At that, Gizer was silent.

"And he fights like it too," I said. "I left King Ormar recovering in a sickbed thanks to Hlod. Hlod is a berserker, just like Hervor. The prince is all smiles now, but I know better. This is a prelude to disaster."

"The blood of Bolmsö comes only in two forms: the noble blood of Hervor, or in the veins of a rabid dog like Heidrek," Leif said ominously as he stared at Hlod.

I followed the jarl's gaze.

There was no mistaking which Hlod was.

And for all of Hlod's jolly pretense, our world was in danger.

CHAPTER 29

The cheer in the tent subdued, many returned to their homes, all whispering about Hlod. I watched as Hlod, Angantyr, and Hofund spoke. Elan also sat with them, seeing to the comfort of Hlod's men. But more, I watched Eyfura.

Wily princess, not only had she said yes to keep the peace, but she was there to listen.

What I did not appreciate, however, was the way Hlod looked at her.

Wolf, indeed. I knew those eyes.

Once, when I was a girl, a man used to watch me when I left the dísarsalr to hunt for herbs in the moonlight. Finally, he plucked up his nerve and grabbed me, pinning me against a tree and grabbing me where his hands didn't belong. He never got to explain his intentions. I cut his throat with my herb knife before he got an opportunity.

The look in Hlod's eyes was the same.

"He needs to leave," Loptr said, his gaze also on Eyfura. "His eyes wander where they aren't wanted."

"Eyfura is there to listen. She may not be a shield-maiden, but that princess is no weakling."

"He's dangerous. Did you hear him? 'Loptr of Hreinnby'," my brother grumbled. "Did you hear that?"

"I did."

"And?"

"And you *are* Loptr of Hreinnby," I said in annoyance.

"You know what I mean," my brother replied with irritation. "I am Hofund's chosen heir. Everyone knows that. I am his grandson and a prince of Grund."

I said nothing. Loptr had always reveled in that identity. I was not one to take it from him. After all, I had long wallowed in the miserable truth, as I saw it, that Loptr and I didn't belong anywhere. Where Loptr had gone high, seating himself on the throne of a great kingdom, I'd seen myself as belonging nowhere. We wore our grief differently.

"If he sees me as jarl of Hreinnby, then he sees me as *his* subject," Loptr went on, his voice full of irritation. "Who is he, filthy stinking horseman, to come in here and stake a claim to things that are not his?"

I turned to my brother, meeting his gaze. I held it for a long time...long enough that Loptr saw the truth.

"You're wrong, Ervie," Loptr said finally. "He is not the rightful heir of Grund."

"He is. But not in any way that truly matters. Hofund won't cast you aside. If Hofund didn't choose Angantyr as his heir, he certainly won't accept Hlod," I said, my tone more bitter than I had intended.

"Hofund loved and raised our mother like his own daughter," Loptr retorted.

"He did, but we are *not* his blood. You *are* Jarl of Hreinnby, whether you like it or not."

"Then I am a jarl of nothing more than shadows."

I laughed. "Now you see the world as I see it."

Loptr huffed.

Dag, who had been sitting with his brothers, rejoined us. "My father learned you rallied Skagen's guards."

"Yes."

"He has added his men to them. And King Jorund has sent warriors as well."

"Good."

"Do you expect Hlod to attack?" Loptr asked, looking alarmed.

"I don't know what Hlod will do," I replied. "He may have a thousand Huns riding hard on Skagen, or burning Jutland's southernmost cities, or sailing in on ships. Or, he may be here with a small company simply to observe us, to check our strength. All options seem equally plausible."

"He is the one who wounded King Ormar?" Loptr said.

I nodded. "They were raiding the cities in the Myrkviðr. Ormar was taken prisoner by Hlod and his men."

"Taken?" Loptr asked.

I nodded. "Taken and tortured. May Jǫrð be thanked, we were able to rescue him."

My brother stared at me.

Beside me, Dag, too, was paying keen attention.

"Ormar has a strong warband, a fierce force. I fought with them. They are mighty warriors, but still, we struggled against the Huns. Hlod is not to be trifled with."

"Have you told all this to Angantyr?" Loptr asked me.

"Yes."

"And Hofund? King Hofund looked like he saw a ghost," Dag said.

"I told him. But knowing and seeing are two different things."

Angantyr rose, the others, including Hlod, along with him. When Eyfura moved to go back to her father, Hlod gently took her hand and implored her to stay.

Eyfura acquiesced.

"I will take that hand from him," Loptr grumbled.

"Friends," Angantyr called. "It is a momentous night. I have taken my crown and bride, and now my brother has come to Skagen. Let us cheer once more for Prince Hlod, our guest under the eyes of the gods."

We lifted our horns. "Skol," the company called politely.

But no one felt the sentiment.

"Prince Hlod, why have you come here?" Gizer called, irritation in his voice. "What do you want from these good people?"

"Only what I am owed, King Gizer. My share of my father's fortunes."

"Your father was a plague upon our people," Gizer replied. "He brought nothing but shame to King Hofund and King Harald. Would you take your share of that?"

Beside him, Queen Kára whispered to her husband, but Gizer had been unnerved by the turn of events. Usually the slick negotiator, Gizer was speaking through his guilt and regret—which made his tongue far too loose. He ignored his wife.

"You are right, King Gizer. I wear the shame of being my father's son—as does my brother and anyone else in this tent whose blood is the same as ours, for we all know Heidrek had many bastards. But I am Heidrek's firstborn son, as I have reminded King Hofund and King Angantyr. I shall have my place and the honors owed to me. I shall have swords and shields, cattle and sheep, horses and women. To the southeast, where your land borders the Myrkviðr, I will have land for my people."

I looked to Angantyr, who kept his expression guarded.

"I will have the things owed to me by my blood," Hlod continued. "Because who among you would not claim what belonged to your father? Who among you would not claim your birthright?"

I hated to admit it, but Hlod had a point.

"And to prove I am one of you," Hlod continued, "I will take a bride. I will marry Eyfura, daughter of King Gizer."

At that, protests rippled through the tent.

Loptr set his hand on his blade and stepped forward. "You will have to come through me if you want her."

"That can be arranged, ergi," Hlod said with a laugh.

Angantyr stepped toward Hlod. "Brother, the princess is already promised to Prince Loptr. There are many other fine women here. I am sure one would be willing to be your bride."

"No," Hlod said. "Princess Eyfura is the most beautiful woman in all of your lands. This company is indebted to me. And I am owed by King Gizer, who insulted my grandfather, King Humli. He shall make amends for those offenses by giving me Princess Eyfura for my bride."

"I will not," Gizer said, stepping forward. "You

upstart boy, willful and cocksure, just like your father. You, who would come amongst your betters and make demands of us. You should have come in here on your knees like the dog you are. King Angantyr is overgenerous to offer you anything. A Hunnish princess is worth no more than a thrall. May the gods curse you for even thinking of my daughter, let alone suggesting you would wed her. Come, Eyfura," Gizer said, motioning for her to return to her father and brothers.

Hlod held Eyfura's arm.

At that, Bjarki pushed forward.

"Remove your hand from my sister, Prince Hlod. Or only the gods will keep me from relieving you of it."

Hlod took the measure of Bjarki and then let Eyfura go. "Forgive me, Princess. My passion for you overran its bounds."

"You are forgiven," Eyfura said, pulling her arm away. "But you can lay no claim to my heart. I am pledged to another. There is no question of it. And I am already as good as married," she added, admitting freely to Hlod and everyone else within earshot that she and Loptr were lovers.

Hlod huffed a laugh. "That is not a deterrent, Princess. It only makes you more trained," he said with a laugh, then looked back to Gizer. "I *will* have your daughter."

"You are little more than a whore's son. Less than

that. I wouldn't wed my dog to you," Gizer spat angrily. "Go from this place."

"Gizer," Hofund said, but the damage had been done.

Hlod's face shifted from one of bemused annoyance to rage. I had seen that look before. The last time I saw it, I'd barely escaped with my life.

"You will pay for those words, old man," Hlod said, pointing to Gizer.

"Hlod, be at peace. We are still—" Angantyr began, but it was too late.

The red rage had taken Hlod. You could see it in every inch of his features.

Had he not been outnumbered, he would have tried to kill us all.

"You, all of you, will pay what is owed. Not in swords and shields, cattle and sheep, horses and women. You will pay in blood. When I am done burning down your world, I will take what is mine. It is easy to step over corpses," he said, then gestured to his men. They turned to leave, but Hlod paused and looked at me. "I will destroy any who get in my way. Tell your burned king that, Reindeer Princess."

With that, Hlod and his men turned and left the tent.

The company stood in stunned silence.

Gizer's tongue had unleashed war on us.

Jarl Leif was the first to speak. "What have you done, Gizer?"

But Gizer looked indignant. "What needed to be done. We will not have that swine undo all we have worked so hard to achieve. I will not allow it! Once was enough. To see my friends die, our loved ones butchered, to watch it all burn because of one man's greed. No. Never again."

And there was the truth.

Gizer felt guilty.

He had not been able to help Heidrek come to terms with the wildness within him. Hervor and Hofund had sent Heidrek to Gizer in the hope he could somehow tame him. But it hadn't worked. Heidrek had still destroyed everything. And Gizer felt he was to blame... for all of it.

"Gizer, what happened with Heidrek was not *your* fault," Hofund said gently. "That blame lies elsewhere."

Within himself.

Still, Hofund blamed himself.

"A curse upon Heidrek," I said, unable to hold my tongue. "Even from his grave, he reaches for your throats, hearts, and spirits. I know what it means to live in the shadow of his misdeeds. I know what he has taken from all of us. But no more. No more of this. He is dead and gone. We must stop living in his shadow. We must put a stop to all this. Now," I said, turning to Angantyr.

Angantyr nodded. "Ervie is right. I will try to fix

this," he said, then turned and quickly made his way from the tent, Magnus following along behind him.

Cursing my leg, I turned back to the room.

"Gizer, the Huns are a mighty force," King Jorund warned.

"They cannot get past the Myrkviðr," Gizer said, waving his hand glibly.

"Yes, they can," I corrected him. "Hlod's blood contains the magic of Bolmsö. The enchantments that kept the Myrkviðr hidden from us and impassible to the Huns, Hlod *can* pass them."

"Then, we won't wait. Let's take the war to him," Gizer said, then turned to Gunnar, who had ridden with the other men from Arheimar as escort to Hlod. "Where did you encounter them?"

"Southeast of Arheimar, near the Myrkviðr."

"Rally the men," Gizer told Bjarki. "We will ride and meet them there."

"We don't even know if he has his army with him," I protested. "We could leave Skagen open to attack."

"Jorund and I will go. Once we find the army, we will send word. Hofund, you keep Grund's warriors in Skagen with Angantyr's forces."

Suddenly, panic swelled up in me. All of this seemed like a terrible idea. "We must wait for Angantyr to decide. Don't be rash, Gizer," I said, then turned to

Hofund, looking for help. "This is for Angantyr to decide," I repeated.

"What is there to decide?" Gizer retorted. "We won't have that Hunnish dog take what we have all worked so hard to win. Will we, Hofund?"

Hofund hesitated.

Gizer took his silence for assent. "Rally the forces," he told Bjarki. "We will not let these insults go unanswered. Jorund?"

"I am with you, Gizer," the king told him.

"Good. Gauti, sound the horn. We prepare for war."

Suddenly, everything had come undone.

CHAPTER 30

By the time Angantyr returned, Gizer had everyone on the move.

"What's happening?" Angantyr asked with annoyance as he met us outside the tent. Warriors were rushing everywhere, preparing to ride out.

"We will follow that dog and cut him down," Gizer growled. "How dare he disrespect you on this night, come asking like a beggar for—"

"For what is owed to him," Angantyr retorted abruptly. "Now, you would bring war to my doorstep, Gizer? A war I did not ask for. A war I was trying to avoid."

"You gain nothing by obliging him, Angantyr. No. There is nothing to be won from the effort," Gizer replied. "What did he want, half your kingdom? Arheimar, which you have already promised to Ervie?"

At that, Loptr turned and looked to me.

"Or maybe my daughter, who is already promised to Loptr. Will you give away all that belongs to Mjord's children? What makes you think he would stop with you, Angantyr? Your heart is good. In that, you are like your mother. She, too, wanted to see the best in people. But there is nothing good to see here. That man is a copy of his father. He must be stopped. Now. The others agree with me," he said, looking to Jorund and Hofund.

Jorund nodded. "Yes. Gizer is right. You must cut off the head of the snake."

Angantyr looked agitated—and conflicted. In a way, Gizer was right. Out of honor, Angantyr was trying to find a way. But Angantyr was good. He would have given Hlod too much, been too generous. And when he was done, Hlod would have stabbed him in the back. The situation was frustrating. But it was not for Gizer to decide. Yet, Angantyr would have chosen peace. Ultimately, Gizer was right, even if it was Gizer's guilt driving him. But still, something felt off here. I couldn't see what, but something irritated my mind, like a scratch in the back of my throat that would not ease.

Angantyr turned to Hofund. "He is your blood as much as I am. What do you say?"

Hofund hesitated a moment, then said, "I listened to Hlod. I heard what he said and what he did not say. Your heart is in the right place, Angantyr, but he would not stop with you. There is greed in his eyes... While he wears her eyes, the spirit behind them is Heidrek's."

"Good. That's settled, then. Should we ride out with Gizer?" Loptr asked Hofund.

I frowned at my brother and then asked, "What do you want to do, Angantyr? This is your city. He is your brother. These are your lands."

Angantyr sighed. "I want to drink another tankard of ale then fall into bed with my new wife," he said, then half-laughed, lightening the mood for the moment. He turned to Gizer and Jorund. "You have rallied your forces to pursue them south?"

"We have," Gizer replied.

Angantyr nodded. "Go, then. When you have located their army, send word," he said then turned to Hofund. "I have my men here to secure the city, but I worry for Arheimar. My southernmost city sits exposed."

"I will rally my jarls and ride south. Jarl Leif and the warriors of Dalr can stay with you to help secure Skagen until Gizer sends word."

Angantyr nodded. "May Freyr watch over us, and all the gods give us strength," Angantyr said, then pulled his horn and blew.

All at once, it was war.

When Gizer's sons left to prepare for battle, Dag moved to go along with them.

"Dag," I called. "Where are you going?"

He paused, then turned to me as I limped in his direction.

"I will ride with my brothers."

"By Freyja, are you mad? The flesh over your wound is barely mended, and your face... You are not recovered."

"Are you worried about me, Reindeer Princess?"

"Of course I am," I replied waspishly.

"I must go," Dag said. "I can't stay here and cower. You understand this."

He was right, but still... "Dag. You are not well."

Giving me a knowing smile, he met and held my gaze.

"Aye, gods. Then go carefully," I said. "You are half-drunk, and you always forget the buckle on your right sleeve. And use your bow. Stay out of the fray."

Dag chuckled lightly. "You need not worry about me, Reindeer Princess. I have the motivation to return, not just to depart."

"And that is?" I asked.

"To hear your proposal," he said with a laugh, then touched my face when he saw hesitation cross my features. He leaned toward me. "I love you, Ervie. Be safe."

"You be safe," I told him, then added in a whisper. "I love you too."

Dag tried to smile but winced. "I cannot smile nor kiss you," he said, then pulled me against him. "See you soon," he whispered into my hair, then turned and hurried off.

My body tingled from head to foot with frustration.

When I turned back, I found Elan standing there. The leaves on her crown had wilted, and she had dark rings under her eyes. Magnus sat beside her, the pair of them watching the chaos unfolding.

"Elan?" I asked gently.

"I..." she said, then paused. "I guess it is a fitting start to this marriage, all things considered."

I looked out at the warriors hurrying to prepare to ride out. Under the light of the moon, metal shone silver. Voices that had been lit up in song mere hours ago were now calling for blood.

"It's better if it's finished now. My cousin has a good heart, but in this case, it would have led him astray. Hlod would not have been satisfied with whatever Angantyr wished to give him. Angantyr will be torn apart by what is happening here, but the other kings are not wrong."

Elan nodded slowly, then exhaled deeply. She looked down at Magnus, who looked up expectantly at her, his tongue hanging from the side of his mouth. She chuckled.

"I am the queen of this city and these people now," Elan told Magnus. "I suppose the wedding feast will serve well enough to feed men at war. Want to help me prepare the provisions?"

The wolf gave her a soft bark.

"And you, Reindeer Princess?"

I gestured down to my leg. "The Norns have woven. I am here to help you wrap up bread and cheese. I suppose I can use my dwarven sword to cut the meat."

Elan laughed.

I joined her, but inside, I was trying to keep a lid on my simmering frustration. Why would the gods hobble me now?

Seven sleeps.

Tonight would be the seventh. With a bit of luck, by the time word came from the south, I would be able to ride and put my blade to better use.

But for now...

I took Elan's arm. "It was a beautiful wedding," I told her as we turned and returned to the tent.

"Yes," Elan said wistfully. "Right up until people started threatening to murder one another."

At that, I laughed. "Yes, right up until then."

CHAPTER 31

Elan and I worked hard, many of the other women from Skagen joining us, packaging up all the food and sending it off to the men in the warbands. When Gizer's horn sounded, indicating that they were about to ride out, a shiver washed over me. Something about all of this just felt...wrong. And it wasn't just because I wasn't joining the other warriors.

There was something else.

Something I couldn't see.

I paused a moment, looking out of the tent.

"Ervie?" Elan asked.

"I... I'll be back in a moment," I said. Setting my crutch aside, I limped my way out of the tent. A woman rushed past me, carrying a large bag of goods. She hurried toward the others. In the fields below, I saw they were preparing to leave.

Overhead, an unkindness of ravens, startled awake by all the noise, squawked loudly.

Awake and at war. War comes again. Bones and meat and flesh. Blood and death.

What was it?

What was I missing?

This all felt too...something.

Hlod was smarter than this. He came asking for things he didn't expect to be given. When Angantyr agreed, he reached for something he knew would be denied—Eyfura. Hlod expected to be chased from our lands. Were our warriors riding into a trap?

As I stood watching, Loptr suddenly appeared by my side.

"Ervie... What are you doing?"

"Thinking."

Loptr's brow narrowed. "About what?"

"Doesn't this all seem too... I don't know. Easy isn't the right word. Expected. Look at everyone. They are all acting exactly as expected. The warhorns have sounded. The armies are gathering. Have we given Hlod exactly what he wanted?"

"Hlod wanted half of Angantyr's lands, the throne of Grund upon Hofund's death, and my future wife."

"Did he, though?"

"What are you talking about?"

"A trap, Loptr. Is this a trap?"

Loptr rolled his eyes. "You can't hide the Hunnish army. It's no trap. We will find his forces and defeat him."

I scanned my brother's armor. He was not dressed for war. "You're not riding with Hofund?"

Loptr shook his head. "No. With Leif injured, Hofund thought it best I stay here."

I looked back toward the warband.

Gizer at the front, they rode out of the city.

"May the All-Father, Freyr, and all the gods watch over them," I said, my eyes drifting to the ravens again. The birds followed the warband. Their black feathers shone with the moonlight on their wings. But at the front of their flock were two large ravens. When I reached out toward them, to feel what they felt, to see what they saw, an enormous presence pushed back.

Huginn and Muninn had come.

The All-Father's eyes were fixed on the warband.

For better or worse, the gods were here.

I SPENT THE REST OF THE NIGHT HELPING THE OTHERS prepare the city. Skagen was in ruins. The walls protecting the city had been burned. The ramparts were gone. While repairs had begun, they were not where they needed to be—especially not in any condition to repel a Hunnish army. In the morning, when the sun came up, much work needed to be done.

Of course, that would not be long now. The moon was high in the sky when I finally came across Angantyr, who looked exhausted and frustrated.

"Ervie," he said. "Thank you for your help. Leif said you were at the docks."

"Yes. We have watchmen and archers stationed there."

Angantyr nodded. "Good."

"Cousin," I said gently. "Take your rest. There are many here ready to watch in your place. Go to Elan. It is your wedding night, after all."

"Elan," Angantyr said, his eyes drifting behind me toward the town. "I... Yes, but only if you agree to rest as well. That leg will not thank you if you don't sleep. I had my people prepare you a tent not far from mine. If you need anything, simply ask."

"Very well. I will check on the wounded at the convalescence tent first, see if the gothar need anything."

"Thank you, Ervie."

"Good night, Cousin. I wish you many sleepless hours."

At that, Angantyr laughed then headed off.

I turned and headed toward the sick tent. As I did

so, I felt the weight of exhaustion finally catching up with me. When I arrived, I found most of the patients sleeping. I joined a gythia who was at a table grinding herbs.

"Reindeer Princess," she said, looking up. "Did you need something?"

"Only to offer my help if you need it."

The woman exhaled in relief. "If you are offering, then I will accept. The shield-maiden there needs fresh salve on her leg. The gods forgive me, but I can barely keep my eyes open. Would you mind finishing for me so I can just take a small rest? If you are able..." she said, her gaze going to my leg.

I reached for the pestle. "Rest. I will wake you if there is a need."

At that, the priestess left me, going to one of the cots and lying down.

I finished her work, grinding the herbs into a fine powder. When I was done, I poured the herbs into a cream and worked them until the salve was ready. Limping across the room, I joined the shield-maiden. She opened her eyes just a crack when she saw me.

"Reindeer Princess," she said.

"The gythia is resting. If it's all right with you, I will change the wrap on your leg and apply a fresh salve."

She nodded then moved to sit up.

I worked carefully, removing the old wrapping on her

leg. When I did so, I discovered a long scar down the side of the girl's leg from her knee to her ankle.

The wound, however, looked like it was healing well. Taking a bowl of warm water and a clean cloth, I first cleaned the tender wound.

"It seems I'm not the only one nursing a bad leg," she said.

I huffed a laugh, then nodded. "The Gauls were fierce fighters."

"That they were."

"Are you from Skagen?" I asked her.

She nodded. "Yes. I was here when Kjar attacked. My father and brother perished in the fighting."

"You went to avenge your family."

"Yes."

"Are you on your own now? Did any of your family survive?"

"I have a small sister. She is staying with my elderly aunt."

"You will be able to rejoin her soon, I think. The wound is healing nicely."

"Princess Eyfura has been tending to it."

"Ah, that explains it. Eyfura's hands are the most gifted in our lands."

The shield-maiden looked toward the tent flap. "I heard the horns. The gothar said the Huns were here, and we are pursuing them."

"Yes."

"I don't understand. Did the Huns come to declare war?"

"The Huns came with demands that cannot be met. War is the natural outcome."

"So it seems," the girl said, then grew silent as I applied the salve. Only when it was done did she speak again. "Thank you, Princess."

"Can I bring you anything for the pain? A mixture to help you sleep?"

She nodded.

I gave her a soft smile and then returned to the workbench. There, I mixed up a tonic to help ease the pain. Returning, I helped the girl drink, then settled her back in bed.

"I'm sorry I can't ride with them," she said.

"As am I. But you will be well soon enough, then the two of us can limp into battle together."

At that, she laughed.

"Good night," I told her.

"Good night."

The shield-maiden settled, and I made my way across the tent, checking on the others. Some of the warriors had taken severe injuries. One warrior had lost an eye. Another had lost his fingers. Many slept. After giving some pain tonics to two more warriors, I returned to the workstation to find the gythia awake.

"It is deep in the night, Reindeer Princess. Here," she said, handing me a steaming cup. "There are herbs here to help your bone mend. Why don't you rest?"

I took the mug from her. "I'll stay here tonight. You can wake me if you need help."

She inclined her head to me.

Going to one of the cots, I sat down. Finally, at ease, I felt the ache in my leg and ankle. I drained the cup and then lay down. The moment I closed my eyes, I drifted off into a restless half-sleep.

In my dreams, I was near the border of the Myrkviðr. There was smoke in the air. Somewhere, something was burning. I hurried through the woods, my bow in my hand, looking in vain for the source of the fire but couldn't find it. Around me, shadows moved. Out of the corner of my eye, I saw people darting about unseen.

My skin rose in gooseflesh.

I paused in the middle of the forest, smoke billowing around me.

In the dark of the woods, I heard Hunnish voices.

Amongst them, I heard Hlod's laughter.

Then, I heard the sound of a woman whispering in desperation.

"Ervie.

"Ervie, hear me.

"Ervie! Help me!

"Ervie, wake up. Ervie. Ervie!" I felt someone roughly

shaking my shoulder.

I opened my eyes to find Loptr standing there. Not far behind him was Queen Kára, who was speaking to the gythia.

"No, Queen Kára, I haven't seen her since before the wedding feast. She didn't return to the tent tonight."

I sat up. "What's happening?"

"Eyfura," Loptr said. "No one can find her."

I rose. "Did she ride with the others?" I asked, turning from Loptr to Kára. "Maybe to help with the wounded?"

"No," Kára told me, a worried expression on her face. "I saw her after her father left. She was going to check on an elderly man in the village, but he said she never arrived. No one has seen her for hours."

My dream came back to me, and a sick feeling rocked my stomach. "I need to go to the temple," I said, rising. I moved past Loptr.

"Ervie, there is no time. What if something has happened—"

"Loptr!" I began in annoyance, then tempered my tone when I saw the anguished expression on his face. "I dreamed of this. I need to go to the temple. Wait for me."

"Ervie," Kára whispered.

"I'll find her," I said, then turned to Loptr once more. "Wait for me," I told him then made my way out of the tent.

When I arrived at the temple, I found the place was silent. Flowers and greens still decorated the space. The previous day had begun in peace and with hope for the future. Now, that was all shattered.

It was the deepest part of the night. The temple was unattended. I went to a bench at the center of the hall and lowered myself onto the seat.

Freyr, be with me. Freyja, be with me. Jǫrð, let me see.

And then, I let myself fall.

Deep within myself.

Deeper still.

Until I was gone.

There was nothing more but bone, and feathers, and the eyes of a raven.

I blinked hard, then flew from the temple. Flying away from the Skagen, I lifted off into the night's sky. In my dream, they were in the forest. They were making their way toward the Myrkviðr. They had been traveling under the cover of darkness. I flew in the direction of the trees. Gizer was marching in the wrong direction, and Hofund wouldn't find Hlod in Arheimar. The Hunnish prince was headed east into the Myrkviðr.

Panic triggered in me, but I silenced it.

There was no time for fear.

I had to find them.

Now.

I reached out, feeling for Eyfura in the space between us.

Where?

What path had they taken?

Where was she?

Feeling the sense of Eyfura, I moved toward it. I was pulled deeper into the forest, following a stream that snaked through the woods. The silver stream wound across the land like veins of blood.

Jǫrð, lead me. Show me. Jǫrð, please help me.

Eyfura, I'm coming.

Eyfura!

I was becoming increasingly desperate. Then, I saw smoke spiraling into the air. I flew toward it, dropping down into the canopy of leaves. Fluttering down onto the branches, I found them.

Hlod and his companions sat beside the fire, all talking and laughing in their language. Also seated beside the fire was Eyfura, her hands and feet bound. There was a red mark on her cheek where she had been struck. Her hair was in knots. She stared vacantly into the fire.

Hlod rose. With an ale horn in his hand, he went to Eyfura and set the drink to her lips. She sipped the liquid then pulled back and spit it at the Hun.

The other two men laughed, but Hlod struck her. "I like your spirit, Princess. But you will not waste our ale.

It will be a long ride," he said, then went and sat back down.

Eyfura's pretty features contorted into a mix of rage and despair.

I didn't want to leave her there, but I knew I must. Even if I shifted form, I was alone and wounded. I needed help.

Turning, I flew quietly back through the trees and into the night sky. Flying high above the clouds, I caught a wind that pushed me back toward Skagen, hurrying my flight. When I came near the city again, I spiraled lower, dropping under the clouds.

The sky had shifted to deep purple and gray. Daylight would soon be upon us.

I slipped down toward the city, spotting Queen Kára as she made her way down the street toward the temple. I flew toward her, pulling myself back to the surface as I did so. Turning quickly, I transformed once more into my human self.

"By the gods, Ervie," Kára gasped.

"Where is Loptr?"

Kára shook her head. "I don't know. He disappeared after you left. Ervie…"

"I found her. She's alive. Gizer has gone in the wrong direction. Hlod must have waited until the army left to sneak back in and abduct Eyfura. I know where she is. We must leave at once."

Kára nodded. "I'll go find Angantyr. He was gathering some people to go look for her."

"I'll meet you at the stables," I told Kára, and the two of us then turned and went our separate ways.

When I arrived at the stables, I found them nearly empty. Utr, who had been brought from Keil, knickered at me.

"There you are," I said, patting the horse's nose. "Now, where is everyone else?"

I spotted a young lad hurrying with a grain bucket on the other side of the stables.

"Boy," I called. "Have you seen Prince Loptr?"

The boy stopped. "Reindeer Princess, your brother rode out not twenty minutes ago."

"Rode out? To where?"

"He said to tell Queen Kára he was riding south to meet up with King Gizer to tell him about Princess Eyfura. What happened to Princess Eyfura?"

Dammit, he's headed in the wrong direction.

"I need my saddle. Quickly," I told the boy.

I opened Utr's stall and brought the horse out. Grabbing his bridle, I quickly readied him. The boy returned a few moments later with the saddle, which was nearly as big as himself. I worked fast, getting the horse saddled. Slipping my good leg into the stirrup, I pulled myself up. My wounded leg and ankle screamed in protest, sending shooting pains from my toes to my head.

"Gah," I exclaimed in agony, unable to hold back.

"Princess," the boy said worriedly. "Your leg."

"There is no time to wait. Tell Queen Kára that Loptr was going in the wrong direction. I've gone to fetch him."

With that, I clicked to Utr and headed out of the stables and down the road away from Skagen in a hard run.

It was not until the great city had fallen out of sight behind me that I remembered the gythia's warning.

Seven nights.

It was not yet dawn. While the sun threatened on the horizon, it was still dark.

I weighed the gythia's—knowing full well that was *not* who she was—words against Eyfura's life and found them lacking.

The woman's threats had been vague. Eyfura was my friend, my brother's true love, Dag's sister, and cherished by all who knew her. I was the only one who knew where Hlod had taken her.

Nothing could have held me back.

"Ervie.

"Daughter of Mjord and Blomma.

"I warned you.

"My weaving is undone.

"Let come what may."

CHAPTER 32

Loptr had taken the main road from the city. Having traveled it often enough, I knew a short cut through a farm and apple orchard that would head him off. Coaxing the horse faster and trying to brace my leg from being jangled too much in the process, I rode hard, trying to catch up with my twin.

When the sun finally rose over the horizon, I left my diagonal path and rejoined the main road. I paused there, letting Utr catch his breath, then listened.

It wasn't long before I heard the sound of hooves thundering in my direction.

A moment later, I spotted Loptr, his cape billowing behind him as he raced down the road.

"Whoa," he called to his horse upon seeing me. The beast struggled to stop but slowed, prancing and breathing hard as it halted its steps. "Ervie... What the... What are you doing here?"

"Loptr," I snapped. "I told you to wait for me."

"There was no time to wait!"

"You are riding in the wrong direction. Hlod has taken Eyfura toward the Myrkviðr."

"How do you know?"

"Because I used seidr to find them. *That* is why I told you to wait."

"Which way?" Loptr asked.

"Follow me," I said, then turned Utr off the trail and into the woods.

Picking our way through the forest, we soon came across a cart path. We took off at a trot, hurrying as quickly as we dared. As the sun rose, we raced toward the Myrkviðr, finally crossing into the forest. Soon, we reached the stream.

"They followed the stream into the woods," I told my brother, directing the horse once more.

When we finally reached the place where Hlod had camped, we dismounted. For a moment, I had forgotten the pain of my leg. When I slid off my horse, I landed too hard on the bone, making me cry out.

"Ervie," Loptr said, rushing to me. "By the gods, you should not be riding. In my haste, I completely forgot. I can go on without you. Just tell me which way they've gone."

"You will take on three Huns alone, including Hlod? As it is…" I began but didn't finish. As it was, Loptr and I might not be enough, especially in the condition I was in. I should have sent for Kára or waited for Angantyr. "We have both acted in haste," I said then limped downstream, bending to look for footprints.

When I did so, the shield-maiden Sigrun's voice reached out to me from memories past.

"Look, Ervie," she would say, squatting down. "See how the leaves are disturbed? Watch for broken twigs, crushed ferns or plants." How many times had Sigrun taken me into the woods to hunt when I was young? First, it was animals. Later, she taught me how to track people. In that moment, and many others, I was grateful for the time I'd spent dogging her shadow.

The path appeared before me.

"This way," I said, then went back to Utr.

Hlod was skirting the borders of the Myrkviðr, but eventually, he would have to cross into Ormar's lands. Loptr and I rode throughout the day. Finally, we passed through a stand of ancient trees.

On the other side, the trail disappeared.

I studied the forest floor. They had crossed the stream and gone into the Myrkviðr.

I signaled to Loptr. "They've crossed here," I said, then urged my horse to step across the rocky stream to the other side. Naturally, the animal took the opportunity to drink, Loptr's horse doing the same.

"By Hel," he whispered, trying to urge his horse on.

"Let him have a moment's rest. Drink something yourself," I told him.

Loptr paused. Of course, he had no waterskin with him. It would have marred his wedding outfit.

With a sigh, I pulled my skin from my belt and tossed it to him.

"We will pass into the Myrkviðr," I told Loptr. "And we will not pass unseen. The woods will whisper. Asa will know."

"Who is Asa?"

"The dís who guards these woods."

"Will she let us pass?"

"Yes," I said. "And hopefully, send help."

Loptr drank then tossed the skin back to me. "Good. We'll need it."

When the horses were finished, we set off once more. As we passed into the Myrkviðr, I sensed a change in the air. It was not long after that when the air grew foggy, and it became hard to see.

"I can't see a foot in front of me," Loptr said, a pinch of panic in his voice.

I signaled to Loptr to stop, then closed my eyes.

Asa, can you hear me? Asa, I need your help. The Huns have taken my friend. I must find her before it's too late. Slow them. Slow them so I can reach her in time. Asa, please help me. Please help us. Send help.

A moment later, a soft wind blew across the forest, clearing the fog and revealing the Huns' hoofprints once more.

"Ervie," Loptr whispered.

"It is Asa," I said, then clicked to my horse.

I bent all my attention on following the hoofprints and getting to Eyfura, but even as I did so, I knew…

Asa would send Ormar.

My heartbeat quickened at the thought of it. But those feelings were quickly coupled with a strange sense of conflict. My feelings for Dag had roared to life in a way I had never expected or hoped for. What did that mean for Ormar and me?

Pushing the thoughts from my mind, I wove deeper into the forest, hunting the Huns. They had taken a sharp turn on their path and were headed southeast toward the ridge. On the other side of the forest, a mountain sat above a wide valley. The other side of that valley was Hunnish lands.

We had to get to Eyfura before they made their way back to their own people.

We rode all day, pushing as hard as the horses could stand. We would catch them by nightfall.

In a pine grove near a pool, we paused to give the horses a moment to rest. Pain shot from my toes to my temples when I set my foot on the ground. I sucked it in, not wanting Loptr to know.

It was going to take everything in me to fight the Huns.

I might die in this battle.

But if I saved Eyfura, it would be worth it.

We could stop there and wait for Ormar and the others, but they were hours behind us now. In that period of time, Hlod would cross into Hunnish territories, and Eyfura would be lost.

I felt a prickle down my spine, and my skin turned to gooseflesh.

"Ervie. Ervie?"

I felt Ormar reaching out to me.

Ormar?

"Ervie, wait. We are coming. Wait."

There is no time.

"Ervie, I'm coming for you. I'm coming…"

Exhaling deeply, I braced myself against a tree and then dug into my pouch, pulling out a small packet of dried widow's cap mushrooms. My leg throbbed. The pain was so bad my head ached, and my stomach rolled with nausea. But there was no time. Breaking off just the tiniest bite of the fungi, I stuck it into my mouth and swallowed. It would stem the pain. The leg was wounded. There was nothing to be done about that, but the pain… at least now, I wouldn't feel it, or anything else, anymore.

I drank water from my skin and then went to Utr, preparing the horse to ride out once more.

Loptr rejoined me.

He had gone pale. I had never seen my brother like that before. Loptr was always so poised. Now, he was undone.

I frowned then said, "When we meet the Huns, do not rush in swords flashing, screaming to the All-Father. We are outnumbered, and the weakest Hun fights like our best men."

"I understand," he said simply. "You… You lead the way, Ervie."

I took Loptr's hand. "We will get her back. You hear me? We will get her back."

Loptr nodded but said nothing more.

With that, we rode on. Day grew into night. As the light began to grow dim, fog crept in around us once more. In the moist air, I smelled a campfire.

"The fog is back," Loptr whispered.

Asa had slowed the Huns down, weaving a mist around them.

"They are close," I replied, then motioned for him to ride toward a small glade.

We were very near the ridge that looked over the valley. The Huns must have been camped along the edge, settling in as close to their own lands as possible. They would not ride down the ridge path until the fog lifted.

Reaching the glade, Loptr and I dismounted and tied up the horses.

Standing still in the fog, finally, I caught the sound of voices in the wind.

"Ervie," Loptr whispered.

I nodded, then motioned for him to be silent.

Moving low, creeping beneath the trees, we followed the sound of voices and made our way to the Huns' camp. When we grew close, I heard the Huns, including Hlod, but there was another voice amongst them. At first, I didn't recognize it. Then, my ears picked up the notes of a prankster's tone.

"Narfi," I whispered.

The boy was speaking in Hunnish, making the men laugh.

"Who is that?" Loptr whispered, moving in beside me.

"Help," I replied.

We moved toward the camp, staying hidden as we went. Narfi started singing a song, clapping his hands as he sang, making the Huns laugh. The noise muffled any sound Loptr and I may have caused.

We drew in close, hiding behind a boulder. When we peered around, we found them collected by a small campfire. Eyfura was there, staring drowsy-eyed into the flames.

Narfi had the two Huns laughing, but Hlod didn't look amused.

After a moment, he grumbled at the boy.

From what I could discern, Hlod had told Narfi to quiet down because Narfi ended his song.

The Huns were preoccupied with their meals. A hare sat roasting over a spit. Already, they were eating another. Hlod handed Eyfura a bite of meat, but she turned away and would not take it.

Hlod merely laughed.

At that, Narfi perked up. He began pointing into the woods a short distance from where Loptr and I were hidden. He jabbered, moving his hands as he spoke, gesturing to Eyfura.

When Narfi grew silent, the two men looked to Hlod.

Hlod nodded, then gestured to one of his men.

The warrior shook his head in annoyance and reluctantly set his plate down. With that, he and Narfi walked into the woods.

I gestured to Loptr to follow me.

Pulling my long dagger from my boot, I followed the boy and the Hun. Narfi led the warrior away from the camp toward a thick patch of blackberry brambles. I gestured for Loptr to hold back.

Narfi chirped happily to the man in Hunnish, waving to the blackberries.

As he did so, his eyes flashed briefly toward me.

In them, I saw a glimmer of silver.

He winked at me, then kept talking, and talking, and talking.

The sound of his voice drowned out my footfalls.

When the man knelt to pick some blackberries, I moved in.

I grabbed the Hun by his hair and pulled my blade across his neck, silencing any cry he could make before he made it.

I held him for a moment, waiting until he grew still, then dropped him.

"Can you lure the other man out?" I whispered to Narfi.

He shook his head. "The prince will grow suspicious. Change hamr, Reindeer Princess. Become the man," he said, gesturing to the dead Hun.

Narfi's gaze went from me to Loptr. "Stay silent, Prince Loptr. You and I will approach Hlod from behind once Ervie has done her work."

Loptr looked at me, a troubled expression on his face. "Can you do it?" he whispered.

I looked down at the dead man.

If I could become an animal, I could become a man.

"Yes," I whispered. "Go with Narfi," I told my brother, then turned to Narfi. "Be careful."

"I would never do anything to risk the rightful heirs of Bolmsö," he replied with a wink. With that, he led Loptr away.

I stared down at the Hunnish man, trying to memorize his face, his clothes, his armor.

Closing my eyes, I reached within.

Jǫrð, in your forest, please be with me. Freyr, at your borders, please be with me.

And then, I shifted form.

The feeling was different than taking on the likeness of an animal. I expanded into the shape of the warrior, feeling both like myself and the man. Moving quickly, I snatched a handful of berries, wrapping them up in the leather the man had been holding. Leaving the corpse behind, I made my way back to the camp.

I set my hand on the hilt of the Hun's sword.

But it was not his blade.

It was Hrotti.

I am here. I am ready.

Steeling my nerve, I rejoined the others.

The second warrior looked up at me, giving me a passing glance as he asked a question.

"Bah," I replied, waving my hand in annoyance.

My guess had been correct, because the warrior merely chuckled.

I went to Eyfura, handing her the berries.

Furious, she looked up at me.

But when she met my gaze, her brow furrowed. She saw...something.

I winked at her.

She suppressed a gasp and then knocked the berries from my hand. "Choke on them, you Hunnish dog."

At that, both Hlod and the other Hun laughed.

I gave Eyfura one last look, my gaze quickly flicking behind Hlod, then turned and moved back toward the spot where the Hunnish warrior had been sitting.

Keeping my nerve, I approached the Hun. Setting my hand on the dagger on my belt—the illusion of the Hun's dagger but really my own—I drew close to the man who was busy eating, meat fat slobbered on his lips, morsels of meat hanging from his mustache.

And then, I pulled my blade.

Hlod said something. I didn't understand his words, but I realized he was talking to me.

The seated man paused. He looked from my leg, his brow furrowing, to my face.

At that moment, I realized I had been limping. That was what Hlod had seen.

Moving fast, I plunged the dagger into the man's neck, then yanked, slicing a hole. I jerked my knife back, and the Hun keeled over.

Turning, I shook off the illusion, returning to my former self once more.

"You," Hlod said, then threw his plate aside and rose. Pulling his sword, he moved to rush me just as Loptr attacked.

My brother's knives whirling, he sliced Hlod's arm with one blade, then went for his neck with the second.

But Hlod was quick.

He ducked in time, turning to block Loptr's advance.

Wanting to make quick work of it, I pulled Hrotti and rushed at Hlod.

Overhead, the sky rocked with thunder.

"Boy, untie me," Eyfura called to Narfi. "Quickly."

Hlod shoved Loptr, pushing him back into the forest, then turned to fight me.

Our blades met, the metal clanging so loudly that an echo rolled through the canyon below.

"You may wield your father's blade and have his magic, but you cannot defeat the blood of the ancient isle of wolves," Hlod yelled, then shoved me back.

Unbalancing my footing, Hlod attacked once more. This time, when his blade hit mine, my whole body protested. The mushroom had dulled any pain I felt, but it was still there, beyond my senses. I somehow managed to push him back. Hlod retreated, steadied himself, then the dance between us began. He swung, but I ducked, darting out of the way in time. Mindful of the cliff nearby, I did everything I could to keep myself on the land side, pushing Hlod toward the ridge's edge.

Behind Hlod, Loptr rallied and launched his attack once more.

Soon, Hlod, Loptr, and I were locked in battle. My brother was quick with his blades, moving fast. Trying to push back against me and defend himself from Hrotti, Hlod left his side exposed long enough for Loptr to stab. Loptr's blade found the Hun's exposed left flank.

The Hun screamed, then turned, punching Loptr in the face.

Blood exploded from my brother's nose. Dazed, Loptr stumbled backward.

With a scream, a knife in his hand, Narfi ran toward Hlod, but Hlod bashed him toward the rock.

Narfi hit the boulder hard and then slumped to the ground, unconscious.

Hlod charged me once more.

Keeping my footing, I held Hrotti in one hand and my dagger in the other.

But the look in Hlod's eyes told me his wound had awakened something mean in him. For the briefest of moments, I saw the flicker of a wolf in his features.

He was Hervor's blood, after all.

A knife in her hands, Eyfura rushed Hlod, but he batted her away like she weighed nothing, flinging her to the ground.

"I will have that sword, Reindeer Princess," Hlod hissed at me. "I will have your sword, that woman, and when I am done, a matching pair of heads to hang from my saddle," he said with a laugh. "I will braid your hair and wear it across my chest, the last blood of Blomfjall falling to the rightful heir of Bolmsö."

"What makes you the heir of Bolmsö?" I asked. "Bolmsö and Blomfjall were once one. It is the vætt of Bolmsö who decides its true ruler. And you... you are a bastardization of everything that island stands for," I seethed.

"And yet, I hear the wolf within me," he said, then let out a howl that was so menacing, I felt it deep within my soul.

But it also woke up something in me.

I was a child of Blomfjall.

But I was also the Reindeer Princess, my father's daughter, and I was not afraid of anything.

I gripped Hrotti firmly, then began whispering to the fire, calling to the element. Speaking the runes, I called to the essence of flame, summoning it to me.

A moment later, Hrotti burst into flames.

Hlod's eyes widened, and the wolf within him looked out again, his features contorting as he snarled.

Then, he came at me.

Our blades clashed as we moved back and forth across the ledge.

Behind me, coming from the shadow of darkness, I saw a flash of silver as Loptr rejoined the fight. The three of us battled, blade upon blade.

Hlod was not able to keep up. For all of his might and the strength of the wolf within him, the Hun was fading.

So, he did what all desperate men do.

Hlod darted away from us and grabbed Eyfura. Holding her roughly, he dangled her over the ledge.

Eyfura tried to fight back, but the ground under her feet loosened. Rocks and earth fell into the ravine below. Yelping, Eyfura struggled to reclaim her footing, then stilled.

"Back away, or I drop her," Hlod told us.

"Drop her, and you will summon the force of every warrior in Scandinavia upon you," Loptr shot back.

"Good," Hlod said. "Let them come. I will slay them all and make a great hall from their bones," he said, then turned to me. "If you want her, Reindeer Princess, toss me your sword. Give it to me, and I will give you the princess."

"My sword?"

"I will have that dwarven blade. Toss it to me now, or I will let her go," Hlod said, shoving Eyfura farther over the brink.

Eyfura struggled, holding on to Hlod's sleeve as the stones beneath her feet shifted. Her eyes grew wide. "Ervie," she whispered.

"Stop. Stop. Take it. Let her go," I said, then tossed Hrotti to him. My father's dwarven blade shimmered in the firelight as it fell before Hlod's feet, the fire on the sword extinguishing. "Now, give her to us."

Loptr moved toward Eyfura, reaching for her.

But Hlod did not let her go.

"Give her to us," I hissed at him again.

The Hun grinned at me.

His eyes sparkled.

"No," I whispered. "Loptr!"

Hlod bent for the sword, and when he did so, he shoved Eyfura toward the brink.

"No!" Loptr screamed.

Everything that happened next occurred so quickly that my heart barely beat in between. Eyfura, against all chance of hope, managed to grab the ledge as she went down.

Loptr threw himself to his knees, grabbing Eyfura with one hand just before she lost her grip.

"Loptr," Eyfura wailed in desperation.

"I've got you," he said, grasping her hand. "Hold on to me. I've got you."

Eyfura safe, I moved with purpose to get my father's sword back. I pulled Riddell and shot an arrow at Hlod. It slammed into the Hun's shoulder.

Working quickly, I nocked another arrow and then shot again.

The Hun lifted my father's blade, deflecting it.

I reached toward the fire, manifesting a ball of flame into my hands. I lobbed it toward Hlod. He dodged, but the fire seared his long locks. His lengthy hair fell to the ground gently, like falling snowflakes.

Furious, Hlod turned toward me. The look in his eyes told me he understood. He was not going to leave here alive with my father's sword.

I would bring down the heavens to stop him.

So, Hlod did the only thing that would stop me.

With a menacing grin, he turned, Hrotti in his hand, toward Eyfura and Loptr.

"Loptr!" I screamed, reaching out for my brother.

But I was too late.

Hrotti sliced through my brother's wrist.

The hand that held Eyfura faltered.

For a single moment, Eyfura lovingly held my brother's gaze, then she fell.

"No!" Loptr screamed, reaching for Eyfura with his intact hand.

"Loptr!" I yelled, rushing to him.

Hlod, having created the moment to escape, took it. He rushed off into the darkness. Moments later, I heard the sound of hoofbeats as Hlod raced away.

"Eyfura! Eyfura!" Loptr screamed, reaching over the cliff—reaching too far.

I got to my brother before he, too, went over. Grabbing Loptr's tunic, I pulled him back from the ledge.

His wrist was gushing with blood.

His face had gone snow white.

"Eyfura," he whispered, staring into the canyon.

Saying nothing, I worked quickly. Pulling a strip of leather from my bag, I grabbed my brother's arm, and quickly tied a tourniquet around his wrist so he didn't bleed to death.

Loptr, in a state of shock, looked from the shadowed canyon to his arm, then let out a scream so loud that a piece of my spirit died upon hearing it.

And then, Loptr fainted.

CHAPTER 33

Feeling numb, I pulled my brother away from the ledge toward the fire. I worked quickly, doing everything I could to stem the flow of blood. My hands shaking, I opened my medicine pouch and began working to clean the wound. Hrotti's cut had been a clean one. Our father's blade had taken Loptr's hand, but it had done so neatly. Our father's sword. Hlod had taken Hrotti. I worked quickly, cleaning the wound. In my satchel, I found a small jar of Eyfura's healing ointment.

I moaned at the sight, willing myself not to break down. Not now. I couldn't think about it now. Working fast, I treated Loptr's wound and then wrapped it.

Once I had done so, I lay Loptr gently beside the fire and then rushed to Narfi. There was a cut by the boy's temple. Perhaps it was the play of darkness and firelight, but the liquid was a strange, dark green color.

"Narfi," I said, gently shaking his shoulder. "Narfi?"

The boy—such as he was—opened his eyes. "Ervie?"

I exhaled in relief.

Narfi touched his fingers to his forehead. When he pulled his hand back, his fingertips were wet with the greenish blood.

"Narfi, Hlod is gone. He has taken Hrotti. Loptr is wounded, and Eyfura is...is dead!"

Narfi looked up at the sky. His eyes suddenly looked like a bank of stars. "The burned king is coming. Stay here. He will find you here. He will help," he said, then looked at me, his eyes still full of stars. "I must rest and recover now," he said, then reached out and touched my cheek. "Ervie, the Norns' wheel is spinning. I can hear it. The world is being remade," he whispered, and then the ground below him shifted.

Startled, I moved back.

The grass and moss under the boy shook and grew, vines and plants creeping up on his body.

"Narfi?"

"I will see you again, Reindeer Princess," he whispered. Then he was slowly absorbed by the leaves, the earth itself, until he was gone.

A moment later, I found myself alone in the forest.

It was silent.

So silent.

All I could hear was the crackle of the flames in the Huns' campfire.

I lifted my hands.

They were covered in blood.

Uncontrollably, my hands shook and shook.

And then I wept.

"Aye, you gods, how you play with us. Eyfura, I'm sorry. Forgive me. Forgive me."

I WAS NOT SURE HOW LONG HAD PASSED WHEN I HEARD the sound of hooves approaching. I was sitting with Loptr, my brother's head in my lap. My mind had stopped working. No rolling thoughts. No feelings. I just sat and prayed to the gods that my twin brother would live.

When Ormar appeared before me, bending down to look into my eyes, I felt like someone had breathed life back into me.

"Ervie?" he asked. I could tell by his tone that it wasn't the first time he'd said my name. "Ervie?" he asked again, reaching out to touch my chin, tilting my face to meet his gaze.

"My brother," I whispered, looking toward Loptr's wounds.

Ormar followed my gaze. "By Freyr," he said in shock. Ormar rose. "We need to get Prince Loptr back to Asa. He's sustained a terrible injury."

Gently setting Loptr down, I rose, my hand in Ormar's.

But the mushroom's effect was beginning to wear off. The pain in my leg was excruciating.

I screamed.

"Ervie," Ormar gasped.

"My leg," I said through gritted teeth. "Ormar, Princess Eyfura, daughter of King Gizer," I said, then looked toward the ledge. "She went over. The Huns… It was Hlod's doing. The princess is dead. And he has taken my father's sword."

Ormar held my gaze for a very long time, then nodded. Turning, he gestured to Arnar.

"Arnar," Ormar called to his housecarl. "Take a party down into the ravine. You will find the body of a woman there. If you are able, bring her home."

"Yes, my king," Arnar said.

"What should we do with this one?" Hrogar asked, gesturing to the Hun.

"There is another in the forest," Hrolf added.

"Leave them for the ravens," Ormar replied, then turned to me. "Come on, Ervie. Let's get you home."

WE RODE THROUGHOUT THE NIGHT, MAKING OUR WAY BACK to Eskilundr. They had lashed Loptr to Thorgud, the largest of the men, to get him back more quickly. I mounted Utr once more and rode in silence alongside Ormar.

The ache in my heart was more than I could bear.

Over and over again, I replayed everything that had happened—what I had done wrong, what I could have done differently.

The look on Eyfura's face in that split second before she fell—she had given Loptr the last of her love.

Now, she was gone.

"Ervie," Ormar said, gently taking my hand.

"She fell before my eyes. Before Loptr's. I...I can never forgive myself for my failure."

Ormar's face twisted into a look of empathy. "I understand," he said, then kissed my hand. "If anyone in the world knows what you mean, it is me."

Unable to shake my misery, I could not bring myself to say more as we rode back to Eskilundr.

I felt a surge of relief when the village appeared through the forest.

"Hrolf, please fetch Asa. Ask her to come."

"There is no need, King Ormar. Look," Hrogar said, pointing toward the king's hall. There, Asa stood on the steps.

"Let's get Prince Loptr inside," Ormar told Thorgud.

Leaving his horse to a groom, Ormar came to me and held my waist, helping me down. "You must get off and stay off of that leg. When Asa is done with Loptr, I will ask her to see to you."

"Angantyr and the others will come looking for us," I told Ormar.

He nodded. "I will send someone to meet them at the border and escort them here."

"Don't kill them," I told him with a broken smile.

"Only because you asked," he said, smiling softly at me.

"Ervie," Auðr called, appearing from the village.

"Ervie and Prince Loptr are injured," Ormar told her. "We must get them inside."

Auðr joined Ormar and me, and the pair helped me into the hall. Ahead of me, Hrogar and Thorgud carried Loptr. Once in the hall, they took Loptr to a room not far from the one where I had stayed.

Freydis, the young maid who'd attended me, appeared from the back. "Princess," she said, looking about in confusion.

"I must see to my brother," I told Ormar.

He nodded, then turned to Freydis. "Freydis, will you see to Ervie's things?"

The girl nodded and then hurried on her way.

Hrogar and Thorgud lay Loptr down on the bed. Auðr and Asa hurried into the chamber. Asa leaned over Loptr, examining his wound.

"You bound it. Good. Much blood lost?" Asa asked me.

"I worked quickly, but there was some. I cleaned the wound and put a salve on it before binding. Asa... his arm," I said, looking at Loptr's arm, which looked swollen and was red and purple.

"I will do what I can to save it."

"It was the dwarven blade that made the wound."

"Good," Asa said. "As tragic as it is, that is good," she said, then turned to me. "The heart of your eyes is black as night, Ervie. You have taken widow's cap, but the effect is wearing off."

"My leg. The bone was injured. I could not abide the pain."

"Get off that leg now. Rest. I will ensure the prince does not wake until his wound is tended to. And you have seen enough blood for one day. Take her away, Ormar."

Ormar nodded.

But then Asa turned to me once more. "The vætt?"

"He was wounded in the fray. He...departed."

At that, Asa nodded but said nothing more, merely waved for us to go.

Ormar took me back to the hall. He helped me into a seat and brought a stool for my leg. Freydis brought me an ale and a blanket.

"The air is cool," Freydis said, covering me. "Let me help you. I am sorry to see you return under such dire circumstances, but I'm glad to have you back, Princess," she told me, then disappeared once more.

A moment later, Ormar and I were alone. Setting the ale aside, I closed my eyes for a moment, taking in the silence of the hall. The smell of the wood, the sound of the fire popping and cracking, the mere peace of it all. For the first time in days, despite all the pain and sorrow, I remembered what it was to be at peace. When I opened my eyes again, they were wet with unshed tears.

"Ormar," I whispered.

The king embraced me, holding me tight, stroking my hair. All the pain and trouble I had held inside me broke loose, and I dissolved into tears. For the first time since I had left the Myrkviðr, I felt free to be who I was, free to feel, free to be in pain. I was free to be weak and need someone else. And at that moment, I needed Ormar.

My head against his chest, I wept and wept.

"Rest, Ervie. Just rest. You are safe now. You're home."

CHAPTER 34

Late that night, I told Ormar about the war with the Gauls and how Hlod had come to Skagen.

"Their forces are moving in and out of the Myrkviðr, but King Gizer will find no one waiting to the south. They have returned beyond the mountains for the coming of winter."

"Then Hlod came to Skagen just to see," I said.

"Perhaps. We can only guess his true intentions."

I frowned. "Whatever they were, he has ignited a war. Gizer will never rest until he has Hlod's head."

"Good," Ormar said.

I nodded in agreement.

Asa returned sometime later, joining us in the great hall. "The prince is sleeping," she told me. "I woke him enough to give him a mixture of heartsbane. It will dull him for the next few days…from the pain in his arm and his heart. I saw in his memories. The princess…"

"Yes," I whispered. "They have loved one another most of their lives. They were soon to wed," I told her, then shook my head. "My brother will be destroyed by this loss."

"Yes," she said then pulled a stool and sat beside me. "It is the Norns' will."

"Eyfura was an innocent in all this. Why would the sisters weave such a tragedy?"

"She is a spark that will ignite an inferno," Asa said. "And in Eskilunder, we know to fear fire. Now, let me see this leg." With that, she unlaced my boots and rolled up my pantleg. Then, Asa undid the wrap on my leg.

I suppressed a gasp when I saw my leg from my knee down. It was a terrible pattern of purple, blue, black, and yellow. When Asa touched the bone where it had been fractured, I cried out.

"You didn't let it mend."

"I had no choice."

"Hmm," Asa mused. "I need fresh bandages," she told Ormar who rose and went to the back.

"You will wear this war all your life," Asa told me.

"So I was warned."

"Skuld told you that they would weave again if you didn't heed their warnings. You did not listen, daughter of Mjord and Blomma."

"But if I hadn't come, my brother would be dead alongside Eyfura."

"Would he? If you had listened and never left Skagen to chase your brother, what would have happened?"

"In that case, the Huns would have escaped with Eyfura. She would have been raped and kept captive."

"Yes, but she would still be alive, and Loptr would have his hand," Asa told me.

"Are you saying this is my fault?"

"No, Ervie. I am saying you were warned. No one can know the consequences of their actions. What if you had stayed in Skagen and waited for help from Queen Kára and King Angantyr? What if you had let someone else ride out and bring Prince Loptr back from the road? The beautiful Eyfura was destined for pain, but her death... I don't know. Only the sisters know."

"I was trying to save them both," I whispered.

Asa nodded. "You have a good heart, Reindeer Princess. You acted out of love, as Skuld knew you would. Which is why she tried to stop you."

I sighed heavily.

"It is not an easy thing to go against your very nature. But the Norns made you. They already know that," Asa told me with a wink.

Ormar returned a few moments later with fresh bandages.

Setting to work, Asa wound the bindings once more.

As she did so, I dug my nails into the handles of the chair and tried not to call out.

"Keep it lifted. No weight on it. I will send a boy with a crutch," she said, then dug into her many-pocketed gown, pulling out a vial. She studied my face once more. "Wait until morning, until the last of the widow's cap leaves your blood, then two drops of this in warm water."

I nodded.

"Put her in bed," Asa told Ormar. "Don't let her get up again this night. Auðr is watching over the prince. I will be back in the morning."

"Thank you, Asa," I told her.

She merely nodded then rose. Ambling along in her long robes, the bones, stones, and bells on her adornments clicking, Asa departed.

"Very well, Reindeer Princess," Ormar said. "I would carry you, but Asa would be back to curse me for pushing my own wounds."

"Ormar, your injury? I'm sorry. My mind is a whirlwind."

"Healing, thanks to your good care. Come," he said, then helped me rise.

Leaning on Ormar, we made our way to the back. The king led me to the chamber he'd prepared for me in the past, but at the door, I paused and looked up at him. "Take me to your bed," I whispered.

He studied my face for a long moment. "Are you certain?"

I nodded.

With that, Ormar and I retreated to the back of the house where the king's chamber sat.

Once we were there, Ormar slipped away a moment, returning with a nightdress for me. Then, he helped me disrobe, pulling off my other boot while I undid the laces on my jerkin. My whole body ached. When I finally pulled off my tunic, I realized I was covered in bruises.

Eyfura was gone.

Loptr was lucky to be alive.

But everything they had dreamed of would never come to pass.

Their love had been snuffed out, their life together ending before it had begun.

So, when Ormar undid the laces on my trousers and helped me pull them off, I was overcome by a sense of certainty. I never wanted what happened to Eyfura and Loptr to happen to me.

"Ormar," I whispered, reaching to touch his scarred cheek as I sat in a light shift and undergarment.

"Shall I ask Freydis to…"

I shook my head. "No. Not tonight."

I held his gaze.

My emotions were a jumble. My body ached, but I never wanted to feel the pain Loptr felt now. Loptr was my twin. I felt his heartache in my bones. I *did* love Dag. I knew that now. But I loved Ormar too. And at that moment, I wanted nothing more than to be with Ormar.

"Ervie?" Ormar whispered.

Leaning forward, I set my lips on his. I laced my fingers through his long hair and pulled him toward me. We lost ourselves to our passion, kissing one another with protective ferocity. Working carefully, I pulled off his jerkin and removed his tunic.

His wound was no longer covered. I could see the pink scar on his stomach. It was still tender.

Moving carefully, Ormar helped me slide back onto his bed.

Cautious not to cause one another pain, we relished the taste and touch of one another's flesh until we could stand it no more.

My heart bursting with love and aching with sorrow, I took my king.

Flesh upon flesh, we became one.

And when we were done, Ormar wrapped me in his arms.

I closed my eyes and inhaled deeply, taking in his woodsy scent.

I was safe.

Home.

I was home.

"Ormar," I whispered.

"Welcome home, my queen. Welcome home."

CHAPTER 35

I woke early in the morning, my body aching. My leg felt like it was on fire. I gritted my teeth and forced myself to sit up. Ormar was gone. A crutch sat at the end of the bed, and a dressing gown hanging on the back of a chair. Rising, I limped to the chair and pulled the nightdress on.

The small vial Asa had left me sat on a table nearby. Pouring myself a mug of warm water, I put two drops of the liquid into the brew. Lifting the jar to my nose, I smelled the contents but didn't recognize any scents. Raspberry, maybe? I wasn't sure. I swirled the brew, then drank.

I heard the sound of voices coming from the main hall. The front door opened and then closed.

Grabbing the crutch, I opened the door and limped to Loptr's room.

Auðr was there. She had poured a mug of herbed water and was about to hand it to my brother.

Loptr lay in bed, staring at the ceiling.

Auðr paused. "He just woke," she told me, then gave me a gentle smile. She handed the mug to me. "It would be good if you spoke with him," she told me in a low voice, then departed.

"Loptr," I said, going to the side of the bed.

He shifted his gaze toward me. A tear rolled down his cheek. "Where are we?"

"You are in the great hall of King Ormar of the Myrkviðr," I said. "Drink. You have lost much blood," I told him, then helped him sit up a little so he could drink.

When he was done, I helped him lie back down, then I set the cup aside.

"Ervie," he whispered, his voice cracking as tears streamed down his cheeks. "All I can think about is her body lying at the bottom of the ravine."

"No, Loptr. I asked Ormar's men to retrieve her. We will send her to her ancestors with all honor."

"Thank you," Loptr whispered. "Thank you," he said, then broke into tears. "My heart will never mend. I am a half-person without her. My hand may be gone, but it is my heart that has been destroyed."

I swallowed hard, feeling tears prick at the corners of

my eyes. "Brother," I said simply, taking his hand and pressing it against my lips.

"I will talk with King Ormar," Loptr said, moving to sit up. "And I should see to Eyfura."

"Loptr," I said, tempering my tone not to scold him harshly. "You *must* rest. Your body is in a state of shock. You must do everything you can to let your wound heal. I will speak to Ormar. We will see her, but not yet. I promise you, she is being tended to with great care. The Myrkviðr..." I began, then paused. "I know you rarely dream of what our life would have been like in Hreinnby if things had gone differently. But here, in this place, I feel like I'm home. And if I feel that, so can you. We are all safe here, Loptr."

Loptr closed his eyes. "Ervie," he said with a heavy sigh. "He has our father's sword."

"Yes. But only for now."

With that, I rose and kissed my brother's head. "Rest now, Brother. I will wake you if there is a need. I promise. I'm not far away if you want anything. Just call."

Loptr nodded, then turned on his side.

He moaned lightly, then wept.

My heart feeling like it was breaking, I left the room, gently closing the door behind me.

When I got to the great hall, I found Ormar talking with Arnar.

"Lady Ervie," Arnar said, bowing to me.

"Arnar, Princess Eyfura's body?"

Arnar's expression grew sad. "I asked Auðr to take charge of it. She and her shield-maidens will prepare the princess. But... It was a long fall, Ervie."

I nodded. He didn't have to say more, nor did I want him to.

"I understand. Thank you."

"We have a crypt in the mountain," Ormar said. "If you think it will be all right, we will prepare a tomb for her there," he said, then glanced briefly at Arnar. "It would not be wise, we don't think, to try to take her back to Skagen."

A wave of nausea rolled through my stomach as I guessed his meaning. "It would be an honor. But... Her family *will* come to see her."

"I understand," Ormar said. "They are welcome here."

"My king, I will go and check with the others, see if there is any word from the borders."

Ormar nodded.

With that, Arnar departed.

When he had gone, Ormar turned to me. "How are you feeling this morning?"

"The pain in my body is nothing compared to the pain in my heart. Eyfura was one of my dearest friends.

My brother…" I said, then shook my head. "Hlod has taken Hrotti. Everything has come undone."

Ormar took me into his arms. "I am sorry. I am sorry for it all," he said as he pressed me against his chest.

"If I had stayed here…"

"If you had stayed here, you would have agonized over what was happening to your family and would have been miserable to live with."

At that, I smiled lightly. "I thought you found me miserable to live with anyway."

"The most difficult, stubborn woman I have ever met," he said, then kissed the top of my head.

I exhaled deeply, then pulled Ormar tighter. "I will not make the same mistake twice," I whispered.

"Good," he replied.

At Ormar's insistence, I went back to bed. The king could see very clearly what I could not—I was injured and in pain. Like Loptr, I wanted to push it all aside and continue on, but the body has a will of its own.

As I drifted to sleep, my mother's words returned to me: *"Watch over Loptr."*

"Aye, Mother. I have failed you. I'm sorry," I whispered, then drifted into a deep, dreamless sleep.

I was not surprised when I woke again to find it was night.

Freydis appeared at the door just as I sat up.

"Ervie," she said. "Thank goodness you're awake. Ormar sent for you. Let me help you up."

"What happened? Is something wrong?"

Freydis shook her head. "Nothing wrong. Let me get you a robe," she said, then helped me dress.

Leaning on my crutch, I made my way to the main hall. From the throne room, I heard voices—it took me only a moment to recognize the man speaking. And if that wasn't enough, a wolf suddenly appeared at the end of the hall, ears perked up, tail on alert.

Freydis stiffened.

"It's all right," I told her. "Magnus," I called to the wolf.

Magnus trotted over to me and licked my hand.

I hurried to the end of the hallway, finding Angantyr and Queen Kára in the hall.

"Ervie," Angantyr said, rushing to me. "By the gods, are you all right?"

I flicked my eyes toward Ormar, who looked decidedly uncomfortable.

Angantyr pulled me into a careful embrace. "You're alive," he whispered in my ear. "Thank the gods."

"I am broken in many places, but yes, I am alive."

"We rode through the night, following your trail. Ormar's men intercepted us, leading us here. We've just arrived," Angantyr told me, then turned to Ormar. "We are grateful, King Ormar, for your hospitality. I am glad to find my cousin in your good care."

"The Myrkviðr is Lady Ervie's home as much as mine," Ormar told him. "Her kin are welcome here."

"Ervie," Queen Kára said, stepping forward. "Thank the gods you are alive and well. Loptr is here too?"

"Resting," I said, more breathing the word than speaking it.

"What happened with Hlod?" Kára asked.

"He escaped," I replied, but my stomach quaked in fear and misery. She didn't know. Soon, she would know, and her whole world would fall to pieces.

"No matter. We'll have him in the end. Now, if King Ormar permits, please take me to Eyfura. She'll want to know I'm here."

"She…" I began, but my words faltered.

"It's no matter if she is sleeping. She's used to her mother needling her day and night," she said with a laugh.

Behind me, I heard a soft noise, then turned to find Loptr there. My brother was deathly pale, his hair and clothes disheveled, his eyes red from weeping. His wounded arm was held in a sling. The stump where his hand had been bound in clean linens.

"Loptr," Kára said in shock.

"Cousin," Angantyr added aghast, looking from Loptr to me. "Ervie, what happened?"

"Hlod," I answered simply, then turned to Loptr.

"Loptr," Kára said, stepping closer to us. "Loptr, Ervie, where is Eyfura?"

My stomach quaked.

I turned to Loptr.

Tears streamed down his cheeks. Not able to bring himself to say it, he shook his head.

Kára stared at him for a long moment, then turned to me. "Ervie?" she whispered.

My voice shaking, I said, "Eyfura is... Oh, Kára... The women of Eskilundr have attended to her. She should be... she should be ready now."

Kára's hands flew to her mouth. Her face contorted into a mask of pain. "No," she whispered.

"It was Hlod," I said, my voice coming out as a crackle. "We tried. We tried, Kára. We tried, but we failed Eyfura," I said, then broke into tears.

At that, Kára began to weep.

I hurried to her, wrapping my arms around her as I pulled her close. "I'm so sorry. We are both so sorry. There are no words."

Kára wept into my shoulder and then pulled back, inhaling a deep, shuddering breath. "Aye, gods," she whispered.

The door to the great hall opened. Dressed in her long robes, her face painted with white and black clay, her tall staff in her hand, Asa appeared.

"Asa," I whispered.

"Queen Kára of Götaland. I am Asa, dís of this forest. The gods are whispering, and the runes have been cast. We must bid farewell to your daughter before the moon is high. Come now with us to the mountain where she will lie with great kings and queens of the Myrkviðr as she prepares for her journey."

Kára turned and looked at me, uncertainty and confusion in her eyes.

"It's all right," I whispered to her. "But if Asa says we must go now, we should go."

Kára looked stunned. She had come to the Myrkviðr expecting that Loptr and I had rescued Eyfura. What she found was much different. I could see from her eyes that her whole world was shifting out from under her. She looked like a woman drowning.

"All right," Kára replied absently, reaching for my hand.

Ormar turned to Asa. "All is prepared?"

She inclined her head to him.

"Cousin," Angantyr said, going to Loptr. "Come. I will help you."

"My thanks," Loptr said in a gravelly voice.

I looked back to him. "Loptr?"

"We should go," he whispered.

I turned to Ormar.

"It is a sad welcome to my hall. I hope you and the gods forgive me for that," Ormar told Kára and Angantyr.

"You will send my only daughter to the gods with your ancestors," Kára said, her voice shaky. "What greater honor can I ask for?"

With that, Asa turned.

Arnar opened the door for us, and we all made our way outside.

The residents of Eskilundr waited for us outside, torches in their hands as they lined the path from the great hall to the mountain behind it. The mountain formed the border between the Myrkviðr and the lands of Alfheim. A path wove through the woods from the village into the forest to the mountainside.

Ormar and Asa went before us.

As we passed the villagers, they bowed to Kára and Loptr, putting their hands to their hearts in gestures of respect and sympathy.

Using my crutch to hold my weight, I walked alongside Kára.

We wound through the woods, finally coming to the mountainside. There, we discovered a gap where there was a cave opening. Several men stood to one side of the entrance. A great stone, which must have been used to seal the cave, had been pushed aside.

At the entrance, Asa took a torch and entered.

Ormar paused, looking back at me.

I gave him a nod, then the king took his own flame and headed inside.

Ducking, I followed behind him, Kára coming after me.

I heard Angantyr whisper to Loptr, concern in my cousin's voice, but Loptr merely mumbled a reply.

Making our way through the narrow cave entrance, we suddenly emerged into a vast chamber. The room was lit with braziers. The tall ceiling, higher than the roof of the great hall of Grund, soared above us. The quartz and other minerals in the stones shimmered in the firelight.

Looking around the room, I saw many bodies laid upon stone altars. Ancient shields, swords, and other grave goods decorated the graves.

These were the former kings and queens of the Myrkviðr.

All these years, Ormar had kept us out. Now, we stood in their most sacred places.

Asa led us across the crypt to Eyfura's altar.

There, on a stone slab, lay the princess. The bottom half of her body was covered with a beautifully embroidered piece of fabric dyed dark blue. From her chest up, she lay exposed, her curly red hair lying about her head and shoulders. Flowers and leaves adorned her hair and her altar. All around her, they had laid vines and flowers.

Beside me, Kára gasped, then stopped.

I reached for her hand.

It was ice cold.

"Kára," I whispered.

Collecting herself, Kára went to her daughter. The queen wept as she adjusted one of Eyfura's curls.

"Oh, my beautiful daughter," she whispered. "We are lost on the sea without you. A beauty, not just in face but in heart. My only daughter, blessed with healing hands. How many live because of your gifts? Ah, Eyfura," she said, then wept.

I swallowed hard. All her life, Eyfura had feared she was a disappointment to her mother. Kára was a fierce shield-maiden who had fought alongside Hervor. Eyfura was not like her mother, but that didn't mean her mother loved her any less.

"May Freyja take you to Fólkvangr and meet you with honor," Kára said, then drew her dagger and laid it at Eyfura's side. "We will see you again, my daughter,"

Kára said, bending to kiss Eyfura on the forehead, then she stepped back.

I looked back at Loptr, but he stood beside Angantyr, too stunned to move.

I went forward then, meeting my friend.

How still she was.

How very still.

No more jokes.

No more jibes.

Now, only silence.

I slipped off the silver ring I wore on my wrist and laid it beside Kára's dagger.

"I'm sorry," I whispered. "I'm sorry, my sister. I will see you again one day."

Wiping tears from my cheeks, I went to Ormar, who held me.

Angantyr stepped forward then. He, too, whispered his farewells to Eyfura, leaving behind the amber and silver pendant he always wore.

I looked back to Loptr, but he was as still as stone.

"Prince Loptr of Grund, son of Mjord and Blomma, the moon is rising. It is time to say goodbye," Asa told him.

Loptr went to Eyfura. He lay his daggers at her side, then removed his neck and wrist rings, the silver rings on his fingers, and even poured out the silver from his pouch.

He was giving her everything.

But Loptr's thoughts were so loud, I could hear him thinking.

Still, it is not enough. Nothing in the world would be enough.

He stared down at Eyfura for a long time. He touched her cheek and then said, "I have a riddle for you," he told her, then leaned into her ear, whispering. When he stood again, he had a broken smile. Tears rolled down his cheeks. "When I see you again, I will have your answer, Princess."

Covering my hand with my mouth, I suppressed a sob.

Loptr stepped back.

Asa raised her hands into the air. "Jǫrð, mother of this mountain, Princess Eyfura is ready to begin her passage to the lands of the Æsir and Vanir. The tomb will be closed so the princess may begin her journey. Travel with her, Jǫrð, for she will not know her way. Take her to her ancestors. Let her be amongst those who love her. We honor her and grieve her passing but set her now into your gentle hands." Asa looked down at Eyfura and then set her finger on Eyfura's brow. "Go now, Princess, to your ancestors. Your time in the land of the living is done. Those you love, you will see again. Go now, to the realm of the gods."

With that, Asa turned to Ormar and nodded.

"Come," Ormar said, gesturing for us to go. "We must seal the tomb."

Angantyr gently took Kára's arm and led her from the tomb.

I went to Loptr, who looked like he was in shock.

"She looks cold," he whispered.

"She is beyond pain now, Brother. She is at peace."

"Then pain is all that is left behind," Loptr said absently.

Not saying more, I led my brother from the cave.

When we moved to exit, I turned back to Ormar.

He had paused a moment at the foot of an altar. Upon it was a body covered with a faded green cloth. Ormar had set the tips of his fingers on the edge of the stone. His lips moving, he whispered to the person thereon.

His first wife…and their child.

After a moment, he turned and looked at me.

His eyes were glossy, but he gave me a broken smile, then came along behind us.

Turning back, I followed the others from the tomb.

Outside, the people of Eskilundr had gathered, their torches aloft.

We exited the cave and joined them.

Freydis was there, a cloak in her hands.

Everything had happened in such a hurry, I was still wearing a dressing gown and simple robe. The maid draped the cloak over my shoulders and then stepped back.

Ormar rejoined me.

When Asa exited, she turned and gestured to the men gathered.

We watched as they rolled the great stone back in place.

In a loud and clear voice, Asa began to sing in a language unfamiliar to me.

The others of Eskilundr joined her.

Confused, I looked up at Ormar.

"It is a funeral lament of Alfheim," he whispered to Kára and me. "We are wishing the princess goodbye."

Kára nodded mutely then wept.

I took Loptr's hand, the pair of us watching as they sealed Eyfura in her tomb.

"Until she is avenged, I will not rest," Loptr whispered. "If it is the last thing I do, I will avenge her."

"I am with you, Brother. We started in this world together. If we must end it together, then so be it."

Loptr nodded. "So be it."

Out of the corner of my eye, I spotted movement in the woods. I turned to look. There, hidden in the shadows, revealed only by the firelight, was a fox. The creature sat on a stone, watching. Its eyes shimmered in the darkness. When it met my gaze, it let out a soft yip, then turned and disappeared back into the woods.

May the Norns weave what they may.

Continue Ervie's adventure in Shield-Maiden: Gambit of Swords, available on Amazon.

ACKNOWLEDGEMENTS

With special thanks to Taylor Stellan and Rachel Malachuk for their help with bringing my characters to life!

Thank you to my ARC team for their feedback and help.

Many thanks to the members of The Clockpunk Reading Room (my Facebook Reader's Group) for their feedback, shenanigans, and all things bookish. Viking Hipster approves of this message.

As well, thank you to Jesikah Sundin, Alisha Klapheke, Elle Madison, and Robin D. Mahle for all of the mushroom emojis.

ABOUT THE AUTHOR

New York Times and *USA Today* bestselling author Melanie Karsak is the author of *The Celtic Blood Series, The Road to Valhalla Series, The Celtic Rebels Series, Steampunk Red Riding Hood, Steampunk Fairy Tales* and more. The author currently lives in Florida with her husband and two children.

amazon.com/author/melaniekarsak

facebook.com/authormelaniekarsak

instagram.com/karsakmelanie

pinterest.com/melaniekarsak

youtube.com/@authormelaniekarsak

tiktok.com/@authormelaniekarsak

ALSO BY MELANIE KARSAK

THE CELTIC BLOOD SERIES:

Highland Raven

Highland Blood

Highland Vengeance

Highland Queen

THE CELTIC REBELS SERIES:

Queen of Oak: A Novel of Boudica

Queen of Stone: A Novel of Boudica

Queen of Ash and Iron: A Novel of Boudica

THE ROAD TO VALHALLA SERIES:

Under the Strawberry Moon (Prequel)

Shield-Maiden: Under the Howling Moon

Shield-Maiden: Under the Hunter's Moon

Shield-Maiden: Under the Thunder Moon

Shield-Maiden: Under the Blood Moon

Shield-Maiden: Under the Dark Moon

THE SHADOWS OF VALHALLA SERIES:

Shield-Maiden: Winternights Gambit (Prequel)

Shield-Maiden: Gambit of Blood

Shield-Maiden: Gambit of Shadows

Shield-Maiden: Gambit of Swords

THE HARVESTING SERIES:

The Harvesting

Midway

The Shadow Aspect

Witch Wood

The Torn World

STEAMPUNK FAIRY TALES:

Curiouser and Curiouser: Steampunk Alice in Wonderland

Ice and Embers: Steampunk Snow Queen

Beauty and Beastly: Steampunk Beauty and the Beast

Golden Braids and Dragon Blades: Steampunk Rapunzel

STEAMPUNK RED RIDING HOOD:

Wolves and Daggers

Alphas and Airships

Peppermint and Pentacles

Bitches and Brawlers

Howls and Hallows

Lycans and Legends

THE AIRSHIP RACING CHRONICLES:

Chasing the Star Garden

Chasing the Green Fairy

Chasing Christmas Past

THE CHANCELLOR FAIRY TALES:

The Glass Mermaid

The Cupcake Witch

The Fairy Godfather

The Vintage Medium

The Book Witch

Find these books and more on Amazon!

Made in the USA
Middletown, DE
27 January 2023